EROTICA III

The third illustrated anthology of erotica takes the reader on a journey through four centuries of erotic literature and art. Part one, 'The libertine imagination', fuels libidinous fantasies. Part two, 'Dreams of empire', concentrates on the underground erotica of the Victorians. Part three, 'Decadent visions', moves on to the Edwardian era, spirited pieces with a theatrical background. Part four, 'After the nightmare', features a wide variety of literary styles including the different approaches to erotic writing of a male and a female writer. Part five, 'Fantasy or reality?', brings us up to date and includes same sex writing.

Once more this is an appealing array of literary and artistic erotica, with the emphasis on the dreams and fantasies that all of us indulge in – or would like to.

EROTICA III

An Illustrated Anthology of Sexual Art and Literature

Charlotte Hill
and
William Wallace

Carroll & Graf Publishers, Inc.
New York

First published in the United States in 1996 by
Carroll and Graf Publishers, Inc.
260 Fifth Avenue
New York, NY 10001

Library of Congress Cataloging-in-Publication-Data
is available on request from Carroll & Graf

ISBN 0-7867-0297-4

AN EDDISON·SADD EDITION
Edited, designed and produced by
Eddison Sadd Editions Limited
St Chad's House, 148 King's Cross Road
London WC1X 9DH

Phototypeset in Caslon ITC No 224 Book by
Dorchester Typesetting, Dorset, England
Origination by Rainbow Graphic Arts Ltd, Hong Kong
Printed and bound by
Paramount Printing Company Ltd, Hong Kong

––––––––––––– ◊ –––––––––––––

FRONTISPIECE
Agnolo Bronzino's (1503–72) painting of *Venus and Cupid*
in the National Gallery, London: one of the most disturbing
explorations of eroticism in all art, operating at many levels.
As an allegory, the personifications of Love and Desire are
surrounded by the nature and consequences of sexuality. Masks
remind us that ambiguity is everywhere: scented rose petals,
flung by Folly. The sweetness of the honeycomb, with the sting
in the tail: are these the pangs of jealousy, or of syphilis? And
Time will one day bring the curtain down on everything. Beyond
the complicated mechanisms of allegory are more unsettling
questions. Should mothers and sons embrace like
this even if they are mythical figures?

––––––––––––– ◊ –––––––––––––

Contents

Our wildest dreams

ABOVE 'The Abbé', from *Under the Hill* by Aubrey Beardsley (1872–98).

T he third anthology of erotica follows the development of sexual art and literature through four centuries and more, from the pyrotechnic creations of the Earl of Rochester and the sophisticated paintings of the French and Italian Renaissance to the art and writing of men and women in our own time. Like the 'Grand Tour' enjoyed by a privileged few during the Age of Enlightenment, this is a journey full of incident. There are extracts from the libertine literature which sizzled in the secret library drawers of the eighteenth-century aristocracy, and selections from the best examples of the erotic novels which their Victorian great-grandchildren took in Gladstone bags to every corner of the British Empire. The images which accompany these texts are just as varied: there are prints and drawings by numerous artists, known and unknown, celebrating the many delights of human sexuality. The development of photography in the mid-nineteenth century opened up an exciting new world of possibilities for the erotic imagination, and we have included a unique collection of rare and beautiful early daguerreotypes as well as many later photographs.

The forbidding shadow of Queen Victoria stretched far into our own century. But sex is too insistent and too important to be denied, and there have always been those who have chosen it as their subject despite the risk of disapproval or even prosecution. As we approach the millennium, it seems incredible that as fine and well-intentioned a book as *Lady Chatterley's Lover* or that cheerful classic *Fanny Hill* could have been hauled through the English courts – but they were. While England struggled to clear its air of the fog from nineteenth-century industries and its mind of murky Victorian hypocrisy, Paris shone like a beacon of reason in the gloom: much of the twentieth-century material we have included was created there. Of course, bright lights attract vicious things as well as beautiful and interesting ones, but then it is the job of anthologists to sort out the glamorous moths from among the mosquitoes and midges.

The creators of erotica have no choice but to tap their own reservoir of sexuality in order to achieve that reciprocal excitement in the viewer or reader which is the whole point of erotic art

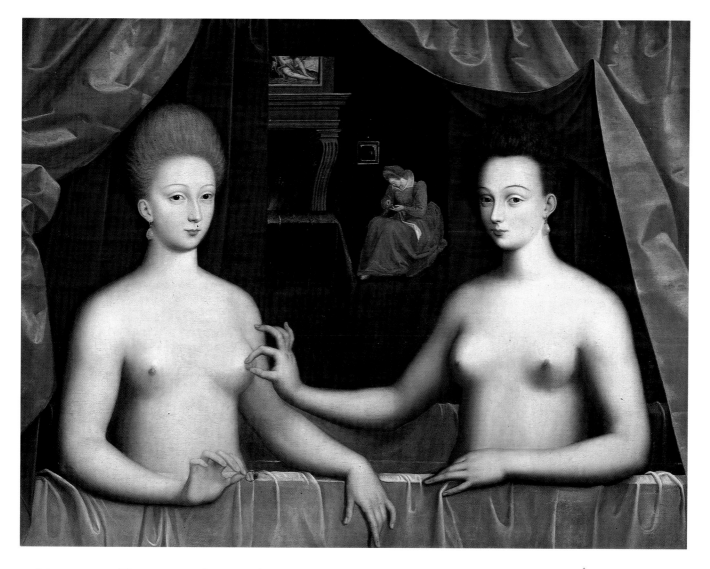

and literature. This means digging deep into the unconscious and far below experience, however wide and varied that may be. Erotic art and literature can then be regarded as akin to dreams: idealized expressions of their creator's urges, obsessions and preoccupations. Dreams – both the profound, sleeping kind and waking fantasies – are of course immensely potent. Fuelled by the limitless power of the unconscious, they can – if they resonate in the imagination of others – go forth into the world like the Golem, full of potential for either good or evil.

If erotica is indeed the stuff of dreams it makes the anthologist's job – choosing a selection of this volatile material – a task requiring care. Are we perhaps taking this task a little too seriously? Let us consult a couple of dreamers. In the summer of 1908 Sigmund Freud wrote the second preface to one of the most important books of the twentieth century, his *The Interpretation of Dreams*: a work which was the foundation stone of psychoanalysis. To complete this project Freud chose a retreat high in the

ABOVE The memorable portrait of the French king Henri IV's mistress Gabrielle d'Estrées (1573–99) with her sister (School of Fontainebleau) is one of the enigmas of art history. Frozen in time and frozen of expression, they seem as surprised as we are to discover them indulging the erotic dreams of their patron in paint as well as in the flesh.

glorious mountains of the Tyrol. Freud did not know – and it would certainly have spoiled his vacation if he had known – that thirty years later another man who understood how to use dreams would make his home on the very same spot. This man once said that he moved towards his destiny 'with the inevitability of a sleep-walker': he demonstrated to the world that mad and evil dreams can wield power if you can make them echo in the minds of others. The place was Berchtesgaden, of course; the man, Adolf Hitler.

The point of this Alpine excursion was to show that a genre which operates at a dream level needs to be properly considered –

not banned, but taken seriously. Erotica plugs deep into the psyche of both creator and user and is potentially powerful stuff. In making this selection we have therefore endeavoured to choose material which celebrates life and gives something back to it. That does not mean that the erotic 'dreams' we have included are always bright and cheerful. Some are dark and disturbing – sex has many faces. But in one respect this selection of erotic material is absolutely clear-cut and unambiguous: the Marquis de Sade and other lesser prophets of cruelty and violence have been left to sweat in their own nightmares.

PART ONE

The libertine imagination

Naked she lay, clasped in my longing arms,
I filled with love, and she all over charms;
Both equally inspired with eager fire,
Melting through kindness, flaming in desire.
With arms, legs, lips close clinging to embrace,
She clips me to her breast, and sucks me to her face.
Her nimble tongue, Love's lesser lightning, played
Within my mouth, and to my thoughts conveyed
Swift orders that I should prepare to throw
The all-dissolving thunderbolt below.
My fluttering soul, sprung with the pointed kiss,
Hangs hovering o'er her balmy brinks of bliss.
But whilst her busy hand would guide that part
Which should convey my soul up to her heart,
In liquid raptures I dissolve all o'er,
Melt into sperm, and spend at every pore.
A touch from any part of her had done't:
Her hand, her foot, her very look's a cunt.

BELOW *The Feeling*, an engraving by the Dutch artist Heinrich Goltzius (1558–1617).

The unmistakable voice of John Wilmot, second Earl of Rochester (1647–80), echoes down the years: the first, and one of the very few, poets writing in English to make sex his principal subject. It is true that Robert Herrick (1591–1674) had already explored every inch of his delicious mistress Julia in verse before Rochester was born, and there is wonderful erotic verse by earlier poets including John Donne, Thomas Carew and of course Shakespeare. But these men had other subjects too, while for Rochester there was really only sex. Three centuries have not dulled his ability to shock and sting us: the words, from his poem *The Imperfect Enjoyment*, still explode like Chinese crackers at a court ball.

One of the brightest stars in the dissolute court of Charles II, Rochester took only 33 years to burn himself out with drink and debauchery. His love lyrics are some of the

most beautiful in the English language, but it is for his bawdy work that he is chiefly remembered. Such was the reputation of this brilliant rake that the Victorian pornographer William Dugdale even produced a phony biography detailing court intrigues and 'the amatory adventures of Lord Rochester in Holland, France and Germany'. Why did he bother? The truth needed no embellishment. Having offended different individuals with his erotic satires at various times, Rochester decided to mark the marriage of the Italian princess Mary of Modena to the Duke of York (later James II) by comprehensively slandering almost every woman in the court. *Signior Dildo* is one of the most outrageous poems ever written, and not the kind of wedding present the Duke and Duchess might have hoped for:

> *You ladies all of merry England*
> *Who have been to kiss the Duchess's hand,*
> *Pray, did you lately observe in the show*
> *A noble Italian called Signior Dildo*

—————— ◊ ——————

ABOVE The word 'lechery' is derived from the verb 'to lick': this powerful evocation of both is by Artur Fischer (1872–1948).

—————— ◊ ——————

This signior was one of Her Highness's train,
And helped to conduct her over the main;
But now she cries out, 'To the Duke I will go!
I have no more need for Signior Dildo.'

RIGHT Priapus, the tireless patron of debauchery, receives an unexpectedly intimate tribute during a parkland orgy. Eighteenth-century sepia print.

Rochester then proceeds to describe the intimate sexual practices of his aristocratic circle:

That pattern of virtue, Her Grace of Cleveland,
Has swallowed more pricks than the ocean has sand;
But by rubbing and scrubbing so large does it grow,
It is just fit for nothing but Signior Dildo!

The unofficial marriage-song ends with the unfortunate Dildo ('. . . sound, safe, ready and dumb/As ever was candle, carrot, or thumb') being chased down Pall Mall by a crowd of jealous penises:

> *The good lady Sandys burst into laughter*
> *To see how the bollocks came wobbling after,*
> *And had not their weight retarded the foe,*
> *Indeed't had gone hard with Signior Dildo.*

Rochester's own end came seven years later. Bishop Burnet maintained that he repented of his wicked ways on his deathbed; visitors to London can see his face in the National Portrait Gallery and judge for themselves if England's first and finest libertine was a man to abandon his principles. Afterwards, if pilgrimages appeal, it is a short walk to the royal park Rochester immortalized in *A Ramble in St James's Park*:

> *Much wine had passed, with grave discourse*
> *Of who fucks who, and who does worse . . .*
> *When I, who still take care to see*
> *Drunkenness relieved by lechery,*
> *Went out into St James's Park*
> *To cool my head and fire my heart.*
> *But though St James has th'honour on't,*
> *'Tis consecrate to prick and cunt.*
> *There, by a most incestuous birth,*
> *Strange woods spring from the teeming earth . . .*
> *Each imitative branch does twine*
> *In some loved fold of Aretine,*
> *And nightly now beneath their shade*
> *Are buggeries, rapes, and incests made.*
> *Unto this all-sin-sheltering grove*
> *Whores of the bulk and the alcove,*
> *Great ladies, chambermaids, and drudges,*
> *The ragpicker, and heiress trudges.*
> *Carmen, divines, great lords, and tailors,*
> *Prentices, poets, pimps, and jailers,*
> *Footmen, fine fops do here arrive,*
> *And here promiscuously they swive.*

BELOW Leather dildos were an important hidden export for Italy during the seventeenth and eighteenth centuries; a contemporary engraving.

On 13 January 1668, Samuel Pepys wrote in his famous diary: 'Thence homeward by coach and stopped at Martin's, my bookseller, where I saw the French book which I did think to have had for my wife to translate, called L'escholle des filles, but when I came to look in it, it is the most bawdy, lewd book that I ever saw.' Nevertheless, by 8 February Pepys had returned 'to the Strand to my booksellers and there staid an hour, and bought the idle roguish book L'escholle des filles . . .' Curiosity had clearly got the better of Pepys, and whether to appease his conscience in purchasing the book, or because he had read more on his second visit, he had moderated his opinion of the work. But the judgement is still unfair. *L'Ecole des filles* is a charming, elegant book and a minor masterpiece. It

Have you beheld (with much delight)
A red rose peeping through a white?
Or else a cherry (double graced)
Within a lilly? Centre placed?
Or ever marked the pretty beam,
A strawberry shows half drowned in
cream?
Or seen rich rubies blushing through
A pure smooth pearl, and orient too?
So like to this, nay all the rest,
Is each neat niplet of her breast.

UPON THE NIPPLES OF JULIA'S BREAST
ROBERT HERRICK (1591–1674)

ABOVE *The digéstif*, anonymous
English copper engraving,
eighteenth century.

employs the dialogue form common to many erotic books of the period, and first used by Pietro Aretino in his *Ragionamenti*. But how different *L'Ecole des filles* is from all the other seventeenth- and eighteenth-century Aretino clones. It takes the woman's view of sex so convincingly, and offers such sound and practical advice to the uninitiated, that it may indeed have been written by a woman. Michel Millot and Jean L'Ange were certainly involved in its publication in 1655, but a rumour has persisted that the real author was Françoise d'Aubigné (c. 1635–1719), better known as Madame de Maintenon, bride of Louis XIV! In reading the following extracts you can make your own decision as to the gender of the writer. The sexually experienced Susanne establishes some first principles with her young cousin Fanchon:

FANCHON: . . . And now that we're on the subject, tell me why on most nights I feel a certain agitation just here – I mean in my cunny – which hardly lets me sleep. I toss and turn from one side to the other without being able to soothe it. What should I do?

SUSANNE: All you need is a big, sinewy yard to penetrate your femininity, to make the sweet sap flow there and soothe the inflammation. Or alternatively, when this happens you should rub it with your finger for a while and then you'll taste all the pleasures of an orgasm.

FANCHON: With a finger? Impossible!

SUSANNE: With your middle finger, using it on the edge, like this.

FANCHON: All right, I'll keep it in mind. But to return to what we were talking about, love, haven't you told me that you sometimes experience this enjoyment with men?

SUSANNE: Certainly, when I feel like it. I owe it all to a boy whom I love very much.

FANCHON: Just as I thought. It must be true that you love him because otherwise, according to you, he wouldn't be able to do it. I'm surprised, though! Has he given you a lot of pleasure like this?

SUSANNE: So much that I can hardly bear it!

FANCHON: And how am I going to find someone who will do this for me?

SUSANNE: Well, you must choose someone who really loves you and who has enough discretion not to say a word about it to anyone.

The importance of love and trust is stressed throughout *L'Ecole des filles*. The practical advice is as systematic as that given in *Kama Sutra*, and in many ways superior. This is what Susanne has to say about touching, male psychology, the sensitivity of the perineum and masturbation:

FANCHON: I never talk to you without learning something. . . . But can't you tell me why men seem to get more pleasure from having their yards caressed by our hands than by any other part of the body? When they have their yards right inside us during intercourse, they still enjoy feeling our hands stroking their stones.

SUSANNE: It's not easy to give an absolute answer. One of the greatest pleasures which they can ever experience is some sign of gratitude from us for what they are doing to us, as I've already mentioned. That's where love's greatest happiness lies, it longs to divide pleasure equally between two lovers, so that one doesn't have more than the other. What better way is there, then, of letting them know how they are exciting us than by using our hands to attend to the instrument which serves us so well? When we caress them, it makes them see that we are in no way half-hearted about it and that we say to ourselves as they watch us doing it: 'I enjoy touching this with my hand because it is an emblem of all my pleasure and happiness, because I have it as it is, and because from this organ I must receive my greatest satisfaction'. This pleases them especially and the touch of the hand is more exciting, a more womanly examination, as with all due care she explores the nature of the instrument, as though it were a limb that seemed strange to her and of which she was going to make use for the first time. This caressing is both pleasurable and soothing for men, thrilling them through and through. The simple, willing grasp of a white, delicate hand which closes round their shepherd's staff is enough to reveal to them the thought of their mistress's heart. The hand working gently on its object is like the symbol of the love which it embodies, just as when it is used too harshly it is a symbol of hostility. As a rule we use the hand to touch those things we love. Two friends seal their friendship by clasping hands, when it's a purely platonic relationship which permits no other kind of contact. Yet contact between a man and a woman should be natural and complete, with body and soul taking part in it. They caress one another's organs as a way of showing their mutual love. A woman who does such things to a man and allows him to do such things to her, shows him more clearly that she loves him than if they had merely shaken hands! There is nothing more precious to us than the stones and I can tell you, what's more, that if she permits kissing, embracing, mounting, riding, insertion – in short, discharging the yard in the cunny – but yet refuses to touch his instrument, she doesn't show her love as clearly as if she had simply put her hand on it out of affection and was too frightened to let him go any further. In fact, this is the summit of love's pleasure: when the woman cannot touch the man's instrument because it is completely engulfed in hers, she can at least caress the nearest thing to it which remains free during intercourse, and stroke the stones which are the source of her pleasure. No form of familiarity is greater than the hand's. Nature, having seen to it that a man can enjoy two pleasures at once, those of the cunny and the hand, has also left a good length and expanse of the yard behind the stones which cannot enter the woman but runs round almost to the rump, so that the woman can caress it, put her hand on it and fondle it during intercourse. This shows clearly that there is nothing in the creation of men and women which

Wo'd ye oyle of blossomes get?
Take it from my Julia's sweat:
Oyl of lillies, and of spike,
From her moysture take the like:
Let her breath, or let her blow,
All rich spices thence will flow.

UPON JULIA'S SWEAT
ROBERT HERRICK (1591–1674)

ABOVE *Riding St George*, anonymous English copper engraving, eighteenth century.

ABOVE Engraving of a drawing attributed to Antoine Borel (1743–1810). In illustrating erotica, the prodigious Paris artist often strayed from the text, using scenes from other books which were graphically more exciting or creating sexual tableaux of his own invention.
OPPOSITE Copy of the oil painting *A Bed in the Corn Field*, attributed to Michael Martin Drolling (1786–1851).

was unintentional and nothing which doesn't have its reasons, if one is curious enough to discover them. It follows from this that it must be a clear abuse of those means of satisfaction which nature has given us not to put them to the purpose for which they were intended. I'm rather preoccupied by this argument because it concerns me in one respect. One of my lover's greatest joys, when we are naked under the sheets, is to see how white my hands are, as I use them in that place which it is absurd to call indecent. (After all, it's the hidden temple of the greatest pleasure in the world, and often makes us flush with excitement just to touch it.) In the same way, I experience a double pleasure when he shows himself eager to bestow the same kind of caresses on me. I ask you, love, what greater happiness is there than to see a little length of limp flesh hanging at the base of your lover's belly – a thing which we take in our hands and which gradually grows stiff and becomes so large that you can hardly get your hand round it. The skin of it is so delicate that it almost makes you swoon with delight just to touch it. After you've squeezed it gently, you find it becomes stiff enough, and then it seems feverish with heat and crimson in colour, which is quite intriguing to watch. You bring your lover to this ecstasy by stroking him and then you see the yard ejaculate a whitish liquid between your fingers, quite opposite in colour to the yard, which is so inflamed. Then we let it fall again as quickly as we took it up, until after a while we begin again.

It is unlikely we will ever know the true authorship of *L'École des filles*. What is certain is that in its tone and content it is quite unlike any other erotic book. In the final extract the admirable Susanne describes a night of passion with Robinet, her lover:

FANCHON: How long is it from the time the tool stands erect until it is beaten down again? And how often can it storm the cunny in a single night?

SUSANNE: Not once, if you keep interrupting all the time! It depends on the people involved, you see, because sometimes they are more eager than at others. . . . Now, where was I when you interrupted me?

FANCHON: Your lover took you when you were half asleep and put his stiff yard into your hand.

SUSANNE: Yes, I remember now, I no sooner felt it, stiff as it was, than I gave up all thoughts of sleep and responded to his

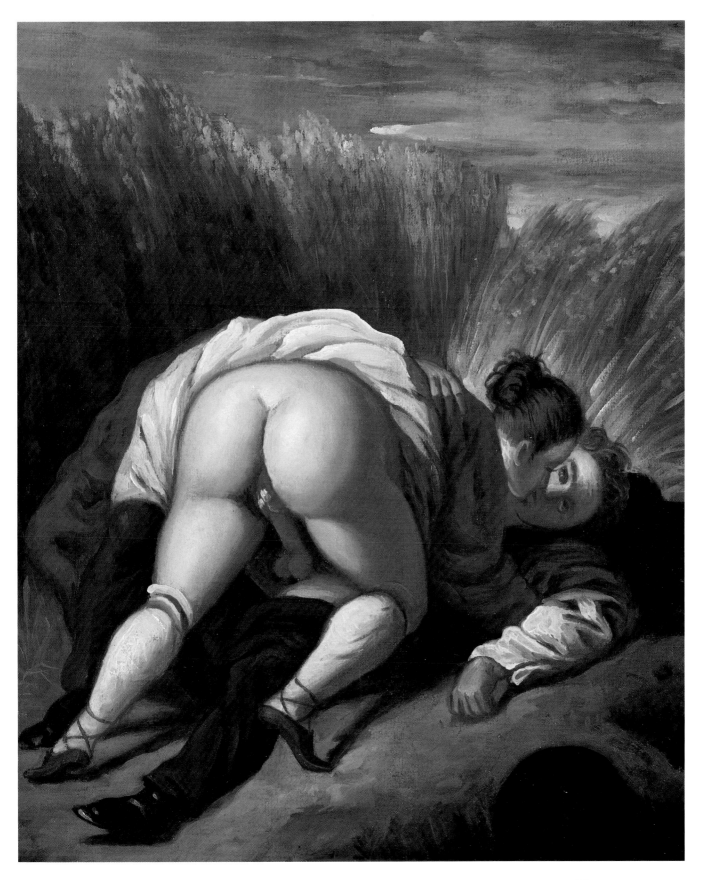

Amelette, Ronsardelette,
Mignonnelette, doucelette,
Tres-chère hôtesse de mon corps.

FROM *A SON AME* (TO HIS SOUL)
PIERRE DE RONSARD (1524–85)

ABOVE Another engraving by
Antoine Borel (1743–1810).

caresses, while he called me his dear heart and soul. We rolled against each other for a long time, arms and legs entwined, and threshed about so much that the bedclothes covering us fell to the floor but we weren't cold by any means so we let them lie there. Growing warmer, he made me take off my nightdress while he took off his own clothes as well, and then he bounded about all over the bed, showing me his yard erect. Then, after asking me to do what he wanted in all respects, he scattered and strewed on the floor a hundred rosebuds. He made me go naked and gather them in the middle of that sumptuous bedroom, turning me from side to side and watching by the light of the fire and the candle in various parts of the room the changing postures which I presented in bending down and rising again. He bathed me all over with jasmine oil and I did the same to him. Back on the bed we rolled over and over to enliven ourselves, turning turtle a score of times. Then he held me on my knees in front of him, gazing at me from top to toe, his eyes ravished with ecstasy. He extolled my belly, then my thighs, bubbies, the swell of my mount of Venus, which he found firm and rounded, running his hand there several times, and I can't pretend that I wasn't absolutely delighted by all these little whims of his.

Turning me away from him, he gazed at my shoulders, my buttocks, and then making me lean on my hands on the bed, he got astride my back and made me move forward. After some time like this he got down from his horse, not at the side but by way of the croup – because he said he had no need to be afraid that I should kick him! At the same time he lowered his yard between my buttocks and thrust it into my cunny. At first I wanted to rear up on my hind legs and show how restive I was, but, in his despair, he begged and conjured me to such an extent that I had to take pity on him. I resumed my posture and felt his pleasure in driving into me and drawing back all in one movement, amusing himself by watching the way it moved in and out. It makes a noise, love, like bakers kneading dough, when they suddenly draw their hands out of it, or like little boys drawing a ramrod from their pop-gun, when they've plugged it with paper.

FANCHON: Oh, Lord! How shameless of you both! And do you enjoy that part of it as well?

SUSANNE: Why not? If you're in love, there are certain little things which are enjoyable however vulgar they may be, and which serve to excite you a little more. It adds pleasure to the way you spend the time and helps to make things still better later on.

FANCHON: Oh, very well, then by all means do it if you find that you like it.

SUSANNE: Anyhow, when he got tired of arousing me in this way, we went naked as we were across to the fire, where he made me sit in a chair near him and went at once to fetch a bottle of mulled wine and some little cakes from the corner of the room. He made me eat and after that I felt marvellously refreshed. While we were still eating, he assumed the most humble and suppliant posture in front of me and wooed me as though he had never set eyes on me before, calling me his martyr, for love of whom he would die. All this was done in the sweetest possible way and it was so convincing that I pretended to have pity on him. So I opened my thighs for him, sitting there as I was, and holding his instrument in my hand I drew him on his knees between my legs. He said that he only wanted to shelter his yard and he soon managed this, holding me impaled upon it but not going any further. We ate like this, passing each titbit gently to and fro, so that when it was half eaten it passed from mouth to mouth. In the end we grew tired of this posture and changed to another and then another, and so on, while he examined me all over as though he would never finish doing it and could never have too much of a good thing. Then he pulled himself together and took a glass from the table, filling it with the mulled wine and insisting that I should be the first to drink. I drained it completely and when I had filled it for him he did the same. We did this two or three times until our eyes twinkled with lechery and gave the signal for love's natural combat to begin. We made a playful truce and, turning again to caress me, he took me by the arms and lifted me. When I was standing up he got ready to ride me in that position, moving towards me and lowering himself while I thrust upwards to meet him. Our two backsides lunged as if the yard was already in my cunny. Then seeing that he could not penetrate me because of the difficulty of standing upright, he explained that what he had done was a sign for me to start moving my bottom so that we could be joined together, moving our buttocks in unison, thrusting and withdrawing in the correct rhythm, which gives a great piquancy to the pleasures of love. He taught me to do several other things later on, and he liked me to do them either before or during intercourse. What else is there to say? All we needed was a mirror so that we could gaze at our own posturing but instead of this he showed me all his limbs – how handsomely made they were! – asking me to caress them, and taking as much pleasure in having them stroked as he did in fondling me himself. To cut a long story short, he never went to such trouble to get me ready to be mounted as he did then, and I begged him to press on to the finale of the affair. He had had enough of kissing, fondling, probing and delving, so he listened to what I said and the climax of our pleasure could no longer be delayed. I took him by his hose and led him towards the foot of the bed, where I lay on my back, drawing him down on top of me. I threaded his yard into my cunny to the very hilt. The bed creaked under the weight and I thrust against him as hard as I could. Soon everything was in full swing between us and our bottoms were going at top speed. In great excitement I felt his two stones beating time against me and at last he threw himself on me in a passion, telling me that he was going to make one last effort which would overwhelm me with ecstasy. I begged him not to keep me waiting and then we murmured a score of times to each other, 'Quickly, my love, my heart, when will you come?' The crisis came on, as he gave me the signal by kissing me and thrusting his tongue into my mouth. It seemed to me as I lay there that he gave me more than six times the quantity of love's fluid that I gave him, and this infusion was accompanied by gentle thrusts, at each of which I seemed to die again. . . . My own

Yet the lusty spring hath stay'd;
Blushing red and purest white
Daintily to love invite
Every woman, every maid:
Cherries kissing as they grow,
And inviting men to taste,
Apples even ripe below,
Winding gently to the waist:
All love's emblems, and all cry,
'Ladies, if not pluck'd, we die.'

FROM *LOVE'S EMBLEMS*
JOHN FLETCHER (1579–1625)

orgasm came simultaneously, and to give you some idea of how much we enjoyed it, just let me say, love, that you would have been in ecstasy just to have seen him gasping and squirming on top of me as we came to the end of the course!

FANCHON: Oh, my dear! I not only believe it but I even get something of the same feeling as in the scene you describe. Honestly, I think I'd rather have that last part than all those preparations you were telling me about.

SUSANNE: You're wrong there. The last part is essential but you mustn't be a spendthrift of your pleasure, since it will last no time at all without the kind of preliminaries that can be devised.

———————— ◊ ————————

ABOVE One of a series of erotic miniatures satirizing French influence in the Catholic cantons; gouache on ivory, Switzerland, c. 1800.

Less than ten years after the publication of *L'Ecole des filles* a very different book appeared: *Satyra Sotadica*. This claimed to be a translation of a work by a Spanish noblewoman from Toledo, Luisa Sigea. In fact, its author was the French lawyer Nicolas Chorier, who was living in Grenoble in 1660, although *Satyra Sotadica* may have been printed and published in Lyons. Superficially similar to *L'Ecole des filles* – an erotic dialogue between two women – the tone and content of *Satyra Sotadica* is completely different. Tullia, the leading character, who represents Luisa Sigea herself, has as much in common with Susanne as La Belle Dame Sans Merci does with Tess of the D'Urbervilles. The prevailing mood is strange and slightly disturbing, as if we are viewing the characters through a lens which distorts them in some subtle way. This quality clearly reflects the preoccupations – perhaps we should say dreams – of the author:

Seeing resistance was in vain, I yielded to the madmen. Aloysio bends forward over my buttocks, brings his javelin to the backdoor, knocks, pushes, finally with a mighty effort bursts in. I gave a groan. Instantly he withdraws his weapon from the wound, plunges it in the vulva and spurts a flood of semen into the wanton furrow of my womb. When all was over, Fabrizio attacks me in the same fashion. With one rapid thrust he introduced his spear, and in less than no time made it disappear in my entrails; for a little time he plays at come and go, and scarce credible as it may sound, I found myself invaded by a prurient fury to such an extent that I have no doubt, that I should get accustomed to it very well, if I chose.

Chorier presides like a literary Alfred Hitchcock over his characters and the wide range of sexual antics they perform, taking every opportunity to shock. He manipulates his characters and they cynically manipulate one another, as in this fevered tale of voyeurism, lesbianism and blackmail:

Enemunda, the sister of Fernando Porcio, was very beautiful, and not less so was a friend of hers, Francisca Bellina. They frequently slept together in Fernando's house. Fernando laid secret snares for Francisca; the latter knew that he desired to have her, and was proud of it. One morning the young man, stung by his desires, rose with the sun, and stepped out upon the balcony to cool his hot blood. He heard the bed of his sister in the next room cracking and shaking. The door stood open; Venus had been kind to him and had made the girls careless. He enters; they do not see him, blinded and deafened by pleasure. Francisca was riding Enemunda, both naked, full gallop. 'The noblest and most powerful mentulas are every day after my maidenhead', said Francisca, 'I should select the finest, dear, but for you; so fain am I to gratify your tastes and mine'. Whilst speaking she was jogging her vigorously. Fernando threw himself naked into the bed; the two girls, almost frightened to death, dared not stir. He draws Francisca, exhausted by her ride, into his arms and kisses her: 'How dare you, abandoned girl' he says, 'violate my sister, who is so pure and chaste? You shall pay me for this; I will revenge the injury done to our house; answer now to my flames

BELOW *Girlfriends*, a copy of a painting attributed to Michael Martin Drolling (1786–1851); oil on canvas.

as she has answered to yours.' 'My brother! my brother!' cries Enemunda, 'pardon two lovers, and do not betray us to slander!' 'No one shall know anything', he answered, 'let Francisca make me a present of her treasure, and I will make you both a present of my silence.'

RIGHT and OPPOSITE More examples from the series of erotic miniatures satirizing French influence in the Catholic cantons; gouache on ivory, Switzerland, c. 1800.

Another Hitchcock device which the author of *Satyra Sotadica* employs is to shock us by suddenly revealing a character's secret history: in this way we learn that Tullia's own sexual initiation was at the hands of Sempronia, the mother of young Ottavia. Naturally, it is not too long before this Freudian motif is repeated:

TULLIA: Pray do not draw back; open your thighs.

OTTAVIA: Very well! Now you cover me entirely, your mouth against mine, your breast against mine, your belly against mine; I will clasp you as you are clasping me.

TULLIA: Raise your legs, cross your thighs over mine, I will show you a new Venus; to you quite new. How nicely you obey! I wish I could command as well as you execute!

OTTAVIA: Ah! ah! my dear Tullia, my queen! how you push! how you wriggle! I wish those candles were out; I am ashamed there should be light to see how submissive I am.

TULLIA: Now mind what you are doing! When I push, do you rise to meet me; move your buttocks vigorously, as I move mine, and lift up as high as ever you can! Is your breath coming short?

OTTAVIA: You dislocate me with your violent pushing; you stifle me; I would not do it for any one but you.

TULLIA: Press me tightly, Ottavia, take . . . there! I am all melting and burning, ah! ah! ah!

OTTAVIA: Your affair is setting fire to mine – draw back!

TULLIA: At last, my darling, I have served you as a husband; you are my wife now!

OTTAVIA: I wish to heaven you were my husband! What a loving wife I should make! What a husband I should have! But you have inundated my garden; I am all bedewed! What have you been doing, Tullia?

TULLIA: I have done everything up to the end, and from the dark recesses of my vessel love in blind transports has shot the liquor of Venus into your maiden barque.

The variety of erotic experience described in *Satyra Sotadica* is enormous, and includes a comprehensive catalogue of sexual positions. In the final extract Tullia describes the standing posture which she and La Tour enjoy as a creeper clinging to a tree: the same metaphor employed by ancient and medieval Hindu sages. Is it pure coincidence, or should we consider the exciting possibility that a scholarly erotomane like Chorier had access to Hindu erotic texts as early as 1660?

La Tour came forward instantly. . . . I had thrown myself on the foot of the bed – (Tullia is speaking) – I was naked; his member was erect. Without more ado he grasps in either hand one of my breasts, and brandishing his hard and inflamed lance between my thighs, exclaims 'Look Madam, how this weapon is darting at you, not to kill you, but to give you the greatest possible pleasure. Pray, guide this blind applicant into the dark recess, so that it may not miss its destination; I will not remove my hands from where they are, I would not deprive them of the bliss they enjoy.' I do as he wishes, I introduce myself the flaming dart into the burning centre; he feels it, drives in, pushes home . . . After one or two strokes I felt myself melting away with incredible titillation, and my knees all but gave way. 'Stop', I cried – 'stop my soul, it is escaping!' 'I know', he replied, laughing, 'from where. No doubt your soul wants to escape through this lower orifice, of which I have possession; but I keep it well stoppered.' Whilst speaking he endeavoured, by holding his breath, still further to increase the already enormous size of his swollen member. 'I am going to thrust back your escaping soul', he added, poking me more and more violently. His sword pierced yet deeper into the quick. Redoubling his delicious blows, he filled me with transports of pleasure, – working so forcefully that, albeit he could not get his whole body into me, he impregnated me with all his passion, all his lascivious desires, his very thoughts, his whole delirious soul, by his voluptuous embraces. At last feeling the

The grasp divine, th'emphatic, thrilling
  squeeze
The throbbing, panting breasts and
  trembling knees
The tickling motion, the enlivening
  flow,
The rapturous shiver and dissolving –
  Oh!

FROM *AN ESSAY ON WOMEN*
JOHN WILKES (1727–97)

All my past life is mine no more;
The flying hours are gone,
Like transitory dreams given o'er
Whose images are kept in store
By memory alone.

FROM *LOVE AND LIFE*
JOHN WILMOT, EARL OF ROCHESTER
(1647–80)

RIGHT Another in the series of
erotic miniatures satirizing French
influence in the Catholic cantons;
gouache on ivory, Switzerland,
c. 1800.

approach of the ecstasy and the boiling over of the liquid, he
slips his hands under my buttocks, and lifts me up bodily. I do my
part; I twine my arms closely round his form, my thighs and legs
being at the same time intertwisted and entangled with his, so
that I found myself suspended on his neck in the air, lifted clean
off the ground; I was thus hanging, as it were, fixed on a peg. I
had not the patience to wait for him, as he was going on, and
again I swooned with pleasure. In the most violent raptures I
could not help crying out – 'I feel all . . . I feel all the delights of
Juno lying with Jupiter. I am in heaven.' At this moment La
Tour, pushed by Venus and Cupido to the acmé of voluptuousness, poured a plenteous flood of his well into the genial hold,
burning like fire. The creeper does not cling more closely round
the walnut tree than I held fast to La Tour with my arms and
legs.

The next landmark of libertine literature – and probably the
most famous erotic novel there has ever been – was *Fanny
Hill*. This minor masterpiece was written in Fleet Prison
between 1748 and 1750 by John Cleland, a journalist and former
diplomat whose debts had finally caught up with him. *Fanny Hill* is

a charming work: a unique combination of vivid descriptions and shrewd insights into human nature, expressed in ornate language encrusted with metaphors. Despite the restrictions of the genre, Cleland even manages to breathe life into some of the minor characters. As for Fanny herself, she is one of those archetypal characters who escape from books and inhabit the realm of imagination and dreams.

We may say what we please, but those we can be the easiest and freest with are ever those we like, not to say love, the best.

With this stripling, all whose art of love was the action of it, I could, without check of awe or restraint, give a loose to joy, and execute every scheme of dalliance my fond fancy might put me on, in which he was, in every sense, a most exquisite companion. And now my great pleasure lay in humouring all the petulances, all the wanton frolic of a raw novice just fleshed, and keen on the burning scent of his game, but inbroken to the sport: and, to carry on the figure, who could better THREAD THE WOOD than he, or stand fairer for the HEART OF THE HUNT?

He advanc'd then to my bedside, and whilst he faltered out his message, I could observe his colour rise, and his eyes lighten with joy, in seeing me in a situation as favourable to his loosest wishes, as if he had bespoke the play.

I smiled, and put out my hand towards him, which he kneeled down to (a politeness taught him by love alone, that great master of it) and greedily kiss'd. After exchanging a few confused questions and answers, I ask'd him if he could come to bed to me, for the little time I could venture to detain him. This was like asking a person, dying with hunger, to feast upon the dish on earth the most to his palate. Accordingly, without further reflection, his clothes were off in an instant; when, blushing still more at this new liberty, he got under the bedclothes I held up to receive him, and was now in bed with a woman for the first time in his life.

Here began the usual tender preliminaries, as delicious, perhaps, as the crowning act of enjoyment itself; which they often beget an impatience of, that makes pleasure destructive of itself, by hurrying on the final period, and closing that scene of bliss, in which the actors are generally too well pleas'd with their parts, not to wish them an eternity of duration.

When he had sufficiently graduated his advances towards the main point, by toying, kissing, clipping, feeling my breasts, now round and plump, feeling that part of me I might call a furnace-mouth, from the prodigious intense heat his fiery touches had rekindled there, my young sportsman, embolden'd by every freedom he could wish, wantonly takes my hand, and carries it to that enormous machine of his, that stood with a stiffness! a hardness! an upward bent of erection! and which, together, with its bottom dependance, the inestimable bulse of lady's jewels, formed a grand show out of goods indeed! Then its dimensions, mocking either grasp or span, almost renew'd my terrors.

I could not conceive how, or by what means I could take, or put such a bulk out of sight. I stroked it gently, on which the

Nanny blushes, when I woo her,
And with kindly chiding eyes,
Faintly says, I shall undo her,
Faintly, O forbear, she cries.

But her breasts while I am pressing,
While to her's my lips I join;
Warmed she seems to taste the
*   blessing,*
And her kisses answer mine.

Undebauched by rules of honour,
Innocence, with nature, charms;
One bids, gently push me from her,
T'other take me in her arms.

NANNY BLUSHES
MATTHEW PRIOR (1664–1721)

BELOW An illustration from the 1784 French edition of *Fanny Hill*, entitled 'Woman of Pleasur or Fille de Joye'. The drawing by Antoine Borel was engraved by F. R. Elluin.

mutinous rogue seemed to swell, and gather a new degree of fierceness and insolence; so that finding it grew not to be trifled with any longer, I prepar'd for rubbers in good earnest.

Slipping then a pillow under me, that I might give time the fairest play, I guided officiously with my hand this furious battering ram, whose ruby head, presenting nearest the resemblance of a heart, I applied to its proper mark, which lay as finely elevated as we could wish; my hips being borne up, and my thighs at their utmost extension, the gleamy warmth that shot from it, made him feel that he was at the mouth of the indraught, and driving foreright, the powerfully divided lips of that pleasure-thirsty channel receiv'd him. He hesitated a little; then, settled well in the passage, he made his way up the straits of it, with a difficulty nothing more than pleasing, widening as he went, so as to distend and smooth each soft furrow: our pleasure increasing deliciously, in proportion as our points of mutual touch increas'd in that so vital part of me in which I had now taken him, all indriven, and completely sheathed; and which, crammed as it was, stretched, splitting ripe, gave it so gratefully straight an accommodation! so strict a fold! a suction so fierce! that gave and took unutterable delight. We had now reach'd the closest point of union; but when he backened to come on the fiercer, as if I had been actuated by a fear of losing him, in the heights of my fury, I twisted my legs round his naked loins, the flesh of which, so firm, so springy to the touch, quiver'd again under the pressure; and now I had him every way encircled and begirt; and having drawn him home to me, I kept him fast there, as if I had sought to unite bodies with him at that point. This bred a pause of action, a pleasure stop, whilst that delicate glutton, my nethermouth, as full as it could hold, kept palating, with exquisite relish, the morsel that so deliciously engorged it. But nature could not long endure a pleasure that so highly provoked without satisfying it: pursuing then its darling end, the battery recommenc'd with redoubled exertion; nor lay I inactive on my side, but encountring him with all the impetuosity of motion I was mistress of. The downy cloth of our meeting mounts was now of real use to break the violence of the tilt; and soon, too soon indeed! the highwrought agitation, the sweet urgency of this to-and-fro friction, raised the titillation on me to its height; so that finding myself on the point of going, and loathe to leave the tender partner of my joys behind me, I employed all the forwarding motions and arts my experience suggested to me, to promote his keeping me company to our journey's end. I not only then tighten'd the pleasure-girth round my restless inmate, by a secret spring of friction and compression that obeys the will in those parts, but stole my hand softly to that store bag of nature's prime sweets, which is so pleasingly attach'd to its conduit pipe, from which we receive them: there feeling, and most gently indeed, squeezing those tender globular reservoirs, the magic touch took instant effect, quicken'd, and brought on upon the spur the symptoms of that sweet agony, the melting moment of dissolution, when pleasure dies by pleasure, and the mysterious engine of it overcomes the titillation it has rais'd in those parts, by

BELOW Another illustration from the 1784 French edition of *Fanny Hill*, drawing by Antoine Borel engraved by F. R. Elluin.

plying them with the stream of a warm liquid, that is itself the highest of all titillations, and which they thirstily express and draw in like the hot-natured leech, which to cool itself, tenaciously attracts all the moisture within its sphere of exsuction. Chiming then to me, with exquisite consent, as I melted away, his oily balsamic injection, mixing deliciously with the sluices in flow from me, sheath'd and blunted all the stings of pleasure, it flung us into an ecstasy that extended us fainting, breathless, entranced.

The sexual episodes in *Fanny Hill* are – despite the flowery language in which they are described – both realistic and nicely observed. We can surmise that some of Cleland's financial problems may have resulted from spending a good deal of time in the company of ladies of the same profession as his heroine. By the simple device of casting Fanny as 'a lady of pleasure' the author is able to describe a large number and variety of sexual encounters,

BELOW *Nature's pleasures*, a watercolour attributed to the German artist Johann Heinrich Romberg (1763–1840).

while retaining a sympathetic heroine who inhabits the real world. And instead of striving for the impression of movement in the narrative by piling excess upon excess (as in *Satyra Sotadica*) Fanny keeps her very human failings within human bounds and is allowed to progress through the novel and out into marriage and happiness at the end – which by that time is just what we want for her. Before finding true love, however, Fanny is obliged to practise her profession. This civilized bathing party is one of her less arduous engagements, even allowing her time to observe her friend Emily in action:

There, setting her on his knee, and gliding one hand over the surface of that smooth polish'd snow-white skin of hers, which now

RIGHT and OPPOSITE Watercolours attributed to the German artist Johann Heinrich Romberg (1763–1840).

doubly shone with a dew-bright lustre, and presented to the touch something like what one would imagine of animated ivory, especially in those ruby-nippled globes, which the touch is so fond of and delights to make love to, with the other he was lusciously exploring the sweet secret of nature, in order to make room for a stately piece of machinery, that stood uprear'd, between her thighs, as she continued sitting on his lap, and pressed hard for instant admission, which the tender Emily, in a fit of humour, deliciously protracted, affecting to decline and elude the very pleasure she sigh'd for, but in a style of waywardness so prettily put on, and managed, as to render it ten times more poignant; then her eyes, all amidst the softest dying languishment, express'd at once a mock denial and extreme desire, whilst her sweetness was zested with a coyness so pleasingly

In a wife I would desire
What in whores is always found –
The lineaments of gratified desire.

WILLIAM BLAKE (1757–1827)

provoking, her moods of keeping him off were so attractive, that they redoubled the impetuous rage with which he cover'd her with kisses.

Thus Emily, who knew no art but that which nature itself, in favour of her principal end, pleasure, had inspir'd her with, the art of yielding, coy'd it indeed, but coy'd it to the purpose; for with all her straining, her wrestling, and striving to break from the clasp of his arms, she was so far wiser yet than to mean it, that in her struggles, it was visible she aim'd at nothing more than multiplying points of touch with him, and drawing yet closer the folds that held them everywhere entwined, like two tendrils of a vine intercurling together; so that the same effect, as when Louisa strove in good earnest to disengage from the idiot, was now produced by different motives.

Meanwhile, their emersion out of the cold water had caused a general glow, a tender suffusion of heighten'd carnation over their bodies, both equally white and smooth-skinned, so that as their limbs were thus amorously interwoven, in sweet confusion, it was scarce possible to distinguish who they respectively belonged to, but for the brawnier, bolder muscles of the stronger sex.

In a little time, however, the champion was fairly in with her, and had tied at all points the true lover's knot; when now, adieu all the little refinements of a finessed reluctance;

BELOW *The Hayloft*, a watercolour by an unknown artist, French, twentieth century.

adieu the friendly feint! She was presently driven forcibly out of the power of using any art; and indeed, what art must not give way, when nature, corresponding with her assailant, invaded in the heart of her capital and carried by storm, lay at the mercy of the proud conqueror, who had made his entry triumphantly and completely? Soon, however, to become a tributary: for the engagement growing hotter and hotter, at close quarters, she presently brought him to the pass of paying down the dear debt to nature; which she had no sooner collected in, but, like a duel-list who has laid his antagonist at his feet, when he has himself received a mortal wound, Emily had scarce time to plume herself upon her victory, but, shot with the same discharge, she, in a loud expiring sigh, in the closure of her whole frame, gave mani-fest signs that all was as it should be.

For my part, I had not with the calmest patience stood in the water all this time to view this warm action. I lean'd tenderly on my gallant, and at the close of it, seem'd to ask him with my eyes what he thought of it; but he, more eager to satisfy me by his actions than by words or looks, as we shoal'd the water towards the shore, shewed me the staff of love so intensely set up, that had not even charity beginning at home in this case, urged me to our mutual relief, it would have been cruel indeed to have suf-fered the youth to burst with straining, when the remedy was so obvious and so near at hand.

Accordingly we took to a bench, whilst Emily and her spark, who belonged it seems to the sea, stood at the sideboard, drink-ing to our good voyage; for, as the last observ'd, we were well under weigh, with a fair wind up channel, and full-freighted; nor indeed were we long before we finished our trip to Cythera, and unloaded in the old haven; but, as the circumstances did not admit of much variation, I shall spare you the description.

Before leaving *Fanny Hill* it is interesting to take a look at two paragraphs included in the second volume of the first edition, pub-lished in 1749, but expurgated from all subsequent editions of the work for centuries, even from the version which was prosecuted in 1964. This is the notorious homosexual encounter which Fanny observes in an inn on the way to Hampton Court. The homophobic outburst which follows the missing paragraphs has always been a surprising blemish in an otherwise tolerant book. Yet it is true to character. And in condemning the 'infamous passion' of the 'male-misses' whom she finds 'scarce less execrable than ridiculous in their monstrous inconsistence, of loathing and condemning women, and all at the same time apeing their manners', Fanny displays an all-too-common prejudice. Here is the scene which sparked a moral tirade from a prostitute who has bored a hole in a partition with a bodkin in order to spy on her fellow guests!

 . . . Presently the eldest unbutton'd the other's breeches, and removing the linen barrier, brought out to view a white shaft, middle sized, and scarce fledg'd, when after handling and playing

BELOW Another illustration from the 1784 French edition of *Fanny Hill*, drawing by Antoine Borel engraved by F. R. Elluin.

with it a little, with other dalliance, all receiv'd by the boy without other opposition than certain wayward counesses, ten times
more alluring than repulsive, he got him to turn round, with his
face from him, to a chair that stood hard by; when knowing, I
suppose, his office, the Ganymede now obsequiously lean'd his
head against the back of it, and projecting his body, made a fair
mark, still covered with his shirt, as he thus stood in a side view
to me, but fronting his companion, who presently unmasking his
battery, produc'd an engine that certainly deserved to be put to a
better use, and very fit to confirm me in my disbelief of the possibility of things being push'd to odious extremities, which I had
built on the disproportion of parts; but this disbelief I was now to
be cured of, as by my consent all young men should likewise be,
that their innocence may not be betray'd into such snares, for
want of knowing the extent of their danger: for nothing is more
certain than that ignorance of a vice is by no means a guard
against it.

Slipping, then, aside the young lad's shirt, and tucking it up

under his cloaths behind, he shewed to the open air those globular fleshy eminences that compose the Mount Pleasants of Rome,
and which now, with all the narrow vale that intersects them,
stood displayed and exposed to his attack; nor could I without a
shudder behold the dispositions he made for it. First, then,
moistening well with spittle his instrument, obviously to make it
glib, he pointed, he introduced it, as I could plainly discern, not
only from its direction and my losing sight of it, but by the
writhing, twisting and soft murmur'd complaints of the young
sufferer; but at length, the first straights of entrance being pretty
well got through, every thing seem'd to move and go pretty cur-
rently on, as on a carpet road, without much rub or resistance;
and now, passing one hand round his minion's hips, he got hold
of his red-topt ivory toy, that stood perfectly stiff, and shewed,
that if he was like his mother behind, he was like his father
before; this he diverted himself with, whilst, with the other he
wanton'd with his hair, and leaning forward over his back, drew
his face, from which the boy shook the loose curls that fell over
it, in the posture he stood him in, and brought him towards his,
so as to receive a long-breathed kiss; after which, renewing his
driving, and thus continuing to harass his rear, the height of the
fit came on with its usual symtons . . .

All I ask of Thee, Lord
Is to be a drinker and a fornicator,
An unbeliever and a sodomite,
And then to die
And then to die very suddenly.

ATTRIBUTED TO CLAUDE DE CHAUVIGNY
(SEVENTEENTH CENTURY)

––––––––––– ◊ –––––––––––

Prisoners have no choice but to dream: waking and sleeping
they must inhabit their own internal landscape. Deprived of
contact, they find their dreams are often sexually charged;
if they can give form to those dreams, that writing becomes a kind
of sexual act in itself. Honoré Gabriel Riquetti, Comte de
Mirabeau (1749–91), inhabited several famous prisons – the Ile de
Ré; Château d'If; Fort de Joux; and the Château de Vincennes –
and while there he produced some famous erotica. Mirabeau's
voice is the last great shout of the libertine soul in Europe. His
erotica gave him a means of sexual expression, but it is also full of
anger and is therefore uncompromising and powerful stuff. Here
is an example of Mirabeau's style: a pitiless description of a
prolonged sexual encounter between a society lady and a gigolo,
from *Ma Conversion*.

A few days later, I run into Madame de Confroid ['cold cunt'],
whom I have had before and who I heard had come into some
money. She is petite with a rather nice figure, but there is nothing striking about her face. Although her love grotto is as cold as
an icy cavern, she does have a remarkable and extraordinary talent for sucking pricks.
  I have never come across any woman even remotely approaching her skill in this art. In my time, I have permitted myself to
be fellated by members of the third sex who certainly are no
amateurs, but Confroid puts the best of them to shame.
  At her coquettish glance, I follow her home where we get into
bed. There she sucks me continually for two hours without taking

the organ out of her mouth. While she drains me, she masturbates and I fondle her pointed breasts, which is about all I can
do.

That is the only way she can get pleasure – sucking a man and
playing with herself at the same time. It takes her at least an
hour at this activity before she can come to a climax.

I have had normal intercourse with her in every conceivable
position without producing any reaction. Once I brought two of
my friends with me and we had her simultaneously in all three
orifices, but when it was over, she was still as motionless as a
rock.

There is nobody like her to get my prick standing up. First she
grazes it with her delicate fingers, and then she breathes on it.

OPPOSITE *The Broken Fan*, French
eighteenth-century colour print.
LEFT *Midday*, after Pierre-Antoine
Baudoin by Emmanuel de Ghendt
(1738–1815). It is interesting to
speculate which particular erotic
book has excited the imagination
of the Rococo lady in this
copperplate engraving.

Her lips wander over my stomach and groin. She nuzzles her nose
in my pubic hair, gets close to my sex, teases it with her blowing,
and finally gives it a fugitive kiss. She is driving me out of my
mind.

When she sees how my prick is throbbing, she knows the precise spot where I am most sensitive. She can judge perfectly the
rise of my seminal fluid, for she stops just when I am ready to
explode.

After letting it calm down for several moments, her mouth
grazes the gland again. She gives it little darts with her tongue.
Then her mouth is wide open to take each of my testicles in turn.

Then she quickly turns her attention back to my virility, running her tongue up and down it, and bestowing little kisses on it.
I am trembling through and through and I feel the sperm rising

RIGHT Cupid looks on nervously at the erotic gymnastics he has instigated in this eighteenth-century sepia print. Unable to join the action, the other spectator has decided to take matters into her own hands.

like the mercury in a thermometer on a hot day.

The vixen senses it. She swallows the tip of my prick for just a moment before spitting it out. A second later I would have come. My prick is in agony from this abortive frustrating pleasure, but it is an agony that I could endure forever.

All this time she is masturbating, violently. Furiously her busy fingers open the lips of her cunt as wide as possible. She squashes her clitoris that springs up red and hard and then scratches it with her fingernails.

Because the gland has quietened down, Confroid renews her oral caresses, inserting it in her mouth down to the very bottom of her throat. Again she rejects it just before the supreme moment to pay attention to her own pleasure. Finally, she is becoming aroused.

This succession of suctions sends delicious shivers running up and down my spine. They are a series of voluptuous vibrations which make me shudder like a palsy sufferer. I hear the rattles in my throat.

This time, I think she has made up her mind. The gland is all the way in her mouth. The tip is touching her tonsils while her tongue is all over it.

I can't stand it any more . . . Now . . . I'm coming.

But again the same confounded frustration. With her extraordinary prescience, she ceases her activities a fraction of a second before my ejaculation.

I remain in that suspended state for I don't know how long. I twitch exquisitely with my nerves taut from the interrupted voluptuousness. It lasts interminably.

During one of the pauses, Confroid masturbates even more vigorously. She passes her thigh on my breast so that the cunt with the busy finger in it is only a few inches from my eyes.

She once told me that she had been playing with herself since she was four years old and has been doing it three or four hours every day since then.

While she is thus engaged with herself, I feel the urge to return the homage she pays my sexuality, but she does not let me, saying it would ruin her pleasure. I content myself by stroking her bottom and sticking my finger in her rear aperture.

Waves of passion rush through my nerves, muscles and veins. My entire body is on fire. I fidget and quiver like a woman in heat. I think my organ is going to expire from the raptures.

Suddenly, my whole being is concentrated in a wild torrent rushing across my stomach and through my prick like an unleashed wild river. It is a marvellous fireworks exploding in a thousand spangles that her mouth avidly gulps down. . . .

Indefatigably, Confroid continues to suck while she thrusts her fingers in her cunt more enthusiastically than ever. I see her wrist and fingers dance in a mad twirl. Her irritated hardened clitoris is a purplish blue.

Again I ejaculate. Two times, three times. And each sensation is more rapturous and more grievous. She never ceases her implacable sucking. I clench my teeth in order not to scream.

I no longer have any control over myself. Again I spurt. Writhing in delirious spasms, I think I am going out of my mind. Now pleasure and pain are inextricably blended, and I no longer know if I ejaculate or not. Finally, I am out of sperm.

Confroid is now near the zenith. Her body throbs, her bosom heaves, and her thighs open and close spasmodically.

Now is the time. Brutally I insert one hand in her cunt and the other in her rear – three fingers in the vagina and two in the anus.

She gives a convulsive jolt. Finally releasing my lifeless sex, she gives a yelp like a mortally wounded animal. Her body becomes taut, arches, relaxes . . . and collapses. Her screech of rapture is muted and prolonged.

Confroid has reached the climax.

When I take my leave of her, she, knowing my insatiable thirst and need for money, gives me a purse containing a hundred louis.

The 'libertine of quality' (the title of another of his works) and hero of the French Revolution spared no one with the salvoes he fired into contemporary society. In another extract from *Ma Conversion*, Mirabeau's *alter ego* spies upon two young nuns in the cell they inhabit.

The door opened and in stepped Angela, one of the more delicious of the novices, who was warmly welcomed with a kiss.
'What lovely hair you have,' Stephanie remarked.
'And how about yours, Sister Stephanie?'

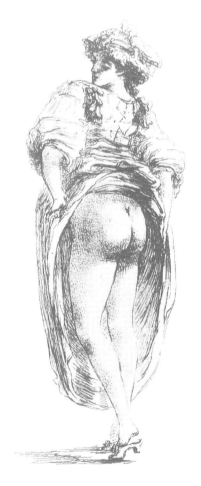

OPPOSITE and BELOW Etchings by Denon Vivant, c. 1790.

OPPOSITE Nuns have featured in both the literary and visual erotica of the West since the Middle Ages. The eighteenth century saw the appearance of politically motivated anti-religious erotica such as Voltaire's *La pucelle d'Orléans* (1762), but this watercolour by C. Bernard (1870) draws on the much older tradition deeply rooted in male sexual fantasies.

*So, when my days of impotence
    approach,
And I'm by pox and wine's unlucky
    chance
Forced from the pleasing billows of
    debauch
On the dull shore of lazy temperance,*

*I'll tell of whores attacked, their lords
    at home;
Bawds' quarters beaten up, and
    fortress won;
Windows demolished, watches
    overcome;
And handsome ills by my contrivance
    done.*

*Nor shall our love-fits, Chloris, be
    forgot,
When each the well-looked linkboy
    strove t'enjoy.
And the best kiss was the deciding lot
Whether the boy fucked you, or I the
    boy.*

FROM *THE DISABLED DEBAUCHEE*
JOHN WILMOT, EARL OF ROCHESTER
(1647–80)

'I am rather vain about it.'

'But I thought when you took your vows, you had to have your head shaved.'

'Yes, you do. But if you get on the good side of the Mother Superior, she gives you permission to let it grow and fix it any way you like. It goes without saying that you can't let it show. Certain nuns would understand these special marks of favour.'

'Show me your hair,' Angela demanded.

Without any hesitation, the woman removed her wimple, and a cascade of tresses tumbled down over her shoulders. Silky curls, elegant waves fell on the white starched collar that formed a part of her costume.

After a gasp of unfeigned admiration, Angela asked permission to brush it.

The girl sat down facing the sister and began to brush the hair with measured strokes. Suddenly, Stephanie kissed Angela's lips with her moist mouth. At first, the girl shrank back but then surrendered her lips and tongue. In a trice her body was embraced. I could see that her sex was being ignited. The sensation must have become even more unbearable when Stephanie caressed the yearning breasts through the blouse. Then, baring them, she took the nipples in her mouth and sucked them slowly and avidly.

'I think I have wet myself,' Angela murmured.

Finally, Sister Stephanie disrobed, exhibiting her nude body with arrogance and hauteur. She possessed opulent round breasts, a thick fleece, smooth thighs, and delicious buttocks.

With deft nimble hands, she quickly divested the girl of her clothing, pushed her back on the bed and began to fondle her ardently.

I could see that Angela had lost touch with reality and I surmised that this was the first time she was experiencing true voluptuousness. Her twitches soon became violent convulsions.

She sank back in a faint from the force of the sensations. But she recovered under the tingling caresses that the sister was bestowing between her open thighs with her agile darting tongue. Then I heard the enamoured sighs, the squeals of joy, and the prolonged moans of pleasure which announced the arrival of the supreme sensation.

Mirabeau spent his last years respectably, as the much-loved Deputy for Aix-en-Provence. The passions he had once channelled into the writing of illicit erotica found expression in public oratory, and he died a popular hero.

Libertinism did not long outlive the eighteenth century. The idea that an individual could be devoted entirely to pleasure, unrestricted by moral laws, was essentially aristocratic. 'Madame Guillotine' played her part in trimming the loose ends of the old order, but it was less gruesome machines which really marked the finish. The new Railway Age was about efficiency and straight lines: libertinism detested the straight and narrow, its devotees enjoyed being off the rails.

PART TWO

Dreams of empire

Once the political aftershocks from the upheavals at the end of the eighteenth century had subsided, the nineteenth century could concentrate on trade and imperial expansion. Powerful new printing presses, trains and eventually steamships rushed erotica to an expanding bourgeois market, which was as eager to consume sex as it was everything else. An early piece of imperial erotica was a slightly absurd book entitled *The Lustful Turk*, published in 1828. Although it contains some cruel and unpleasant material, it is all so over the top that it has a certain period charm. After the intrepid Emily Barlow finally falls for her abductor the wicked Dey of Algiers – a kind of fierce prototype for Rudolph Valentino's Sheikh – she is rather badly let down by her chum and fellow captive: 'The first object that met my eyes was a naked female, half reclining on a table, and the Dey with his noble shaft plunged up to the hilt in her. . . . Imagine to yourself . . . what must have been my emotions on my beholding in his arms my friend Silvia!'

The Dey eventually suffers a fate appropriate to his crimes when a spirited Greek girl – baulking at one of his more exotic sexual ideas – delivers the unkindest cut of all. It was of course only four years since the 'mad and bad' Lord Byron had died at Missolonghi, and the popular imagination was filled with the heroic struggle of the Greeks against the Turks in their War of Independence. The book was even said to have been written by a Greek: a theory borne out by the pickling of the Dey's testicles in glass jars after his emasculation, in a manner normally reserved for Kalamata olives. This extract is typical of the rather overheated style:

> . . . After refreshing myself with a few hours' rest, I returned to my captive with recruited strength for the night's soft enjoyment. The smile of welcome was on her lovely countenance; she was dressed from a wardrobe I had pointed out to her, containing everything fit for her sex. With grateful pleasure I instantly perceived that her toilet had not been made for the mere purpose of covering her person, but every attention had been paid in setting off her numerous charms. The most care had been given to the disposing of her hair, whilst the lawn which covered her broad voluptuous breasts was so temptingly disposed that it was

impossible to look on her without burning desire. She sprang off the couch to meet me; for a moment I held her from me in an ecstasy of astonishment, then drawing her to my bosom, planted on her lips a kiss so long and so thrilling, it was some moments ere we recovered from its effects. My passions were instantly in a blaze. I carried her to the side of the couch, placed her on it, and while sucking her delicious lips, uncovered her neck and breasts, then seizing her legs lifted them up, and threw up her clothes. A dissolving sentiment struggled with my more amorous desires. I stooped down to examine the sight! Every part of her body was ivory whiteness, everything charming; the white interspersed with small blue veins showed the transparency of the skin whilst the darkness of the hair, softer than velvet, formed most beautiful shades, making a delicious contrast with the vermilion lips of her new-stretched love sheath. . . .

ABOVE *The Harem* by the great London caricaturist Thomas Rowlandson (1756–1827). Rowlandson's art epitomizes the uniquely English tradition of satire: moral and idealistic at heart, but taking a ribald, almost affectionate delight in detailing the very sins and excesses it mocks and denounces.

ABOVE *In the bathhouse*, painted in gouache on card, French school.

Tired of admiring without enjoyment, I carried my mouth and hand to everything before me, until I could no longer bear myself. Raising myself from my sloping position, I extended her thighs to the utmost, and placed myself standing between them, letting loose my rod of Aaron, which was no sooner at liberty but it flew with the same impetuosity with which a tree straightens itself when the cord that keeps it bent towards the ground comes to be cut; with my right hand I directed it towards the pouting slit, the head was soon in; laying myself down on her, I drew her lips to mine; again I thrust, I entered. Another thrust buried it deeper; she closed her eyes, but tenderly squeezed me to her bosom; again I pushed – her soft lips rewarded me. Another shove caused her to sigh deliciously – another push made our junction complete. I scarcely knew what I was about, everything now was in active exertion, tongues, lips, bellies, arms, thighs, legs, bottoms, every part in voluptuous motion until our spirits completely abandoned every part of our bodies to convey themselves into the place where pleasure reigned with so furious but still with so delicious a sentiment. I dissolved myself into her at the very moment Nature had caused her to give down her tribute to the intoxicating joy. My lovely prey soon came to herself, but it was only to invite me by her numberless charms to plunge her into the same condition. She passed her arms round my neck and sucked my lips with dovelike kisses. I opened my eyes and fixed them on hers; they were filled with dissolving languor; I moved within her, her eyes closed instantly. The tender squeeze of her love-sheath round my instrument satisfied me as to the state she was in. Again I thrust. 'Ah!' she sighed. 'The pleasure suffocates me – I die! – ah, me.' I thrust furiously; her limbs gradually stiffened, she gave one more movement to the fierce thrusts made into her organ; we both discharged together.

Our next excursion explores *My Secret Life*, that rarest of all documents – a genuine erotic memoir which spares no one, least of all the author. This vast book – eleven volumes and more than 2,500 sexual encounters – certainly passes George Orwell's test that 'autobiography is only to be trusted when it reveals something disgraceful'. *My Secret Life* is disgraceful from beginning to end; it is disgraceful in scope, in content, in expression (even in spelling) – but it is also one of the most important documents to survive from the Victorian era. The reason that the veracity of this legendary autobiography is so often discussed is complicated. Most of those who have read *My Secret Life* in its entirety feel that it is as true as any autobiography can be. But it is the series of extraordinary coincidences which led to the creation of the work that seem 'unbelievable'. Let us look at the facts, if facts they are. 'Walter', as the unknown author calls himself, was born in about 1825. His life therefore coincided with the Victorian era: fortuitous but not unusual. Walter wrote a very long and detailed memoir about one aspect of his life: again, not unusual. So did Victorian clerics, botanists and others. Walter had a near-perfect photographic memory: very unusual, but there certainly are people with that gift. Walter was a sex maniac, not violent or cruel by the standards of his times, but voracious; he lived out his erotic fantasies tirelessly, and it is that obsession which he chose to write about. Can we believe in you, Walter? Should we? Readers must judge for themselves if *My Secret Life* is fact or fantasy. The orgy described in the following extract would have occurred in the early 1850s. Amateur detectives might like to see if a Lord A, late of the Guards, lived in what must be Bolton Street off Piccadilly at that time . . .

An intimate friend of Fred's was Lord A***, he lived with a lady who was called Lady A***. I don't think she had been gay [i.e. a

LEFT A coloured daguerreotype from the studio of the French photographer Bruno Braquehais, c. 1858. The fact that he could not speak, and therefore could not communicate with his models, gives his nude studies a uniquely intimate, almost voyeuristic quality. The colourist was the daughter of the photographer Alexis Gouin, and later became Mrs Braquehais.

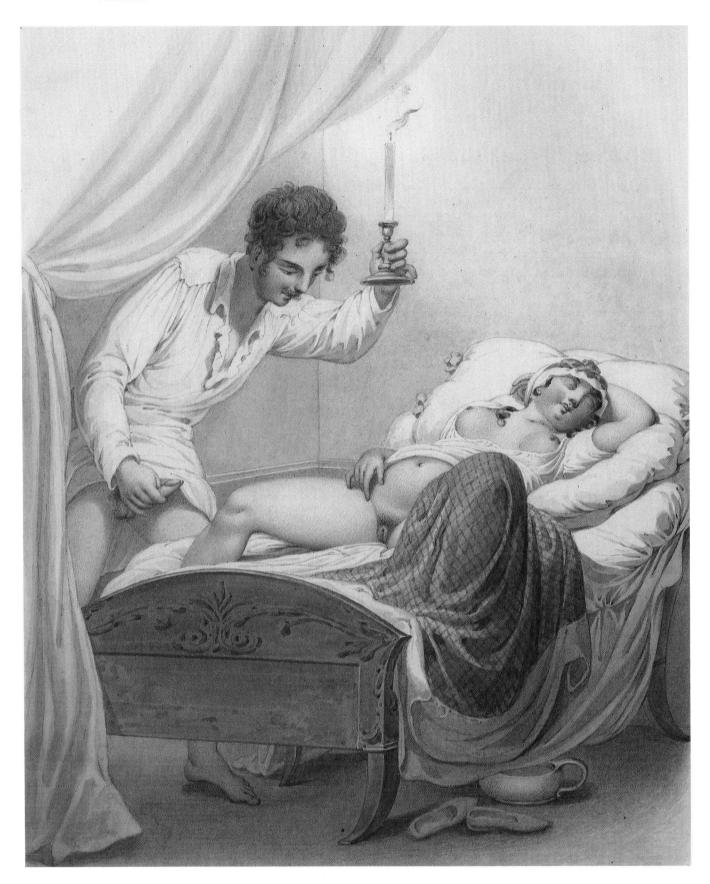

prostitute], and in that respect resembled Laura and Mabel. The three women were much together. We often saw Lord A***, and all became friends. Lord A*** was not very true to his lady. He lived in B*t*n Street, where he had at that time the whole of a handsomely furnished house, but only could half occupy it. His indoor servants were a middle-aged woman who cooked, a maid who was her niece, and his valet, who waited at table as well. A woman who did not sleep in the house came daily. He had grooms and a coachman, but not in the house. Lord A*** had quarrelled with his father. He had been in the Guards, and drank very freely. . . .

On the night in question our conversation got to open voluptuousness. Fred and Lord A*** went in for it, Mabel laughed, Laura hished and hished, said she would leave, but at last gave way, as did Lady A***; then we men got to lewdness. Whenever any sensuous allusion was made, my eyes sought Laura's, hers seeking mine; we were both thinking of the quiet and quick fuck we had with Mabel snoring by our side. We compared our thoughts on the night, but at a future day.

Just at that time a case filled the public journals. It was a charge of rape on a married woman, against a man lodging in the same house. She was the wife of a printer on the staff of a daily paper, who came home extremely late; she always went to bed leaving her door unlocked, so that her husband might get in directly he came home. The lodger was a friend of her husband's, and knew the custom of leaving the door unlocked, – in fact he was a fellow printer.

She awakened in the night with the man between her thighs – had opened them readily, thinking it was her husband. It appears to have been her habit, and such her husband's custom on returning home, or so she said. The lodger had actually all but finished his fuck, before she awakened sufficiently to find out that it was not the legitimate prick which was probing her. Then she alarmed the house, and gave the man in charge for committing a rape. The papers delicately hinted that the operation was complete before the woman discovered the mistake, – but of course it left much to the reader's imagination.

Fred read this aloud. I knew more, for the counsel of the prisoner was my intimate friend. He had told me that the prisoner had had her twice, that she had spent with him; that he had often said he meant to go in, and have her, that she had dared him to do it, and that she only made a row when she thought she heard her husband at the door on the landing, although it was two hours before his usual time of return. His prick was in her when she began her outcry.

With laughter and smutty allusions we discussed the case. 'Absurd,' said Laura, 'she must have known it was not her husband.' 'Why?' 'Why because – ', and Laura stopped. 'If you were asleep, and suddenly felt a man on you of about my

OPPOSITE and BELOW *Candlelight* and *Learning by example*, watercolours by Georg Emmanuel Opitz (1775–1841).

size, and his prick up you, very likely you would not tell if it were mine or not,' said Fred. Laura threw an apple at his head. Decency was banished from that moment, a spade was called a spade, and unveiled baudiness reigned.

'I should know if it were not you,' said Lady A*** looking at Lord A***. 'How?' 'Ah! I should, – should you not know another woman from Laura, if you got into bed with two women in the dark?' said she to Fred. 'I am not sure for the moment if with a woman just for size, and as much hair on her cunt,' said he. 'I tell you what Fred, I won't have it,' said Laura ill-tempered, 'talk about someone else, I won't have beastly talk about me.' 'I'll bet,' said I, 'that if the ladies were to feel our pricks in the dark, they would not tell whose they each had hold of.' Roars of laughter followed. 'I should like to try,' said Mabel. 'So should I,' said another. 'Would you know, if you felt us?' said one woman. 'If I felt all your cunts in the dark, I'll bet I should know Marie's,' said Lord A***. 'That is, if you felt all round and about,' said Fred, 'but not if she opened her legs, and you only felt the notch.' 'I think I should.' 'Why? – Is she different from others?' Lord A*** was going to say something, when Marie told him to shut up.

So we went on, the men in lascivious language, the women in more disguised terms, discussing the probabilities of distinguishing cunts or pricks by a simple feel in the dark. Each remark caused roars of laughter, the women whispered to each other, and laughed at their own sayings. Lewdness had seized us all, the women's eyes were brilliant with voluptuous desire. More wine was drunk. 'Call it by its proper name,' said Lord A*** when Marie remarked that a woman must know her own man's thing. 'Prick then.' 'I will bet five pounds that Mabel would not guess my prick in the dark, if she felt all of us,' said I. 'And I'll bet,' said another. 'Shall we try?' said Fred. 'Yes,' said Mabel, more fuddled than the rest. Baudier and baudier, we talked, laughed, and drank, and at length set to work to make rules for trying, all talking at once.

One proposed one way, one another. 'I can't tell unless I feel balls as well,' said a woman. 'Will they be stiff when we feel?' said another. 'Mine will,' said Fred, 'it's stiff already.' 'So is mine,' added I. . . .

After lewed squabbles we arranged that each man was to give the woman if she guessed the prick right, ten pounds; the men were to be naked, the women to feel all the men's cocks, and give a card to him whose prick she thought she knew. The room was to be dark. No man was to speak, or give any indication by laughing, coughing, or any other way, under penalty of paying all the bets. The women were to lose if they spoke, or gave indications of who they were.

I took three cards, and wrote the name of a lady on each of them. Then each lady took her card, and they went upstairs to the bedroom pell-mell and laughing. The women were to stand of a row in a certain order against a side of the room, we to follow in an order they did not know. They were to feel all pricks twice, each giving her card to the man at the second feel, if she knew the prick. We undressed to our shirts, took off our rings, so as to

OPPOSITE *The helping hand*, watercolour by Georg Emmanuel Opitz (1775–1841).

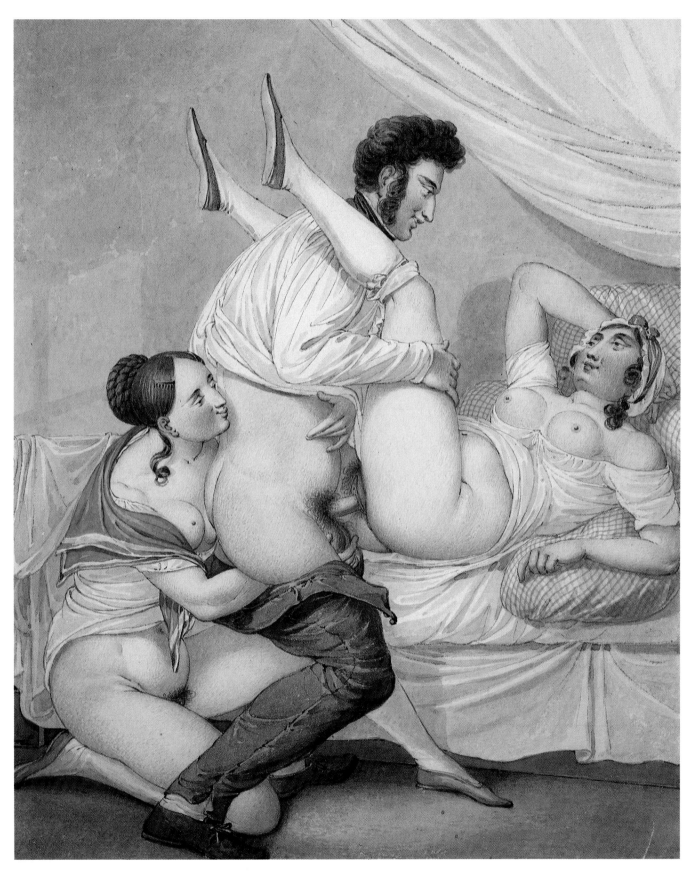

RIGHT To be confronted with an intimate nude photograph of a woman who lived during the Second Empire is in itself astonishing. But this daguerreotype by Louis Jules Duboscq-Soleil has another shock for us: there is a tradition that the model is Blanche d'Antigny, the real Nana, Emile Zola's 'golden fly'.

leave no indications, and in that condition entered the room. The dining room door we closed, there was no light on the first-floor lobby, nor in the bedroom, for we had put out the fire there. So holding each other by the shoulder, we entered, closed the door, and we were all in the room together in the dark.

We lifted our shirts, and closed on the women, each of whom in her turn felt our pricks. One felt mine as if she meant to pull it off. On the second feeling, we got somehow mixed, a slight tittering of women began, some one hished, and the tittering ceased. Two hands touched me at the same time, but one withdrew directly she touched the other's hand. A card was put into my hand, afterwards another card touched me, and was withdrawn. After waiting a minute I nudged the man next me. 'Have you all given cards?' shouted out the man. 'Yes,' shouted the three women at once. Then we all burst out laughing, and the men went downstairs, leaving the women all talking at once like Bedlam broke loose.

Looking at our cards, we found that each woman had guessed

rightly her man's prick; but we changed our cards, and called out to the women who came rushing down like mad. 'Not one of you has guessed right,' said I, 'you have all lost your bets.' 'I'll swear I'm right,' said Lady A***, 'it's Adolphus that I gave my card to.' This set us all questioning at once. 'What makes you so sure?' 'She says it's very long and thin,' said Mabel, 'and so it is.' 'Hold your tongue,' said Marie. 'I felt it,' said Mabel. 'They all seemed the same to me,' said Laura, 'and one of you pushed my hand away.' 'It was I,' said Fred, 'you wanted to feel too much, you nearly frigged me.' 'Oh! What a lie.' Then we told the truth, and that each woman had won, which caused much noisy satisfaction, then we had more wine, we men still with naked legs.

I have told all I can recollect with exactitude, but there was lots more said and done. Fred pulled up Lord A***'s shirt, his cock was not stiff. 'That's not as it was when I felt it,' said Mabel. 'You've guessed pricks, but for all that you would not know who fucked you in the dark.' 'We should,' cried out all the women. 'Let's try,' said Lord A***. 'All right,' said Mabel. 'We are not prostitutes,' said Laura. 'A little free fucking will be jolly, let's

BELOW His ability to draw out the personality of his sitters heightened the eroticism of Félix Jacques-Antoine Moulin's work. Early in his career this skill brought him into conflict with the authorities, who were unused to such personal nudes. Coloured daguerreotype, Paris, 1851–4.

take turns about all round,' said Fred. Then the room resounded with our laughter, all spoke baudily at once, every second, 'prick,' 'cunt,' 'fuck,' was heard from both men and women, – it was a perfect Babel of lasciviousness.

'I'll bet ten pounds a woman doesn't guess who fucks her,' said Lord A***. We echoed him. The women laughed, but led by Laura, refused, and squabbled. All wanted the bet to come off, but did not like to admit it. We had more champagne, the men put on their trowsers, we kissed all round, and talked over the way of deciding such a bet, the women got randier, one showed her leg to another, and at length all the women agreed to take part in the orgie. . . .

The women were to lie down in an order known to us, Lady A*** nearest to the door, and so on. There was to be absolute silence. Each man as he knelt between the woman's legs was to put a card with a number on it under her pillow. We men knew which number each had, the women were not to know which man was to have her, directly we had fucked we were to return, each woman was to produce her card, and guess who had been up her, they were to be in their chemises, we in our shirts. I never shall forget the looks of the women as they went upstairs to arrange

BELOW and OPPOSITE Anonymous French etchings, c. 1860. French sexual imports – books, art, even courtesans – were an established feature of London's underground life during the nineteenth century, with frequent references in *My Secret Life*.

themselves for the fucking, but think that they scarcely knew the rules of what they were to do.

The women undressed quickly enough, for we had scarcely had time to tie up our faces in napkins to prevent our whiskers being noticed (Lord A*** had none), before a voice shouted out, 'We are ready.' Then with shirts on only, up we men went. I only recollect kneeling down between Lady A***'s legs (we had agreed among ourselves how to change our women), giving a card, feeling a cunt, and putting my prick into it, then hearing the rustling of limbs, hard breathing, sighing, and moans of pleasure of the couples fucking fast and furiously; of my brain whirling, of a maddening sensuality delighting me as I clasped the buttocks of Lady A***, and fucked her.

We must have spent nearly all together, none when we compared after recollected more than his own performance. All were quiet. I was feeling round my prick which was still in Lady A***'s cunt, when a light flashed powerfully through the room. That devil Fred had risen, and lighted several lucifers, which then was done by dipping them in a bottle, – they were expensive. What a sight was disclosed at a glance!

All three women lay with chemises up to their navels, Lady

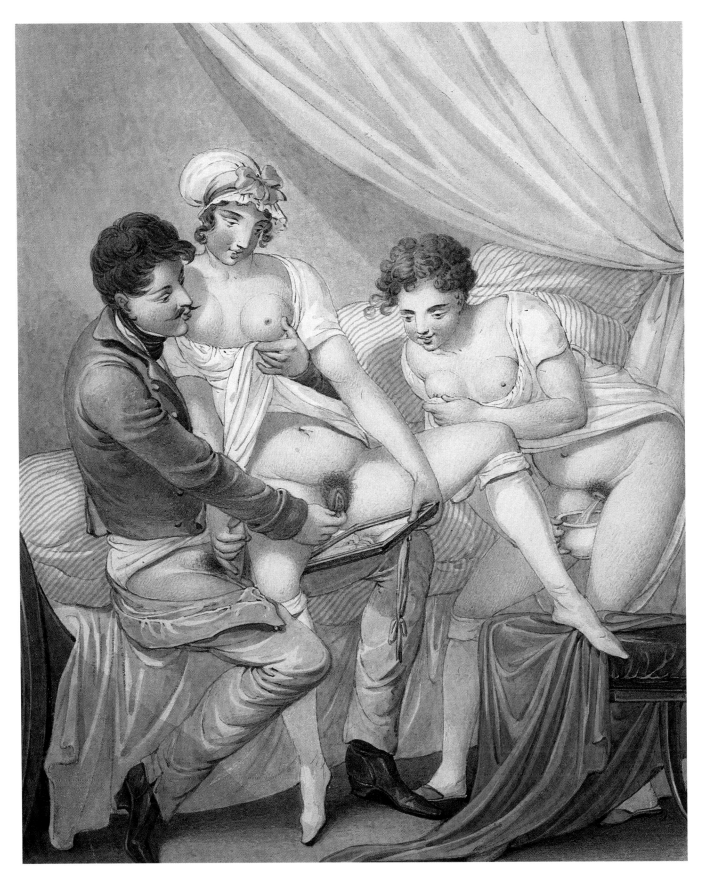

A*** on her back, I on the top of her (rising rapidly at the light). Next to her Mabel seemingly asleep with thighs wide open. Fred kneeling between them, holding the lighted matches, Laura on her back with open thighs, eyes closed, Lord A*** cuddling, but nearly all of her by her side, and his prick laying on her thigh. The women shrieked, and began pulling down their chemises. I swore at Fred, the women joined chorus. 'Most ungentlemanly,' said Laura, getting up. That got up Lord A***. Mabel lay still on her back as if ready to be stroked again. But all was said. In a minute the lucifers burnt out, and it was dark again. Scuffling up, we men went downstairs, leaving the women chattering. Soon after, down they came, looking screwed, lewed, and annoyed that the bets were off, and all chattering at once.

Mabel was quarrelsome. 'You,' said she, turning to Lady A***, 'said that your husband's thing was long and thin, you tried to mislead me in the bed, you wanted to make me lose.' They had evidently been discussing their men's pricks.

'So you have been telling how each of us fucks,' said Fred. Laura denied it. 'We did,' said Mabel. 'It's a lie, Mabel, if you say it again, I'll tell something more than you will like to hear about yourself.' Mabel retorted, Lady A*** chimed in. It was a Babel of quarrelsome lewed women, with their cunts full.

I feared a row, and that Mabel might after all know more about my having had Laura, the night we all three slept in the same bed, than I cared for; so I pacified them. Fred said we had better try again. Laura objected. 'Oh! Yes, Mrs. Modest,' said Mabel. 'When you found it was not Fred, why didn't you cry out?' 'I didn't know,' said Laura. 'Ah! Ah! the printer's wife,' we shouted, then more baudy talk, recriminations, and squabbling. Laura said she should go home, Fred said she might go by herself. Lord A***, who had half fallen asleep, said it was too late, and we had better stop. Some one said we could soon again make the beds comfortable in the upper rooms. 'That be damned,' said Fred, 'we will all sleep on the floor as they are now.' 'Free fucking forever,' said I. Laura said I was a blackguard, Mabel said she should like it, Lady A*** said she didn't care, if Adolphus didn't, Adolphus said any cunt would suit him. He was reeling drunk as he spoke.

All this time we were in shirts and chemises. One woman had thrown a shawl over her, one a petticoat, but their breasts flashed out, their arms were naked, their legs showing to their knees, the men were naked to their knees in their shirts. The scene was exciting, the women hadn't washed their cunts, Fred said so. Mabel asked him if he was sure of it. No, he would feel. Laura told him he must be drunk, and was a beast. 'Drunk?' said he, 'look here.' He turned a somersault, and stood on his hands and head, his heels against the wall, his back-side in the air, his prick and cods falling downwards over his belly, his shirt over his head. Lady A*** took up a bunch of grapes, and dashed it on his ballocks. Then we chased the women round the room, tried to feel them, and they us. It was like hell broke loose, till we agreed to sleep on the floor together, anyhow. . . .

To satisfy Laura, and keep up a sort of appearance, we had said we would only have our own women, who were again to lay in a

OPPOSITE *The looking-glass,* watercolour by Georg Emmanuel Opitz (1775–1841).

So I determined to write my private life freely as to fact, and in the spirit of the lustful acts done by me, or witnessed; it is written therefore with absolute truth and without any regard whatever for what the world calls decency.

FROM THE PREFACE TO *MY SECRET LIFE* 'WALTER'

certain order. Directly they had left the room, we agreed to change. A*** doggedly insisted on having Mabel, so I was to take Laura, and Fred Lady A***. It was such a lark. My prick was up Laura, when she cried, 'It's not you, Fred.' Then were simultaneous exclamations, 'I'm not Mabel,' – 'What a lovely cunt!' – 'Leave me alone,' – 'Feel my big prick,' – 'Damn, a cunt's a cunt,' hiccupped Lord A***. 'Oh! – ah!' – 'Ha! My love fuck, – My darling, oh!' – kiss, kiss, – spending, – 'aha!' – sighs of delight, – 'cunt', – 'fuck,' – 'Oh!' – 'Ah! Ah!' And I fell asleep on Laura amidst this.

Awake again. By my side a wet cunt, a heavy sleeper. Turning round, my legs met naked legs. I stretched out my hand, and felt a prick, perhaps Fred's, I don't know. Getting up, I felt my way, stumbling over legs to the wall to the furthest woman, and laid myself on her. 'Don't Adolphus, I'm so sleepy,' said she. The next instant we were fucking. Others awakened. 'Where are you?' said someone. Then all moved, one man swore, a hand felt my balls from behind. I was spending, and rolled off the lady, turning my bum to her. Then I touched Mabel, and put my hand to her cunt. A man dropped on her, and touched my hand with his prick. Ejaculations burst out on all sides, the couples were meeting again, then all was quiet, and the fucking done. Then all talked. All modesty was gone, both men and women told their sensations and wants. 'You fuck me, – Feel me, – No, I want so and so,' Laura as lewed as the rest.

Again awaking. A hand was feeling my prick. 'Is it you, Laura?' 'Yes.' I felt her cunt. 'Oh! Let me go and piddle.' But I turned on to her, and we fucked. 'How wet your cunt is.' 'No wonder.'

Again I awakened, someone got up, and fell down. 'Hulloa! Who is that?' 'I want to piss, and can't get up,' said Lord A*** in a drunken voice. Someone opened the door, a feeble light came across from the back-room, we helped him up and he stumbled along with us men to piss. Then he insisted on going downstairs. He could scarcely stand, so we helped him to the dining room, we lighted more candles, he swilled more wine, tumbled on to the sofa, where we left him drunk and snoring, and found him snoring the next morning with the hearth-rug over him. We two went back to the women. 'I've fucked all three,' said Fred. 'So have I.' 'Laura's a damned fine fuck, ain't she?' Someone shut the room-door opposite, as we reached the landing. We pushed it open. Two ladies were pissing; Marie and Laura. 'Where is Mabel?' 'Drunk,' replied one. The two were past caring for anything, pissed and went back with us to the bedroom. I took a light there. Mabel was on her back nearly naked, we covered her up, for it was cold. Then I fucked Laura, and Fred, Lady A***. The light we left now on the wash hand-stand, so we looked at each other fucking and enjoyed it, and then we changed women. There was no cunt-washing, we fucked in each other's sperm, no one cared, all liked it, all were screwed, baudy, reckless, Mabel snoring.

Never have I been in such an orgie before, never since, and perhaps never shall be; but it was one of the most delicious nights I ever spent. So said Fred, so said Mabel; and Laura

admitted to me at a future day that she thought the same, and that since, when she frigged herself, she always thought of it, and nothing else.

I thought of nothing else for a long time. Nothing has ever yet fixed itself in my mind so vividly, so enduringly, except my doings with my first woman, Charlotte. At the beginning of my writing these memoirs, this was among the first described. The narrative as then written was double its present length, and I am sorry that I have abbreviated it, for the occurrences as I correct this proof seem to come on too quickly. Whereas we dined at seven o'clock, and it was one o'clock I guess before we all went to bed together, and the stages from simple voluptuousness to riotous baudiness and free-fucking were gradual. At eight o'clock not one of us would have dared to think of, still less to suggest, what we all did freely at midnight.

ABOVE Félix Jacques-Antoine Moulin (active in Paris 1849–61) preferred to work with amateur models. In this image we can see Moulin's special ability of capturing nuances of mood. Coloured daguerreotype, Paris, 1851–4.

The courtesans of the Second Empire held sway in Paris like despotic queens: their hunger for luxury and money was exceeded only by their ability to squander and spend it. On their chosen battlefields – their beds – and with the politicians, bankers and aristocrats who kept them, these warrior queens were invincible. But each secretly feared the prowess of her fellow courtesans and the rivalry between them was intense. In *The Memoirs of Cora Pearl*, the famous English courtesan recalls her irritation on hearing that Anne de Chassigne had received a coterie of important admirers while bathing luxuriously in asses' milk. Commenting that cows' milk would have been more appropriate, Cora prepares a suitable response.

A week later I invited six gentlemen to dinner. The irritating but indispensable M. Goubouges was one, for his tattle I was in need of; then came the Duc de Treage, the Prince C—, Colonel Marc Aubry, M. Paul of the Banque National, M. Perriport (the brother of the owner of the Restaurant Tric), and the actor Georges Capillon, a friend of Henri Meilhac, Offenbach's librettist, on whom I was eager to make an impression. I let it be known that the chief purpose of the occasion was to display the talents of my chef, Salé, formerly with the Prince d'Orléans, but I hinted to Goubouges that the final dish was likely to be one of an unusual nature.

I received the gentlemen in my finest style, and entertained them to a dinner of excellent quality; the conversation was agreeable, the wines accomplished. When we had finished all but the final course, I excused myself, in order to supervise its presentation. Slipping to the kitchen, I stepped out of my gown (when entertaining gentlemen it is never my habit to wear quantities of underclothing, and especially was this the case on this occasion) and mounting a chair lay upon a vast silver dish which Salé had borrowed for me from the Prince d'Orléans' kitchen. I lay upon my side, my head upon my hand.

Salé stepped forward, accompanied by Yves, a footman I had employed only recently, carrying as it were his palate [*sic*] – a large tray upon which was a set of dishes filled with marzipans, sauces and pastes, all of different colours. With that deftness and artistry for which he was so famed, Salé began to decorate my naked body with rosettes and swathes of creams and sauces, each carefully composed so that the heat of my body would not melt them before I came to table.

As Salé was laying long trails of cream across my haunches and applying wreaths of tiny button flowers to the upper sides of my breasts, I could not help noticing that Yves, chosen like all my servants for a combination of personal charm and accomplishment, and a young man of obvious and ever-increasingly virile promise, was taking a peculiar interest in the chef's work. The knuckles of his hands were whiter than would have been the case had the tray been ten times as heavy, and the state of his breeches proclaimed the fact that his attitude to his employer was one of greater warmth than respect.

I love prostitution in and for itself. . . . In the very notion of prostitution there is such a complex convergence of lust and bitterness, such a frenzy of muscle and sound of gold, such a void in human relations, that the very sight of it makes one dizzy! And how much is learned there! And one is so sad! And one dreams so well of love!

GUSTAVE FLAUBERT (1821–80)

Having finished the decoration by placing a single unpeeled
grape in the dint of my navel, Salé piled innumerable *meringues*
about the dish, completing the effect with a dusting of icing
sugar. The vast cover which belonged to the dish was then placed
over me, and I heard Salé call the other two footmen into the
room. Shortly afterwards I felt myself being raised, and carried
down the passage to the dining-room. I heard the door opened,
and the chatter of voices cease as the dish was carried in and
settled upon the table.

When the lid was lifted, I was rewarded by finding myself the
centre of a ring of round eyes and half-open mouths. M. Paul, as I
had expected, was the first to recover, and with an affectation of
coolness reached out, removed the grape, and slipped it slowly
between his lips. Not to be outdone, M. Perriport leant forward
and applied his tongue to removing the small white flower that
Salé had placed upon my right tit; and then all, except for M.
Goubouges, who as I expected was as usual content simply to
observe and record, were at me, kneeling upon their chairs or

upon the table, their fingers and tongues busy at every part of me as they lifted and licked the sweetness from my body. The Prince was so inflamed by the circumstances that nothing would content him other than to have me there and then upon the table, to the ruination of the remaining decoration upon my body, and the irritation of the other gentlemen, in whom only reverence for rank restricted violence.

So speedily did the Prince fetch off that they had not to wait long – *le laurier est tot coupé*, as my friend Théo used to say. Since the centre of a dining-table and a mess of *meringues* together with wine-glasses and forks is not the most convenient nor comfortable of pleasure-beds, the price of my comforting the other members of the party was that they should give me time at least to dispose myself on one of the nearby couches, where the Duc continued where the Prince had left off; M. Capillon as was his wont contented himself with an energetic frigging (often the taste of members of his profession, I have frequently been disappointed to observe), while M. Paul offered his shaft to my lips and Colonel Aubry his to my sufficiently practised manual manipulation. Finally, M. Perriport, in a desperate fit of agitation, was attempting to displace the Duc when his ecstasy overflowed, together with an excess of language which seemed to me to betray a youth spent in less than polite circles.

Cora Pearl's own youth had also been spent in less eminent, though perfectly respectable circles: she had been born Eliza Emma Crouch at 5 Devonshire Place, Plymouth, in 1837. The witty account of her rise (some might say descent) to being a courtesan who could command the equivalent of £10,000 a night makes enjoyable reading. It glosses over the less savoury aspects of high-class prostitution but nevertheless appears to be a reasonably reliable account – except in relation to her rivals. Cora maintains that she alone among *les grandes horizontales* was allowed to drive her carriage through the enclosure at Baden races – in fact Hortense Schneider shared that privilege. She also suggests that she was the model for Zola's Nana, which is downright silly since she herself is referred to in the novel (in less than flattering terms); and Blanche d'Antigny is generally regarded as the original Nana. In most matters, however, we can rely on the book's accuracy. It is a matter of record that Cora Pearl included among her lovers Prince Napoléon, Prince Achille Murat, Prince William of Orange, the Duc de Morny, and Khalil Bey. It is also a possibility – though she never claimed it – that the Emperor himself was no stranger to her bed. In this episode, the Emperor's cousin – His Imperial Highness Prince Napoléon – arranges a little entertainment for Cora, having annoyed her by falling asleep on the previous evening.

'My dear,' said the Prince, 'I am sorry that my conduct last night left you unsatisfied; but as you see I have brought you two of my best beasts, and I hope that they will provide some compensation. Look!' said he, wacking Brunet lightly upon the buttocks

'I wish I had feathers, a fine sweeping gown,
And a delicate face, and could strut about Town!'
'My dear – a raw country girl, such as you be,
Cannot quite expect that.' 'You ain't ruined,' said she.

FROM *THE RUINED MAID*
THOMAS HARDY (1840–1928)

OPPOSITE This superb daguerreotype by an unknown photographer achieves a perfect balance between beauty and eroticism.

I have never deceived anybody, because I have never belonged to anybody; my independence was all my fortune, and I have known no other happiness . . .

CORA PEARL (1837–86)
FROM HER FIRST AUTOBIOGRAPHY

◊

BELOW From the very beginnings of photography, in 1839, nudes became a favourite subject. Such studies covered the entire aesthetic spectrum, from harsh pornography to artistic creations of great beauty. This cheerfully bawdy image from the studio of Félix Jacques-Antoine Moulin falls between the two extremes.

◊

with his cane, 'Charles here is fine enough for any filly, while André' (making a gesture in the direction of Hurion's already swelling person) 'has flanks and loins only less formidable than mine own once were. Gentlemen, please don't mind me . . .' At which he took himself off to an armchair with a bottle of brandy and a glass, to watch events.

First the two men, with infinite solicitude and many murmurs of appreciation, undressed me. By the time they had completed their task, Hurion's manhood stood out proudly, an enormous tool not as massive perhaps as the Prince's, but evidently much more vigorous and ready for the fray. Sturdy and thick, with the bag beneath supporting two stones of concomitant size, it rose from a belly thickly matted in black, curly hair, the line of which was continued to sprout across his chest. Brunet on the other hand was of a small but perfect frame, so that he looked the very model of a Greek statue, the hair of his body so light that it was almost invisible, lying in tight curls around the root of his tool, which was classically shaped rather than large, an object of beauty which could have failed to attract the admiration only of the insensitive. . . .

At first somewhat deterred by the Prince's suavity, when his two friends showed themselves so eager to enjoy me at his command, it would have been ill-natured of me not to show my gratitude for his solicitude. So I led both men to the bed, where they lay one on either side of me, toying with tenderness with my breasts and thighs, while I enjoyed the play of candlelight upon the skin of their bodies, one so dark that it might almost have been that of an Indian, the other utterly pale and white, almost that of a young girl. At last, Hurion placed himself between my thighs and slowly pressed himself into me, filling me with the utmost pleasure. As he moved gently and in a full, plunging motion, he raised his chest so that Brunet could kiss my breasts, running his tongue about my nipples while I stroked his back and butt-ocks, feeling what I could not see, the light down upon his body. Presently, I felt his fingers as they moved between my body and Hurion's, to caress us both at the extreme point of pleasure.

After a while, careful to afford Brunet the pleasure that his friend and I already enjoyed, I encouraged Hurion to raise himself upon his knees, so that while I still lay impaled, my thighs supported on his own, he was in an upright position, allowing Brunet to throw his leg over and kneel in front of his friend, presenting my lips with the opportunity of embracing him. By this time we were all three at a pitch of pleasure, and within a moment we together reached our goals and spent our passion in mutual delight. So caught up were we that we were equally startled at the applause with which the Prince, observing us from across the room, greeted our endeavours.

We now fell into a pleasant lethargy, and then into a doze; from which, when I woke perhaps an hour later, I saw the chair across the room to be empty, but three glasses of brandy placed upon the bedside table. Waking my two companions, I handed them each a glass, and we toasted our past pleasure and our coming delights, the glass warming us to these, for Hurion immediately took my hand and placed it between his thighs, in the hairy coverts of which a limber something was already astir. A moment's stroking, without even the application of my lips, restored him to full life. Brunet, however, showed no sign of recovery, and even my careful mumbling of his perfect tool had no effect; whereupon to my surprise Hurion bent to do my office with his friend, and the first touch of his tongue performed that office so effectively that Brunet was restored to a pitch of excitement in so brief a time that it was only a moment before I invited him to claim me. Taking my legs behind the knees, the beautiful boy pulled me to the side of the bed, where standing he shot the mark, throwing my legs over his shoulders and leaning his hands behind my head. The perfection of his form had quite a different effect upon me than Hurion's animal strength, and I closed my eyes for a moment in ecstasy when, feeling a tension in Brunet's body, I opened them to see with surprise Hurion's face peering over his friend's shoulder, his hands clutching his forearms, and his body moving in an unmistakable motion. He had entered his friend from behind, and the three of us were moving as one creature. Placing my hands between us, it was with the strangest sensation that I felt two pairs of stones moving in enthusiastic concert, while the ecstatic expressions on my lovers' faces showed that they were fully in accord as to the pleasure of the occasion. I was to learn that Hurion in fact had no special bent towards the enjoyment of boys, nor Brunet towards the enjoyment of women; in fact upon one occasion when at my own request I made love with Brunet alone, I was unable to rouse him sufficiently to employ himself conventionally with me, and it was only by encouraging him to come at me from behind (though still conventionally) that we were able to achieve a conclusion. Both men, however, were so devoted friends that they were willing to support each other in roles which some men would have considered strange or even improper. Upon this occasion, it was the Prince's offer of his services in obtaining promotion for Brunet which had encouraged him to engage his friend on my behalf, which, though he loved him, he knew was his natural bent.

ABOVE Louis Jules Duboscq-Soleil impressed Queen Victoria at the Great Exhibition of 1851 with a photograph he had made especially for her. It is unlikely to have been this particular image from his studio.

Although the *Memoirs of Cora Pearl* provide a good read, and an interesting if idealized account of her life, there must be a very large question mark against the book's authorship. But does that really matter to anyone except bibliographers? The main facts are correct, the history is sound and the sex is well described. Literary sex, like its counterpart in the flesh, contains such a large

Professed curtezans, if they be any good, it is because they are openly bad.

SIR THOMAS OVERBURY (1581–1613)

I may say I have never had a preferred lover. . . . Blind passion and fatal attraction, no! Luckily for my peace of mind and happiness, I have never known either. I have always looked upon the favourite lover as a myth, or empty word. . . . A handsome young and amiable man who has loyally offered me his arms, his love, and his money, has every right to think and call himself my favourite lover, my lover for an hour, my escort for a month, and my friend for ever. This is how I understand the business.

CORA PEARL (1837–86)
FROM HER FIRST AUTOBIOGRAPHY

component of fantasy that it is not always possible to tell where reality ends and dreams begin. Even the real, historical, flesh-and-blood Cora Pearl was an invention – her own. We will leave this extraordinary Devonshire girl – whose courage during the Prussian siege of Paris in 1870 was not forgotten by her French obituarists – where she most liked to be: in the arms of a Prince.

I never learned of the Prince the extent of his previous amorous adventures, but either they had been keener than his years and aspect suggested, or his instinct for the arts of love was more than commonly sharp, for within five minutes he had shed his dressing-gown (under which he wore only a pair of drawers beneath which a powerful manhood betrayed itself), and had undressed me to my shift; whereupon, with difficulty it seemed, he drew back, and offering me his hand led me into the next room, where a bed awaited us upon which, taking me in his arms with more strength than a youth of his age might seem to possess, he softly laid me, then drawing my shift over my head and removing his drawers, set to work in earnest.

There is ever a special delight in teaching the arts of love to the young, and in all my passages in that most enjoyable of pastimes, those I remember with the keenest pleasure have been in just such cases, for however much pleasure the attentions of a practised lover may give to a woman whose profession might tend to make her jaundiced in the art, there is a peculiar pleasure in instructing a young man in subtleties of which he has hitherto been ignorant.

That Prince Achille's previous adventures had been with servants and the like cannot be doubted, for he placed himself between my legs without preliminary and busied himself with gaining entry with all the simplicity of a dog with a bitch. However, his figure was so slight that strong though he was I was able by placing my hands on his shoulders to turn him upon his back and pin him there with my superior weight, kissing him the while to still his protests. Surprise then kept him quiet as I traced with my tongue the line of his neck, then moved downward to his paps, the little springy black hairs around them the only ones to decorate the platform of his chest, teasing each one so that the tiny nipple became like an orange pip beneath my tongue. I could feel him shiver with pleasure as he realized for the first time that the art of love as I practised it had more to offer than the welcoming of his tool by my own tender part.

After a while, I moved yet further down, my tongue making a snail's trace down his belly, pausing to thrust into that delightful knot, his navel, and then yet lower, whence black curls marked a broad path to his tool, now hard as ivory and as white, that had almost bruised my breasts as it sprang between them. He began to make little movements with his loins, as though to thrust himself at me; yet I ignored this, and simply feeling his upright instrument soft on my cheek, passed it by and kissed the tops of his thighs, where still there was only the faintest mat of hairs, which I caught between my lips; then parting his thighs placed myself between them, lifting his stones so that I could caress each one with my tongue, even pressing them with my lips, before finally running my tongue up his instrument and parting my lips to slip it between them.

I knew that as with most inexperienced lovers, the pleasure of this was too keen to be long maintained. As my lips passed over the knob of his tool, and I tickled with my finger the part between his balls and fundament, I felt his whole body quiver, and before I had drawn my lips more than three or four times up the shaft, he roughly threw me off – a politeness which spoke of his natural tenderness and concern as well as of his inexperience – as the convulsion came, and ample proof of his passion exuded from him with the celerity and force of a shot from a gun!

He seemed speechless as he bent over to kiss me, then wiping his body with the sheets before drawing me up to lie with him, embraced me tenderly and with many endearments. So resilient is youth that before his tool had seemed to shrink at all, it began to recover its strength, and this time I did not object as he slipped between my thighs and entered me, for the pleasure of bringing him off had brought me to a pitch of eagerness almost matching his own. Still, his passion was such that he was finished almost before I began; but again youth recovered him speedily, and for the rest of the afternoon our pleasure was mutual, for three more times he roused himself, and for the two final attacks was able to maintain himself for such a time as allowed me to the ample happiness he himself was experiencing.

It was now the time at which the Duc would be coming to call at the Rue de Ponthieu, and so I rose and dressed,

BELOW The influence of Ingres and the other great painters of the female nude is clearly evident in the lighting and poses of many of the finest daguerreotypes. This magnificent study is unattributed.

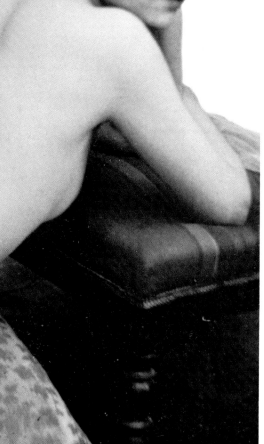

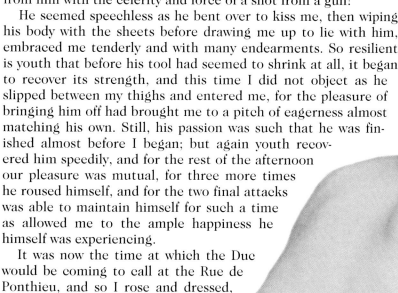

Prostitution is essentially a matter of lack of choice.

CHARLES BAUDELAIRE (1821–67)

ABOVE *La Diligence de Lyon*, a watercolour by Henri Monnier (1799–1875).

while the Prince lay naked upon the bed in happy exhaustion, his adoring looks speaking of his gratitude while the limp prostration of his manhood told of the utmost satisfaction. So I took my leave of him, though not without protestations of renewing the pleasure of his acquaintance.

———————◊———————

Originally published in four volumes between 1873 and 1876, *The Romance of Lust* is the erotic equivalent of a patchwork quilt: diverse material sewn together to form a whole. And like a patchwork quilt it travelled in cabins and sleeping cars to every corner of the British Empire. *The Romance of Lust* tells the story of Charlie – or rather the editor/author William Simpson Potter uses the priapic Charlie like a needle to stitch together different tales. Apart from this remorseless and unsympathetic character, the fundamental link between the parts is just that – links between fundaments and parts. However, *The Romance of Lust* did represent extraordinary value for money; the ratio of couplings (orifice optional) to pages was unbeatable. During the last quarter of the century this action-packed novel, written in vigorous language, was an underground bestseller.

Miss Evelyn at last concentrated all her attention on my well-developed member, which she most endearingly embraced and fondled tenderly, very quickly putting him into an ungovernable state of erection. I was lying on my back, and she partially raised herself to kiss my formidable weapon; so gently putting her upon me, I told her it was her turn to do the work. She laughed, but at once mounted upon me, and bringing her delicious cunt right over my prick, and guiding it to the entrance of love's grotto, she gently sank down upon it and engulphed it until the two hairs pressed against each other. A few slow up and down movements followed, when becoming too libidinous for such temporizing delays, she sank on my belly, and began to show most wonderful activity of loins and bottom. I seconded her to the utmost, and finding she was so excited, I slipped my hand round behind and introduced my middle finger in the rosy and very tight orifice of her glorious backside. I continued to move in and out in unison with her up and down heavings. It seemed to spur her on to more vigorous actions, and in the midst of short gaspings and suppressed sighs, she sank almost senseless on my bosom, I, too, had quickened my action, and shot into her gaping womb a torrent of boiling sperm. . . .

'Oh! my beloved Charlie, what exquisite delight you have given me; you are the most delicious and loving creature that ever could be created. You kill me with pleasure, but what was that you were doing to my bottom? What put such an idea into your head?'

'I don't know,' I replied. 'I put my arm round to feel the beautiful globes of your bottom, and found in grasping one that my finger was against a hole, all wet with our previous encounters,

and pressing it, found that my finger slipped in; you gave it such a delicious pressure when in that the idea entered into my head that, as it resembled the delicious pressure your enchanting other orifice gives my shaft when embracing you, this orifice would like a similar movement to that which my shaft exercised in your quim. So I did so, and it seemed to add to your excitement, if I may judge by the extraordinary convulsive pressures you gave my finger when you died away in all the agony of our final rapture. Tell me, my beloved Miss Evelyn, did it add to your pleasure as much as I fancied?'

'Well, my darling Charlie, I must own it did, very much to my surprise; it seemed to make the final pleasure almost too exciting to bear, and I can only account it a happy accident leading to an increase to pleasure I already thought beyond the power of nature to surpass. Naughty boy, I feel your great instrument at full stretch again, but you must moderate yourself, my darling, we have done enough for to-night. No, no, no! I am not going to let him in again.'

Passing her hand down, she turned away its head from the

ABOVE An illustration by Achille Deveria (1800–57) from *Gamiani ou Deux Nuits d'excès*.

There are only nine original
humorous stories in the world, eight
of which you cannot tell to a lady.

RUDYARD KIPLING (1865–1936)

charming entrance of her cunt, and began handling and feeling it
in apparent admiration of its length, thickness, and stiffness. Her
gentle touch did anything but allay the passion that was rising to
fever heat; so sucking one of her bubbies, while I pressed her to
me with one arm under her, and embracing her on the other
side, I passed my hand between our moist and warm bodies,
reached her charming clitoris, already stiff with the excitement
of handling my prick. My titillations soon decided her passions,
and gently prompting her with the arm under her body, I turned
her once more on the top of me. She murmured an objection,
but offered no resistance; on the contrary, she herself guided my
throbbing and eager prick into the voluptuous sheath that was
longing to engulph it. Our movements this time were less hurried and more voluptuous. For some time she kept her body
upright, rising and falling from her knees. I put my finger to her
clitoris, and added to the extatic pleasure she was so salaciously
enjoying. She soon found she must come to more rapid and vigorous movements, and lying down on my belly embraced and
kissed me. Toying with our tongues I put an arm round her waist,
and held her tight, while her glorious buttocks and most supple
loins kept up the most delicious thrust and pressures on my thoroughly engulphed weapon. I again stimulated her to the highest
pitch of excited desire by introducing my finger behind, and we
both came to the grand crisis in a tumultuous state of enrap-
tured agony, unable to do ought, but from moment to moment
convulsively throb in and on our engulphed members. We must
have lain thus languidly, and deliciously enjoying all the raptures
of the most complete and voluptuous gratification of our passions, for fully thirty minutes before we recovered complete consciousness. Miss Evelyn was first to remember where she was. She
sprang up, embraced me tenderly, and said she must leave me at
once, she was afraid she had already stayed imprudently long. In
fact, it was near five o'clock in the morning. I rose from the bed
to fling my arms round her lovely body, to fondle and embrace
her exquisite bubbies. With difficulty she tore herself from my
arms. I accompanied her to the door, and with a mutual and loving kiss we parted, I to return and rapidly sink into the sweetest
slumber after such a delicious night of most voluptuous fucking.

———————— ◊ ————————

In the 1870s and 1880s a plethora of new magazines and
periodicals were published, reflecting both technical advances
in printing and the development of a widening middle-class
market. These periodicals covered a wide range of subjects, but
just as erotica had been represented among the first lithographs
and one of the earliest of all photographs was a nude, so sex reared
its head among the new journals. The first and most notorious of
these was *The Pearl – a Journal of Facetiae and Voluptuous Reading*. Eighteen volumes were published between July 1879 and
December 1880 when it finally disappeared. Although an urban
and élitist production, scattered with literary references and Latin
phrases, which no doubt pleased its university readership, its

largest market was in the new middle-class suburbs. Goodness knows what they made of its subversive tone. The editor explains his choice of *The Pearl* as the title:

> . . . in the hope that when it comes under the snouts of the moral and hypocritical swine of the world, they may not trample it underfoot, and feel disposed to rend the publisher, but that a few will become subscribers on the quiet. To such better disposed piggywiggys, I would say, for encouragement, that they have only to keep up appearances by regularly attending church, giving to charities, and always appearing deeply interested in moral philanthropy, to ensure a respectable and highly moral character, and that if they only are clever enough *never to be found out*, they

LEFT A Victorian mass-produced erotic postcard. During the *Belle Epoque* rival companies vied to produce 'souvenirs' that were beautiful as well as sexy.

may, *sub rosa*, study and enjoy the *philosophy of life* till the end of their days, and earn a glorious and saintly epitaph on their tombstone, when at last the Devil pegs them out.

There was something for everyone in *The Pearl*, although the comprehensive sexual menu had a bias towards maidenheads and bottoms. Readers in service could confirm their worst suspicions with 'Belgravian Morals': 'The Countess's dress was raised to her navel and I could see the jewelled hand of Miss Courtney groping between her lovely thighs.' Readers who had not travelled could read 'The Sultan's Reverie' and be transported to some very exotic places: 'not there, not there, I never would allow the Sultan to do that!' *The Pearl*'s largely urban readership were offered an alternative *Country Life* in 'Sub-Umbra, or sport among the She-noodles'; this extract gives some idea of the journal's torrid style:

> For fear of damaging her dress, or getting the green stain of the grass on the knees of my light trousers, I persuaded her to stand up by the gate and allow me to enter behind. She hid her face in her hands on the top rail of the gate, as I slowly raised her dress; what glories were unfolded to view, my prick's stiffness was renewed in an instant at the sight of her delicious buttocks, so beautifully relieved by the white of her pretty drawers; as I opened them and exposed the flesh, I could see the lips of her plump pouting cunny, deliciously feathered, with soft light down, her lovely legs, drawers, stockings, pretty boots, making a *tout ensemble*, which as I write and describe them cause Mr. Priapus to swell in my breeches; it was a most delicious sight. I knelt and kissed her bottom, slit, and everything my tongue could reach, it was all mine, I stood up and prepared to take possession of the seat of love – when, alas! a sudden shriek from Annie, her clothes dropped, all my arrangements were upset in a moment; a bull had unexpectedly appeared on the opposite side of the gate, and frightened my love by the sudden application of his cold, damp nose to her forehead. It is too much to contemplate that scene even now.
>
> Annie was ready to faint as she screamed, 'Walter! Walter! Save me from the horrid beast!' I comforted and reassured her as well as I was able, and seeing that we were on the safe side of the gate, a few loving kisses soon set her all right.

OPPOSITE *Country Pleasures*, a coloured lithograph by Peter Fendi (1796–1842). This Austrian artist delighted in cheerful celebrations of erotic games and the generous female form.

Not long after the disappearance of *The Pearl* from London's streets *The Oyster* mysteriously appeared. Although some of the same contributors seem to have been involved in this production, it was a quite different publication, less abrasive and subversive than its predecessor. The preface to the first edition of *The Oyster* suggests a change of editor:

> What is it that causes my lord to smack his chops in that wanton, lecherous manner, as he is sauntering up and down Bond Street,

with his glass in hand, to watch the ladies getting in and out of their carriages? And what is it that draws together such vast crowds of the holiday gentry at Easter and Whitsuntide to see the merry rose-faced lassies running down the hill in Greenwich Park? What is it causes such a roar of laughter when a merry girl happens to overset in her career and kick her heels in the air? Lastly, as the parsons all say, what is it that makes the theatrical ballet so popular?

There is a magic in the sight of a female leg, which is hardly in the power of mere language to describe, for to be conceived it must be felt. . . .

Your editor never sees a pretty leg but feels certain unutterable emotions within him, which as the poet puts it:

Should some fair youth, the charming sight explore,
In rapture he'll gaze, and wish for something more!

Whether by popular demand or because its production was a rich man's fun, *The Oyster* continued publication until 1889. In this extract a pastiche of John Cleland's erotica raises a fever which even an improbable glass of lemonade cannot cool:

'Her secret orifice opened to the probing of my ardent tongue. Her rounded bottom began to move in rhythm with the explorations of my own. Sensing that it was time to leave off this occupation, pleasurable though it was, I retraced my steps, kissing again the delicate outer lips, the still-wet moss, the bluish-white skin of her inner thighs, and concentrated myself upon the main enjoyments. Inch by inch, I impaled her with my sturdy rod, now

BELOW A French sepia postcard, late nineteenth century. The creators of 'naughty postcards' used the latest developments in photography and printing techniques to produce erotic ephemera which has never been surpassed.

grown to even greater dimensions by preceding excitations. This time with her mount of pleasure fully receptive to the aggressions of my member, she did not gasp with pain but moaned with pleasure.

'I thrust; she answers; I stroke, she heaves; our rhythms join and our passions grew. I push so deep into her that I think I must rend the wench in twain but her sole response is yet another moan, this low in the throat as our breathing deepens to a growl, then, in unison, to a roar. The bed shudders with the weight and fury of our entwined violence. Then with a shriek she adds her juices to my own and I discharge in an enormity of passion, my juices boiling over, searing her deepest vitals.'. . .

I ended my reading and sipped slowly at my glass of cool lemonade. The passionate words of Mr Cleland had certainly achieved the desired effect. Louella and Lucy were entwined in a passionate embrace and their mouths met as Lucy's hands examined the large breasts of the dark-haired Louella who unbuttoned her blouse to let Lucy enjoy free play with her plump bubbies. She continued to play with those magnificent breasts while Louella's hands were under Lucy's skirts doing all kinds of things to her clitty. Louella eased down her partner's underdrawers and Lucy's rounded bottom cheeks were naked to my eyes, which feasted upon them as Louella's hands probed the cleft between them, making the blonde girl gasp with joy.

During the 1880s *The Oyster* had to compete with a rival: *The Boudoir*. Although a superior publication – or perhaps for that reason – *The Boudoir* lasted for only six issues before sinking without trace. The editorial style is quite different from its crustacean rivals – *The Pearl* and *The Oyster* – and although some of the contributors may be the same, it is a more literary production full of classical allusions and cheerful anecdotes and less reliant on four-letter words for its pyrotechnics. This extract from the serial 'Voluptuous Confessions of a French Lady of Fashion' is, despite its title, a very English piece of erotic writing:

Yet, I was far from depraved! I loved my husband as a sure friend, as the companion of my existence, and if he had possessed the manly vigour that was necessary for me, or if even he had known how to subdue my clever caresses, I should never have dreamt of being unfaithful to him! I resolved to spare him all sorrow and I have fully succeeded, as he has never had the least suspicion!

This revolution demanded much care, trouble, and even privation; the town I inhabited was much inclined to scandal, and it was very difficult for me to hide my connection, so I had to take endless precautions.

I warned my lover, who, wishing above all to save my

ABOVE An illustration by Félicien Rops (1833–98) from *The Lesbians*. This Belgian artist's strict Catholic upbringing, eclipsed by ideas from Baudelaire and his own sexual appetite, produced a technically brilliant, darkly erotic œuvre that was to influence Beardsley, von Bayros and many other artists. Rops has been called 'the last painter of sins'.

Mrs Drummond, the famous preacher among the Quakers, on being asked by a gentleman if the spirit had ever inspired her with thoughts of marriage, 'No, friend,' says she, 'but the flesh often has.'

FROM *THE BOUDOIR*

The daughter of Pythagoras used to say that the woman who goes to bed with a man must put off her modesty with her petticoat, and put it on again with the same.

FROM *THE BOUDOIR*

ABOVE *Au bois*, a coloured lithograph from *Gamiani* by Louis André Berthomme-Saint-André (1905–77).

reputation, promised to do all in his power not to excite suspicion, and I knew I could rely on his honour.

A few days went by without our meeting; I suffered greatly and he as much as I! A sign, a look during our walks was our only consolation for eight long days!

At last F. could bear it no longer, and came to pay us a visit; we chatted in an ordinary friendly way; someone else called, F. went away; my husband showed him out and returned to the room. I know not what instinct warned me that F. had not left the house! I got up, with some excuse that seemed all the more reasonable as the visitor was keeping up a technical conversation with my husband, and went into the vestibule. I was not mistaken; F., seeing no servants about, was waiting by the street-door.

As soon as he saw me, he threw himself upon me, clasped me in his arms and with violent passion exclaimed: 'Darling angel, how I suffer!'

'And I? . . .'

We were once again between the double doors. Before I knew where I was, our mouths were glued together, my petticoats were up to my navel, his finger pushed itself into my burning slit, that opened beneath its pressure. My hand had seized the darling object.

What more can I say? In a second or two – a few movements of our hands took place – I swooned with joy, and drew away my hand, bathed all over with an abundance of the warm liquid.

Yet a few moments went by without our being able to meet, till at last a happy moment of liberty was granted to us. A whole hour was ours.

Ah, how we profited by it! My lover came into my boudoir. I rushed to receive him, and I devoured him with caresses. . . .

I tore myself from him, pulled up my clothes behind, and, getting onto the sofa on my knees, presented my bottom.

He put it in at once, and I very soon swooned beneath his copious discharge.

We then sat down, but my lover was not satisfied, and despite my fears I could not refuse. He went on his knees between my legs, then he made me stretch wide apart. I took his vigorous firebrand in my hand; it was already as hard as ever. I stroked it a second, then pushed it gradually into myself, while I savoured slowly the delightful pleasure. . . .

I used to vastly like to change the way of doing it. For instance, sometimes when plugged from behind, one of my favourite positions, would unhorse my cavalier, turn round quickly, give a kiss to my rosy conqueror, wet with my spendings, and escape to the other end of the room, I would place myself in an easy chair, my legs upraised, and my pussey quite open, while I gave it a provoking twitching movement. My lover was hardly in me again, when by a fresh whim I would draw it out, make him sit on a chair, get on his knees, my back turned towards him, and taking his courser, plunging in my body to the very hilt, let his burning jet finish our sweet operation.

My dear Minet, as I generally called the splendid instrument of my joy, had become my passion, the object of real worship. I was

never tired of admiring its thickness, its stiffness, and its length, all equally marvellous. I would dandle it, suck it, pump at it, caress it in a thousand different ways, and rub it between my titties, holding it there by pressing them with both my hands. Often when captive in this voluptuous passage, it would throw out its dew.

My lover returned all my caresses with interest. My pussey was his god, his idol. He assured me that no woman had ever possessed a more perfect one. He would open it, and frig it in every conceivable way. His greatest delight was to apply his lips thereto, and extract, so to speak, the quintessence of voluptuousness, by titillations of the tongue, that almost drove me mad.

PART THREE

Decadent visions

... 'Sweet youth
Tell me why, sad and sighing, thou dost rove
These pleasant realms? I pray thee speak me sooth
What is thy name?' He said, 'My name is Love!'
Then straight the first did turn himself to me
And cried, 'He lieth, for his name is Shame,
But I am Love, and I was wont to be
Alone in this fair garden, till he came
Unasked by night; I am true Love, I fill
The Hearts of boy and girl with mutual flame.'
Then sighing said the other, 'Have thy will,
I am the Love that dare not speak its name.'

We two boys together clinging,
One the other never leaving,
Up and down the roads going, North
    and South excursions making,
Power enjoying, elbows stretching,
    fingers clutching
Arm'd and fearless, eating, drinking,
    sleeping, loving . . .

FROM *CALAMUS*
WALT WHITMAN (1819–92)

These lines, taken from 'Two Loves' by Lord Alfred Douglas, were read aloud by the prosecution at the trial of his friend Oscar Wilde. Asked to explain the love that dare not speak its name, Wilde (1854–1900) said it was 'a great affection of an elder for a younger man such as there was between David and Jonathan, such as Plato made the very basis of his philosophy, and such as you find in the sonnets of Michelangelo and Shakespeare. It is that deep, spiritual affection that is as pure as it is perfect . . . on account of it I am placed where I am now . . . the world mocks at it . . . puts one in the pillory for it.' The world has indeed mocked Oscar for his sexual orientation. It mocked him in the savage sentence of two years' hard labour, which ruined his health. It mocked him with a premature death in exile, living in poverty ('I am dying above my means') with – thank God – his old love Robbie Ross there to hold his hand at the end ('either that wallpaper goes or I do'). And the world still remembers Oscar Wilde as much for his homosexuality as for his astonishing brilliance as a dramatist, wit and poet.

The decision to include extracts from *Teleny* – the homosexual novel written by Wilde and others – could be criticized for perpetuating the link. After all, the year 1995 marked the anniversary of his trial and the placing of a long overdue memorial in Westminster Abbey. However, there was a powerful self-destructive tendency in Oscar, embodied in his own paradoxical assertion that 'each man kills the thing he loves'. If he did not seek martyrdom, he certainly did not avoid it as many others had done, and his actions were often those of a man courting disaster. Oscar took the

ABOVE 'Then afterwards came
Egypt, Antinoüs and Adrian. You
were the Emperor, I was the slave
. . . Who knows, perhaps I shall die
for you one day' (*Teleny*).
A lithograph, hand-coloured in
watercolour, by the French artist
Paul Avril (1849–1928).

original risk of involving himself in the creation of *Teleny*: it seems
fair to include it. Published in 1893, *Teleny* is arguably the first
modern homosexual novel. The pity is, of course, that it is not the
novel it would have been if Wilde had written it all. Yet his voice is
there, and worth hearing on a subject with which he will for ever
be associated.

The main character, Des Grieux, first falls under the spell of
Teleny at a concert. The young pianist's playing stimulates vivid
hallucinations of Ancient Egypt, Greece and, portentously, 'the
gorgeous towns of Sodom and Gomorrah'. That night Des Grieux
has a dream that Teleny is his own sister, and not a man, yet he
desires her. The forbidden passion in this piece of *grand guignol* is
all the more disturbing (and Freudian) since Des Grieux does not
actually have a sister!

'One night, unable to overcome the maddening passion that was
consuming me, I yielded to it and stealthily crept into her room.
'By the rosy light of her night-lamp, I saw her lying, or rather,
stretched across her bed. I shivered with lust at the sight of that

Of man's delight and man's desire
    In one thing is no weariness –
To feel the fury of the fire,
    And writhe within the close
        caress
      Of fierce embrace, and wanton
        kiss,
And final nuptial done aright,
     How sweet a passion, shame, is
       this,
A strong man's love is my delight!

To feel him clamber on me, laid
     Prone on the couch of lust and
       shame,
To feel him force me like a maid
     And his great sword within me
       flame,
     His breath as hot and quick as
       fame;
To kiss him and to clasp him tight;
     This is my joy without a name,
A strong man's love is my delight.

FROM *WHITE STAINS*
ALEISTER CROWLEY (1875–1947)

RIGHT A Rococo fantasy by Franz
von Bayros (1866–1924).

pearly-white flesh. I should have liked to have been a beast of prey to devour it.

'Her loose and dishevelled golden hair was scattered in locks all over the pillow. Her lawn chemise scarcely veiled part of her nakedness, whilst it enhanced the beauty of what was left bare. The ribbons with which this garment had been tied on her shoulder had come undone, and thus exhibited her right breast to my hungry, greedy glances. It stood up firm and plump, for she was a very young virgin, and its dainty shape was no bigger than a large-sized champagne bowl. . . .

'I quietly drew near the bed on the tip of my toes, just like a cat about to spring on a mouse, and then slowly crawled between her legs. My heart was beating fast, I was eager to gaze upon the sight I so longed to see. As I approached on all fours, head foremost, a strong smell of white heliotrope mounted up to my head, intoxicating me.

'Trembling with excitement, opening my eyes wide and straining my sight, my glances dived between her thighs. At first nothing could be seen but a mass of crisp auburn hair, all curling in tiny ringlets, and growing there as if to hide the entrance of that well of pleasure. First I lightly lifted up her chemise, then I gently brushed the hair aside, and parted the two lovely lips which opened by themselves at the touch of my fingers as if to afford me entrance.

'This done, I fed my greedy eyes upon that dainty pink flesh that looked like the ripe and luscious pulp of some savoury fruit appetizing to behold, and within those cherry lips there nestled a tiny bud – a living flower of flesh and blood.

'I had evidently tickled it with the tip of my finger, for, as I looked upon it, it shivered as if endowed with a life of its own, and it protruded itself out towards me. At its beck I longed to taste it, to fondle it, and therefore, unable to resist, I bent down and pressed my tongue upon it, over it, within it, seeking every nook and corner around it, darting into every chink and cranny, whilst she, evidently enjoying the little game, helped me in my work, shaking her buttocks with a lusty delight in such a way that after a few minutes the tiny flower began to expand its petals and shed forth its ambrosial dew, not a drop of which did my tongue allow to escape.

'In the meanwhile she panted and screamed, and seemed to swoon away with joy.'

We may feel instinctively – and we may be right – that Oscar Wilde did not write that piece. But deciding what he did contribute to the book is difficult: the nicely crafted but over-embellished links which carry the plot forward, heavy with the scent of heliotrope and anguished passion? Or the compelling and fearful brothel scene, like the drawings of Félicien Rops transformed into words? Perhaps it was the descriptions of passionate, physical love between two men. These are probably the best thing in *Teleny or The Reverse of the Medal* – a suggestive subtitle which also reminds us that here is simply another face of love.

'. . . our knees were pressed together, the skin of our thighs seemed to cleave and to form one flesh.

'Though I was loath to rise, still, feeling his stiff and swollen phallus throbbing against my body, I was just going to tear myself off from him, and to take his fluttering implement of pleasure in my mouth and drain it, when he – feeling that mine was now not only turgid, but moist and brimful to overflowing – clasped me with his arms and kept me down.

'Opening his thighs, he thereupon took my legs between his own, and entwined them in such a way that his heels pressed against the sides of my calves. For a moment I was gripped as in a vice, and I could hardly move.

'Then loosening his arms, he uplifted himself, placed a pillow under his buttocks, which were thus well apart – his legs being all the time widely open.

'Having done this, he took hold of my rod and pressed it against his gaping anus. The tip of the frisky phallus soon found its entrance in the hospitable hole that endeavoured to give it

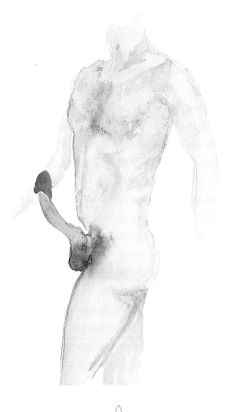

ABOVE *The Phallacy*, a watercolour sketch by a contemporary artist.

admission. I pressed a little; the whole of the glans was engulfed. The sphincter soon gripped it in such a way that it could not come out without an effort. I thrust it slowly to prolong as much as possible the ineffable sensation that ran through every limb, to calm the quivering nerves, and to allay the heat of the blood. Another push, and half the phallus was in his body. I pulled it out half an inch, though it seemed to me a yard by the prolonged pleasure I felt. I pressed forward again, and the whole of it, down to its very root, was all swallowed up. Thus wedged, I vainly endeavoured to drive it higher up – an impossible feat, and, clasped as I was, I felt it wriggling in its sheath like a baby in its mother's womb, giving myself and him an unutterable and delightful titillation.

'So keen was the bliss that overcame me, that I asked myself if some ethereal, life-giving fluid were not being poured on my head, and trickling down slowly over my quivering flesh.

'Surely the rain-awakened flowers must be conscious of such a sensation during a shower, after they have been parched by the scorching rays of an estival [summer] sun.

'Teleny again put his arm round me and held me tight. I gazed at myself within his eyes, he saw himself in mine. During this voluptuous, lambent feeling, we patted each other's bodies softly, our lips cleaved together and my tongue was again in his mouth. We remained in this copulation almost without stirring, for I felt that the slightest movement would provoke a copious ejaculation, and this feeling was too exquisite to be allowed to pass away so quickly. Still we could not help writhing, and we almost swooned away with delight. We were both shivering with lust, from the roots of our hair to the tips of our toes; all the flesh of our bodies kept bickering luxuriously, just as placid waters of the mere do at noontide when kissed by the sweet-scented, wanton breeze that has just deflowered the virgin rose.

'Such intensity of delight could not, however, last very long; a few almost unwilling contractions of the sphincter brandle the phallus, and then the first brunt was over; I thrust in with might and main, I wallowed on him; my breath came quickly; I panted, I sighed, I groaned. The thick burning fluid was spouted out slowly and at long intervals.

'As I rubbed myself against him, he underwent all the sensations I was feeling; for I was hardly drained of the last drop before I was likewise bathed with his own seething sperm. We did not kiss each other any further; our languid, half-open, lifeless lips only aspired each other's breath. Our sightless eyes saw each other no more, for we fell into that divine prostration which follows shattering ecstasy.

'Oblivion, however, did not follow, but we remained in a benumbed state of torpor, speechless, forgetting everything except the love we bore each other, unconscious of everything save the pleasure of feeling each other's bodies, which, however, seemed to have lost their own individuality, mingled and confounded as they were together.'

BELOW An allegorical self-portrait of Aubrey Beardsley published in *The Savoy* magazine. Tethered to the phallic god Priapus, is the artist carrying a pen or a whip to flog us with? Perhaps for him they are one and the same thing?

After his release from prison in May 1897, Oscar Wilde went to live in the village of Berneval in Normandy. Close by was Dieppe, a favourite resort for the English, who could combine the joys and economies of France with the familiar comforts of an expatriate community. While Oscar was engaged in the therapy of writing *The Ballad of Reading Gaol* he hoped, therefore, to receive visits from old friends who were holidaying in Dieppe. Some came, but some did not. Among those who did not come, for fear of further scandal, was the brilliant young artist Aubrey Beardsley, who had done the illustrations for Wilde's *Salome*. After his arrest it was reported that Wilde had been carrying a copy of *The Yellow Book*, the controversial magazine Beardsley had helped to found. As a result the artist lost his job and found employment difficult. Beardsley's avoidance of Wilde might then have been entirely understandable but for their friendship. In a letter from Reading, Wilde wrote of Beardsley's deteriorating health: 'Poor Aubrey: I hope he will get alright . . . Behind his grotesques there seems to lurk some curious philosophy.' On hearing that Beardsley had avoided him in Dieppe, Oscar said simply: 'That was cowardly of Aubrey.' It was, especially as the main concern of Beardsley's art was to explore the ambiguities of gender while attacking Victorian sexual hypocrisy. His own sexuality was unconventional in the extreme, and perhaps that was the main reason for his cowardice. Beardsley was visiting Dieppe with his sister Mabel, whose close relationship with the artist was already the subject of unpleasant rumour. He was to die from tuberculosis in the following year, before his twenty-sixth birthday. So little time and so much still to do: no time for the distractions of scandal? Perhaps; we shall never know.

In his short life Aubrey Beardsley produced a large body of extraordinary art. Largely self-taught, he took what he needed from a wide range of artistic traditions: the erotic art of Japan, Shunga; Greek vase decoration; eighteenth-century masters such as Gillray and contemporaries including Félicien Rops. The unique and highly innovative style which Beardsley developed is instantly recognizable as his own. It was also the ideal vehicle for his exploration of his special subject: sex.

We know from his contemporaries that the prodigiously talented erotomane also wanted to become a writer. From the experimental work that remains, some poems and the unfinished novel *Under the Hill* – a version of the *Tannhäuser* story – it is fair to assume that his graphic art would have remained the best expression of his genius. The poems are complicated erotic cyphers, as dull as his drawings are exciting. Beardsley said that *Under the Hill* was an exercise

BELOW 'The Toilet of Lampito', from *Lysistrata* by Aubrey Beardsley (1872–98).

in 'rococo eroticism with peeps into the exotic underworld of amorous fantasy'. In this extract the draughtsman uses language to make us see, forming words with a drawing pen:

> Poor Adolphe! How happy he was, touching the Queen's breasts with his quick tongue tip. I have no doubt that the keener scent of animals must make women much more attractive to them than to men; for the gorgeous odor that but faintly fills our nostrils must be revealed to the brute creation in divine fullness. Anyhow, Adolphe sniffed as never a man did round the skirts of Venus. After the first interchange of affectionate delicacies was over, the unicorn lay down upon his side, and, closing his eyes, beat his stomach wildly with the mark of manhood. Venus caught that stunning member in her hands and laid her cheek along it; but few touches were wanted to consummate the creature's pleasure. The Queen bared her left arm to the elbow, and with the soft underneath of it made amazing movements upon the tightly strung instrument. When the melody began to flow, the unicorn offered up an astonishing vocal accomplishment. Tannhäuser was amused to learn that the etiquette of Venusberg compelled everybody to await the outburst of those venereal sounds before they could sit down to *déjeuner*.

The nineteenth century closed, but the party went on. Edward VII presided over the feast like a reformed satyr, eager to prove – as he did – that he could be a king as well. Most of the important guests – Wilde, Verlaine, Beardsley, Rops – had already left, but in the heat and clamour of the moment they were hardly missed. With the benefit of hindsight, knowing that young men were rushing towards Passchendaele and the Somme, we are tempted to read into their gaiety some unconscious understanding that the end was near. We are probably wrong.

Of course, erotica flourishes in so humid an atmosphere – and it did. Like lewd orchids raised secretly in the conservatories of the middle classes, a whole crop of colourful erotic novels appeared.

This Edwardian erotica was literate, but not much of it was literature. It was as if the well-educated, robust journalists who wrote quality boys' magazines such as *The Captain* had turned their hands (anonymously) to a different genre; perhaps they had. *Eveline* was first published in 1904. The aristocratic, very English heroine of this fast-moving adventure has trouble keeping her hands off the servants:

> I rang the bell.
> 'I want some tea, John. What time is it?'
> 'It's not ten yet, miss.'
> 'Where is the butler?'
> 'Sir Edward has sent him out, miss, to see the painter. He is not to send his men in the morning unless it is quite fine.'
> 'How is poor Robin, John? I am afraid he is drooping.'

You cannot expect a boy to be depraved until he has been to a good school.

SAKI (H. H. MUNRO) (1870–1916)

The footman came closer. He bent cautiously down to me.

'Drooping? Miss Eveline, I wish he was! Why he stands up in the mornings and looks at me in the face. It's shocking how he suffers. I'm quite ashamed to look at him, miss.'

'So am I, John. All the same, let me see the poor thing. I might be able to do him some good.'

The door was shut. John looked all round. He listened. All seemed in order and quiet. He saw his chance. In another instant, he had opened his flap. He twisted his big limb out from under his shirt. My hand closed on it. It was already stretching itself out, and half erect. I loved to feel it thus – so warm, so soft!

I bent my head over it as I sat. I kissed the red tip. The impulse was too strong for my resistance in the condition in which I was. I opened my moist lips. I let the big nut pass in. I sucked it. It swelled and stiffened. John involuntarily moved himself backwards and forwards. It very quickly attained its extreme stiffness and dimensions. I withdrew my face a little to look at it. The big round top shone as if it had been varnished.

'Take care what you do, miss. He's not to be trusted. He's in such a condition. What you have just done has made him more rampageous than ever.'

I rubbed his member up and down quickly. He put down his hand and stopped me.

'Oh, Miss Eveline, mind your dress, miss.'

'Is it so near, John? Poor Robin! He must have all the pleasure I can give him to make him more tractable.'

I put down my head. I applied my lips again. I only released his limb to whisper:

'Let it come so, John! I want it!'

The idea made him mad. He pushed forward, breathing hard. He moved his loins again. I took into my mouth the whole of the big nut. I tickled it with my tongue. I moved both hands in little jerks upon the white shaft.

'Oh, Miss Eveline! Oh, my good Lord! I shall come! Oh!'

He discharged. My mouth was instantly filled with a torrent of his sperm. I swallowed as much as I could. It flew from him in little jets. It must have given him immense pleasure. Soon all was over.

'Now fetch the tea, John. I hope Robin will be better. If it had not been a cock – your Robin – I should have said it had laid an egg and broken it.'

Eveline's highly individual answer to the problem of keeping servants meets with the approval of the groom, if not of her horse, Goorkha:

I suppose my expression reassured the young fellow. He put his hat on the table and grinned with the restless, uneasy grin of a

ABOVE *The Unexpected Gift*, a coloured lithograph of a drawing by 'Onyx'.

man whose will is under restraint and who is afraid to let his inclination run riot.

'Come here, Jim! Help me to take off my habit. Undo those hooks. So – that's a good fellow! Do you like to feel my breasts, Jim? You shall stroke me as much as you like. Let me look at your tool once more, Jim. Undo your breeches – pull it out! I should like to see it again.'

His restraint vanished. His trembling hands aided me to get rid of my habit. I was almost undressed. At my lewd invitation he opened his flap and exposed the monstrous limb already stiffly erect at the idea of enjoying me. I put my hand upon it. We stood closely together.

'Oh, Jim! Oh, what a big one it is!'

We both breathed hard and fast as we pressed our bodies together. His huge limb was in my grasp. His hand was up my legs. His fingers arrived at the centre. I was fearfully excited. I goaded him on.

'Oh, Jim, you shall stroke me now! You shall violate me again. Won't it be nicey nicey? Do you like feeling there, Jim? You shall push this tool of yours in there, dear Jim. We will have such pleasure. I will roger with you, Jim.'

I put my hot lips up to his. I sucked humid kisses from his mouth. He was wild with passion. His limb was immense and very hard. I quite dreaded it. I like large-made men. I forced him to take off his coat and breeches. I stood up in my *chemise*. I seized his member again in my grasp. The big nut delighted me. We were both impatient to commence the lewd act of enjoyment. I leant against the soft bed in the corner. I raised my *chemise* with both hands.

'Look there, Jim – do you like that?'

I showed him my body naked to the waist. Half mad with the intensity of his passion, he rushed upon me. I mounted upon the bed. He placed himself kneeling between my legs. His monstrous limb stood erect and menacing. I anointed the knob with cold cream and also applied a little to my slit. He came down on me. I put the thing in between the nether lips. He pushed. I threw up my legs. I arched up my loins. It entered my belly. It passed slowly up my vagina.

'Oh, my goodness! Jim – you're into me?'

'My God! How lovely it feels – oh! Oh! Ugh!'

'Push, push! I can take it all! Do it slowly, Jim! Is it nicey nicey?'

Jim grunted and thrust as if his life depended on it. I was gorged with the monstrous thing. I had it up to the balls. Oh, how he worked me! How he slipped his huge member up and down! How the bed shook as he thrust in his pleasure!

'Oh, Jim! Stroke me slowly – so – slowly! Oh! Oh! It's lovely – it's heavenly now! Oh, Jim! Dear Jim! Stroke – stroke me! Oh!'

'My God! Oh, Miss Eveline, it feels as if I was up to your waist! I never had such pleasure! Ugh! Ugh!'

'Finish me, Jim! You're too big – but it's lovely all the same! Oh, my! I can feel it throbbing!'

Neither could articulate now. I clutched the bedclothes. I

ABOVE A print from a series by 'Jean le Pêcheur'. The artist's name is a pun on a word which can mean both 'sinner' and 'fisher'.

rolled my head from side to side. My limbs quivered under the furious shocks of my ravisher. He sank upon me. His thrusts became harder and shorter. He discharged. Thick jets of semen inundated my womb. He was a long time finishing. I received the whole flood of his sperm. . . .

At last he let me slip from the narrow bed. He had stroked me

LEFT *The Lovers*, a coloured print by the Danish artist Gerda Wegener (b. 1889).

twice without withdrawing. What happened during the next three quarters of an hour I do not know. He seemed like one possessed by a demon of carnal lust. He kept me in a constant whirl of copulation. He must have discharged five or six times in all. I was almost unconscious when he at length desisted. I returned to the park. I remounted. I could hardly sit my horse. I fancied Goorkha looked at me reproachfully. I reached home. I threw myself upon my sofa – my ride had much fatigued me.

Edwardian readers who wanted different adventures from those described by Henty and Rider Haggard could follow Eveline through three volumes packed with sexual derring-do. In this final extract our intrepid heroine wrestles with the mysterious Theodore (who can only communicate by writing on a slate) and discovers hidden treasure!

ABOVE and OPPOSITE Two prints from the series by 'Jean le Pêcheur'. The caricatures of knowing ways which the artist creates lend a curious atmosphere to this strange group of erotic prints.

His eyes shot flames of lust. He took the slate.
'You are no less sensual than beautiful. We will drown ourselves in pleasure. I love pleasure. With you it will be divine.'
He threw off his coat. He assisted me to remove my bodice. Soon I stood in my corset of pale blue satin and a short skirt of the same colour and material. He rapidly divested himself of his outer things. He caught my hand. He carried it under his shirt.
'Oh, good heavens! What a monster!'
His instrument was as long as Jim's. It was even thicker. It was stiff as buckram. It throbbed under my wanton touches.
He pressed my hand upon it and laughed a strange silent laugh. Then he wrote on the slate:
'What do you call that?'
This was evidently intended as a challenge. Not bashful, I took it up.
'I call it an instrument – a weapon of offence – a limb.'
'I call it a cock!'
'Well, he certainly had a very fine crest. He carries himself very proudly – his head is as red as a turkey-cock – he is a real beauty!'
The slate was thrown on one side. Theodore drew me on his knee. He tucked up my short, lace-trimmed *chemise*. I made only just sufficient remonstrance to whet his appetite. He lifted me in his strong arms like a little child. He bore me to the bed. He deposited me gently upon it. He was by my side in an instant minus all save shirt, which stuck up in front of him as if it was suspended on a peg – as indeed it was. Theodore laid his handsome head on my breast. He toyed with my most secret charms. My round and plump posteriors seemed specially to delight him. I grasped his enormous member in my hand. I ventured to examine also the heavy purse which depended below. His testicles were in proportion to his splendid limb. I separated them from each other. There seemed to be something I did not understand. I felt them over again. Surely – yes, I was correct – he had *three*! He led me eagerly to the soft couch. Once on the bed he recommenced his amorous caresses. I seized him once more by his truncheon.

It was so nice to feel the warm length of flesh – the broad red nut – the long white shaft, and the triangle of testicles which were drawn up tight below it. It was so strange too that this fine young fellow could neither hear nor speak! The spirit of mischief took possession of me. The demon of lust vied with him in stimulating my passion. I slipped off the bed. Theodore followed me. I raised my *chemise* up to my middle and laughingly challenged him to follow. The view of my naked charms was evidently appetising. He tried to seize me again. I avoided his grasp. He ran after me round the table which stood at one end of the room. His expression was all frolic and fun, but with a strong tinge of sensuous desire in his humid eyes and moist lips. I let him catch me. He held me tight this time. I turned my back to him. I felt him pressing the brown curls of his hairy parts upon my plump buttocks.

He pushed me before him towards the bed. His huge member inserted between my thighs. I saw its red-capped head appear in front of me. I put my hand down to it. To my surprise he had placed an ivory napkin ring over it. It reduced the available length. It certainly left me less to fear from its unusually large proportions. I had already taken the precaution to anoint my parts with cold cream. I adjusted the head as I leant forward, belly down, on the soft bed. The young fellow pushed. He entered. I thought he would split me up. He held me by the hips. He thrust it into me. It passed up. I groaned with a mingled feeling of pain and pleasure. He was too excited to pause now. He bore forward, setting himself solidly to work to do the job. I passed my hand down to feel his cock, as he called it, as it emerged from time to time from the pliable sheath. Although I knew he could not hear, yet it delighted me to utter my sensations – women must talk – they can't help it. I was every bit a woman at that moment! Besides, I could express my ideas in any language I liked, as crudely as I chose – there was no one to hear me – no one to offend – no one to chide. I jerked forward.

'Oh! Take it out! Don't spend yet! I want to change – it's so delicious! How sweetly you poke me – you dear fellow!'

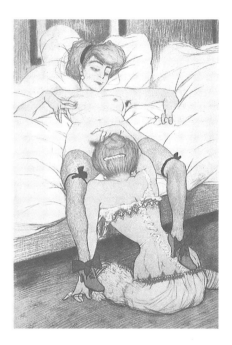

The huge instrument extricated itself with a plop! Theodore divined my intention. He aided me to place myself upon the side of the bed. I took his cock again in my little hands. I examined it voraciously. It was lovely now – all shining and glistening, distended and rigid in its luxury.

'I want it all – all – all!'

He evidently understood. He slipped off the napkin ring. He presented it again to my eager slit. It went up me slowly.

'Oh, my God! It is too long now. Oh! Oh! Never mind – give it me all – all – oh! Ah! Oh! Go slowly! You brute – you are splitting me! Do you hear? Poke! Oh! Push – push now! I'm coming, do you hear? You cruel brute! Coming – oh, God! Oh!'

He perceived my condition, he bore up close to me as long as my emitting spasms lasted. My swollen clitoris was in closest contact with the back of his weapon which tickled ecstatically.

I clung to him with both thighs. I raised my belly to meet his stabbing thrusts. I seized the pillow. I covered my face. I bit the

pillowcase through and through. When I had finished he stopped a little to let me breathe.

'You have not come yet, but you will soon. I know it. I can feel it by the strong throbbing of your cock. I want it – oh! I want it! I must hold your balls while you spend. I want your sperm!'

He became more and more urgent. He was having me with all his tremendous vigour. His strokes were shorter – quicker – my thighs worked in unison. His features writhed in his ecstasy of increasing enjoyment. He was nearing the end. I felt every throb of his huge instrument.

———◊———

Edwardian London saw the publication of a group of erotic novels which were evidently the work of the same anonymous writer: *The Confessions of Nemesis Hunt*, *Pleasure Bound Afloat*, *Pleasure Bound Ashore* and *Maudie*. Who this man was is uncertain, but he seems to have had links with the theatre. Not only is the heroine of *Nemesis Hunt* an actress, and the novel full of background detail; but all the books are theatrical both in their presentation and their pacing. *Pleasure Bound Afloat* even has pirates to provide some action, as did J. M. Barrie's *Peter Pan*, which had first appeared four years earlier, in 1904; but John Tucker, ex-MD of Edinburgh, who left 'for an unmentionable offence in Princes Street Gardens', has none of Captain Hook's problems with foreplay.

John Tucker began to think: he *must* show his manhood. He pulled her over him as tenderly as he knew how, and swept his strong hand over her deliciously rounded breasts to the opening in her drawers. He knew all the time that he was thinking about the boat coming in, and he knew that Helena knew it, but his penis stiffened automatically.

She, always all readiness, guided his great prick, not without some difficulty, into her moist little cunt. She wriggled delightedly, closed her eyes, and bit him savagely on the cheek. Then she flung herself violently up and down on his vibrating cock, uttering little cries of joy. Her fingers dug into his ribs, her naked legs clasped in a vice-like grip round his, her little tongue darted in and out of his mouth, and together they spent voluminously and savagely. For those few seconds all thoughts of mines and dividends had fled from John's brain; he saw only the lovely angel face pressed close to his, felt only the vicious clasp of her cunt muscles. It was the first time she had been so madly passionate with him. Perhaps, he thought, that little talk had done good. He made up his mind to keep her straight.

'Promise me, little angel,' he whispered as she slowly raised her cunt from off his cock, and looked down with those lovely turquoise eyes into his, 'promise me to be true.'

'If you can always do it like that, I'll think it over.'

They strolled on, hand in hand, the lovely, semi-naked girl, and the brutally strong-looking buccaneer, through the soft groves.

———◊———

OPPOSITE and BELOW Etchings by an unknown German artist illustrating the *Steps of Love* by the playwright Frank Wedekind (1864–1918). He was famous for his plays *Pandora's Box* and *Spirit of the Earth*, on which Alban Berg based his opera *Lulu*; the heroine is the spirit of destructive sexuality.

———◊———

The dialogue in all the books is also handled in a way that suggests familiarity with scripts, and much attention is given to costume and the appearance of each erotic tableau.

The Sisters Lovett were just his style: they made him remember with a sigh the jolly chorus girl supper parties of the old days, the merry moments in the dressing-rooms, and the frank impropriety of the conversation.

He was rather sorry just now to find the sisters nude; he would have liked them better in their daringly suggestive music hall frocks, he liked to see pretty legs emerging from a sea of fluff.

He apologized with a laugh for his unannounced intrusion.

'We are rather free and easy here, you know,' he said.

RIGHT A studio photograph, Paris, early twentieth century.
OPPOSITE A French erotic postcard of the *Belle Epoque*. The care and imagination with which much of this erotic ephemera was produced raised the status of the postcard to a new art-form.

'Oh, don't mind us,' said Tilly, 'we've soon tumbled to your habits.'

'*And* we like 'em,' added Cissie.

Mike knew his girl, and had not come empty-handed.

'I know you theatre girls like jewels and pretty things,' he said, and emptied his pockets.

They were pretty things with a vengeance, and the sisters went into openly expressed raptures. Bracelets, rings, necklaces, all of beautiful designs, mingled with brooches, combs, jewelled garters, and a score of dainty ornaments.

'You'd best just divvy 'em up equally,' said Mike, 'only you ought to have your clothes on to show 'em off.'

'Shall we dress, then, in our music hall frocks?' asked Tilly, 'and after that we'll thank you *ever* so prettily.'

ABOVE and OPPOSITE Two more etchings by an unknown German artist illustrating Wedekind's *The Steps of Love*. Both technique and composition are daring and original.

This story has no moral. If it points out an evil, at any rate it suggests no remedy.

SAKI (H. H. MUNRO) (1870–1916)

She was clever enough to see that this was just the way the young man wanted to be made randy, and didn't attempt to kiss him.

They chose rather simple dresses, those in which as *les deux demi-vierges* they had electrified even Paris.

Firstly they had to do their hair, which now was all flowing loose. In two twin plaits it went, with a little bow at the end. In front a deep wave swept their foreheads. The corsage was not very *décolletée* in front, but at the back the V cut down to the waist. They wore no corsets.

The skirts were short, well above the knee, distended by a mass of underskirts. They had very short drawers, and very long black stockings with a golden stripe down the side: the whole note of the costumes was black and gold. Their shoes were golden, with very high black heels.

'Well?' said Tilly, when the attire was complete.

'Like to kiss us?' said Cissie.

'Wait till I put all the pretty things on, and then you'll see what I want to do,' answered the young earl excitedly.

He just loved them like this, and all the old *joie de théâtre* came back to him. When Cissie did a high kick and Tilly slipped gracefully into the 'splits' he was in a seventh heaven.

'We oughtn't to have 'em on with those clothes,' said Cissie, 'we're supposed to be dear little darlings who've never had our windows broken. We ought to keep 'em for our second costumes, but we'll do that when we give our real show at the theatre.'

The jewels pretty well smothered the girls, and they danced for delight before the long cheval glass.

'Now then, you darling,' said Tilly, 'we've both got to thank you, but you can't have us both at once; which'll you have first?'

It was an *embarras de richesses*, and Mike looked uncomfortable.

Eventually the toss up made it Cissie.

'Do you want me to undress?' she asked.

'No, no, I'm sick of naked women.'

'Well, *you* must undress,' said Tilly. 'I'll boss this fuck, Cis, you just go and lie on that couch.'

Cissie obeyed, and lay back, her legs wide apart, a ravishing vision.

Tilly undressed Mike to the buff. She did it slowly, for she was very randy, and took an especially long time in undoing his fly.

He was a finely made young fellow and his cock stood proudly up. Tilly took it in her mouth for a moment, then kissed him, smacked his bottom and told him to do his duty.

He dived lasciviously into Cissie's mass of *dessus*, his white naked body making a wicked contrast to the black and gold of the girl's clothes.

It was a couch that could be raised at either end, and Tilly, knowing the joy for a man of fucking a really acrobatic girl when her head is on a lower level than her body, raised the front of the couch.

Cissie curved up her legs right round his shoulders, and a very loving fuck began. She kissed and bit him and squeezed him and

they finished in a frenzy, Cissie giving a piercing scream as she
felt the juice spurt into her.

In *Maudie* (1909) the unknown author describes an incident in
which the heroine shows off her collection of erotic photographs.
It also gives him an opportunity to display his own knowledge of
the incidents in Biblical history which artists have traditionally
depicted in order to deal with erotic subjects safely. It is an interesting list, and another insight into the mind of the author.

    '*Voilà*: hey, presto!' exclaimed Maudie, pressing a button at the
side of the proscenium.
    The walls altered as if at the touch of a fairy's wand, and a
most gorgeous vista of photographic voluptuosity met Charlie's
astonished and delighted eyes. . . . First in numbers came the
nudes. They were none of them of the blatantly crude, erotic,
fucking, all-ends-up type, but they were – well – not the sort that
Aunt Lavinia ought to see.
    There were many single nudes, very nearly always the model
being Maudie herself. For this she apologized.
    'You see, Charlie,' she said, 'I have a paucity of models. . . . I
want more girl models for the *single* figures. It doesn't matter so

much for the groups, as long as we have good principals.'
    The single figures were very beautiful. There was a complete
set of Maudie's life – Maudie in her bath – Maudie drying herself
under the trees – Maudie in varying stages of dressing – Maudie

riding, cycling, rowing, and in various gowns. The nearest approach to being very suggestive was Maudie with only her stockings and shoes on, but every strip of jewellery she possessed.

There were a number of pretty girl pictures, but nearly all the same models again.

'We *must* have more flappers,' said Maudie, vehemently.

The groups, however, were of the more surpassing interest, very many depicted great – and small, but interesting – events in the world's history. Biblical subjects were quite prevalent there; for instance, we had Susanna and the Elders. A lovely Susanna, mother naked, admiring herself in the well water, and the most lascivious-looking Elders admiring; in the middle distance, a pretty girl and boy, quite naked, were playing prettily with each other. The scenic effects were splendid. Maudie confessed that she had the help in that line of a very well-known French actor manager, and that an English actor manager had put his scenic stock at her disposal.

Potiphar's wife was well treated. A naked Mrs. Potiphar had just rent the garment from the fleeing Joseph, who, with one hand attempting to conceal his parts, was rushing from the room.

Mrs. Potiphar, who blazed with jewels, was of a pronouncedly Egyptian type, sinuous and wicked-eyed. In Joseph, Charlie had not the slightest difficulty in recognizing a prominent young stock-jobber.

'Where had he been in London all this time, and never heard

BELOW A studio photograph, Paris, early twentieth century.
OPPOSITE Half of a stereoscopic photograph taken by Eugène Agelou and reprinted in 1910.

The Western custom of one wife and hardly any mistresses.

Saki (H. H. Munro) (1870–1916)

of this place and their goings-on?' he wondered.

Samson and Delilah – God bless my soul – it was the famous wrestler, and *very* little clothes on, and *what* a Delilah – Maudie herself this time.

In Samson Agonistes, Samson was unencumbered with clothing. In the fight between David and Goliath, the giant had been, by some ingenious photographic trick, made to look a very real giant, and his John Thomas was a thing like a quarter-staff, his balls like melons.

A sweetly-pretty little David stood boldly forth in the foreground, aiming the sling.

There were some pictures of the historic intimacy between David and Jonathan, which left little to the imagination.

We have missed the earlier episode of the Garden of Eden. Adam and Eve were very frankly naked and unashamed in several positions, and there were the dearest possible Cain and Abel.

The scene where, after the fall (which, by the way, was realistically treated), the man and woman get themselves clothed was admirably arranged.

The strange behaviour of Lot's daughters, when they sat in turn on their poor old father's prick and got themselves in the

family way, was reproduced in detail, as also was Onan's strange behaviour to his sister, when he foolishly spilt it on the floor.

King David and Bathsheba on the roof, and later the same pair in bed, were fully illustrated.

Although all the erotic books in what we might call the 'Edwardian Theatrical' series are pure escapism, written to order for an eager public, they are good examples of their kind. The books are humorous and well-paced; it is even true to say that some of the characters occurring in the books give a strange impression that they are drawn from life. Who was their creator? The biography of 'Charlie Osmond' in *Maudie* is written as something of a joke, but is it only that?

> A gentleman by birth, he had most of the right instincts and per-versions. He had left Eton for the usual reason, and he regretted it. He did *not* want to bugger other boys, but some did, and he somehow hated to be out of the fashion. Unfortunately, he was found out.
>
> At Oxford his career had been meteoric. He could not go to a very good college, owing to his school troubles, and his good allowance made him a star at – (we will suppress the name). He did many things he should not have, and his final exploit of sow-ing the word 'CUNT' in mustard and cress in the front quad grass, which came up under the astonished eyes of the dean's daughter, led to his final exit. His defence – that he had meant the word as a moral admonition to those of the Varsity who had leaned to malpractices in the sodomitical line – was not accepted, and he went.
>
> The home-coming was as usual – nobody to meet him at the station but the chauffeur, and father in the gun-room.

> > Your son's devotion to landscape gardening [ran the dean's note] is undoubtedly commendable, but we must remind you that the grass in the front quadrangle at — has for 500 years preserved its virginity, and the word inscribed makes not only a blemish on the grass, but con-veys a reflection on the locality. We are only pleased that no word has found its way to the American papers. – We are, etc.,
> >
> > HY. CHARTERIS (*DEAN*)

> Charlie Osmond came to town with £300 a year, and a paternal kick on the arse.

It has been suggested by P. J. Kearney, the authority on erotic lit-erature, that the true identity of the writer who produced this cheerful corpus of erotic work in the decade before World War I was the journalist George Reginald Bacchus (1873–1945). He cer-tainly seems to fit the evidence. Bacchus had been a close friend of Leonard Smithers, the well-connected publisher of erotica whom Oscar Wilde called 'the most erudite erotomane in Europe'. He

OPPOSITE and BELOW Another two etchings by an unknown German artist for the edition of Wedekind's *The Steps of Love*. Expensively produced limited editions of illustrated erotica have always found a small, discriminating connoisseur market.

A woman whose dresses are made in Paris and whose marriage has been made in Heaven might be equally biased for and against free imports.

SAKI (H. H. MUNRO) (1870–1916)

had been at Oxford ('the homecoming was as usual'). Improbably, Bacchus wrote for a weekly religious paper ('Biblical subjects were quite prevalent there') and, most important of all, he was married to Isa Bowman (1874–1958), the well-known actress. Bacchus certainly had the right name for the job: wine and other delights of the table abound in the novels. But if he was the author, what did his wife – one of the theatrical Bowman Sisters – make of it all?

———————— ◊ ————————

One evening, during Christmas 1914, Lytton Strachey (1880–1932) read his novel *Ermyntrude and Esmeralda* to his friend David Garnett. The book had been written two years earlier for the artist Henry Lamb, with whom Strachey was then very much in love. Garnett saw at once that the light comedy – delivered in Strachey's piping falsetto voice – disguised a stinging satire on contemporary attitudes to sex and sex education.

Ermyntrude and Esmeralda is written as an exchange of letters between two privileged young ladies whose sexual education has been sadly neglected. By pooling their experiences – Ermyntrude lives in London, her friend in the country – they hope to solve the mystery.

In an early letter Ermyntrude reports on the questioning of her governess, Simpson, and decides on an absurd nomenclature for the sexual organs, which both girls adopt.

I've tried to go on with our enquiries about love and babies, but I haven't got much further. The other day I began edging round the conversation in that direction with old Simpson, and naturally that didn't succeed. She shut me up when I was still miles off. Everyone always does – that is, everyone who knows. What can it mean. It is very odd. Why on earth should there be a secret about what happens when people have babies? I suppose it must be something appallingly shocking, but then, if it is, how can so many people bear to have them? Of course I'm quite sure it's got something to do with those absurd little things that men have in statues hanging between their legs, and that we haven't. And I'm also sure that it's got something to do with the thing between our legs that I always call my Pussy. I believe that may be its real name, because once when I was at Oxford looking at the races with my cousin Tom, I heard quite a common woman say to another 'There, Sarah, doesn't that make your pussy pout?' And then I saw that one of the rowing men's trousers were all split and those things were showing between his legs; and it looked most extraordinary. I couldn't quite see enough, but the more I looked the more I felt – well, the more I felt my pussy pouting, as the woman had said. So now I call ours pussies and theirs bow-wows, and my theory is that people have children when their bow-wows and pussies pout at the same time. Do you think that's it? Of course I can't imagine how it can possibly work, and I daresay I'm altogether wrong and it's really got something to do with W.C's.

As the correspondence develops Ermyntrude asks if the bow-wow of her brother's tutor, Mr Mapleton, 'pouts' for Esmeralda. Alas for the eager young lady, we soon learn that it does not:

There has been the most awful row. Papa went in by accident yesterday morning to get a shoe-horn, and found Mr. Mapleton in Godfrey's bed. He was most fearfully angry, told Mr. Mapleton that he would have to go away out of England and live abroad for ever and ever, or he would have him put in prison, and stormed at Godfrey like anything, and said he would flog him, only he was too old to be flogged, but he *ought* to be flogged, and that he had disgraced himself and his family, and that it could never be wiped out, never, and that he couldn't hold up his head again with such a son, and that as Godfrey wasn't to be flogged he would have to

be punished in some even worse way – but none of us know what yet. It was too dreadful for words. Godfrey told me all about it. Mr. Mapleton went away that very morning, immediately after breakfast, but he didn't come down to it, so perhaps he didn't have any, and Mama has been almost in tears ever since, and Papa has hardly spoken to anyone. The Dean has been looking very grave. . . . Poor Godfrey is in such dreadful disgrace, and I am very sorry for him. I suppose it was a frightfully wicked thing to do, but the curious thing is he doesn't seem at all wicked, and I really do believe I'm fonder of him than I've ever been before. I talked to him for quite a long time yesterday before dinner. I went into the morning room, and he was there, so I began to say how sorry I was. But before I'd said very much he turned round and walked towards the window, and then I saw that he was crying. I hardly knew what to do, so I went on talking for a little,

He belonged to that race of beings who are in effect, since it is precisely because their temperament is feminine that they worship manliness, at cross-purposes with themselves.

MARCEL PROUST (1871–1922)

How different, how very different from the home life of our own dear Queen.

AN OVERHEARD REMARK BY AN ANONYMOUS BRITISH MATRON DURING A PERFORMANCE OF *ANTONY AND CLEOPATRA*

ABOVE A book illustration by G. de Sainte-Croix (active 1949–59 in France); drypoint, hand-coloured in aquatint.

and at last I threw my arms round his neck and kissed him a great many times, which seemed to comfort him although he began to cry harder than ever at first. But in the end he told me all about Mr. Mapleton, and how fond he was of him, and how unhappy he was to think he'd never see him again, and when I asked him whether he was in love with him, he said yes, he was, and why not? – that he loved him better than anyone in the world and always would as long as he lived, and then he began crying again. And he said he didn't think he'd done anything wicked at all, and it seems the Greeks used to do it too – at least the Athenians, who were the best of the Greeks – which is very funny, don't you think?

Contemporary attitudes towards homosexuality at all levels of society caused Strachey much pain. Behind his amusing and skilfully constructed satire is considerable private anger at the hypocrisies and prejudices of his peers.

As for the girls, their sexual education is at last completed when Ermyntrude encounters the handsome footman, Henry.

He didn't say anything, but put out his hand, and looked at my eyes, and I looked at his eyes, and then – well, it didn't seem to be me any longer, but it was like something else that made me do things, and I put my arms round his neck all of a sudden, and he hugged me so hard that I could only just breathe, and it felt as if he was hugging me with the whole of his body. And then the candle fell over and went out, and it was pitch dark, and after that I hardly know what happened, because it was so very exciting, but somehow I began to half lie down on the stairs, which are quite steep and nothing but wood, and Henry was on the top of me, hugging me just as much as ever, so you can imagine that it wasn't particularly comfortable. I forgot to say that directly he hugged me I felt my pussy pouting so enormously that I didn't know what to do – except hug him back, which seemed only to make it pout more. But when we were lying down it did it even more still. Then Henry began pulling up my skirt and even my petticoat, and I began helping him, and it was very funny – we were both in such a hurry, and his body twisted about so much and he breathed so hard that I half began to feel frightened. But he held me too tightly for me to have possibly got away, even if I'd wanted to, and then all of a sudden my pussy began to hurt most horribly, and I very nearly screamed. It was as if something was going right through me, but though it hurt my pussy so, it made it stop pouting at the same time and begin to purr instead, as if it liked it, and I think it did like it better than anything else in the world. I can't understand why pussies should like so much being hurt. And the curious thing was that I suppose I liked it too, because I went on kissing Henry more and more, and although I was so uncomfortable and hot and all squashed-up and disarranged and I believe nearly crying, I didn't at all want it to stop, and I was very sorry when Henry said he would have to go and lay the dinner. . . .

He said that his bow-wow had begun to pout so much, especially when he was handing me the vegetables, that he couldn't have
stood it any longer. But that night, when he handed me the vegetables, it was a great lark, because my pussy was pouting, too.
After dinner, when I'd gone up to bed, it was still more of a lark.
I'd arranged it with Henry. When all the lights were out I opened
my door a very little, and then he came in, and after we'd kissed
each other a great deal we took off our clothes. I was very excited
to see what his bow-wow was like, but I was astonished to see that
he hadn't got one, but a very funny big pink thing standing
straight up instead. I was rather frightened, because I thought he
might be deformed, which wouldn't have been at all nice, so I
asked him what it was. Then he laughed so much that I thought
every one would hear, and at last I discovered that it *was* his
bow-wow after all, and it turns out that that is what they get like
when they pout! I was very pleased indeed, and so was my pussy
when his bow-wow went into it, and after that we went to bed.
Ever since then he's come every night, and I've enjoyed myself
very much.

ABOVE Another illustration from
Les Délassements d'Eros by the
Danish artist Gerda Wegener
(b. 1889). When an artist's
personal style is so distinctive, his
or her creation of 'anonymous'
erotic work becomes something of
an open secret.

PART FOUR

After the nightmare

ABOVE *Eve* by Eric Gill (1882–1940), first-class artist, typographer and – so it appears from a recent biography – practitioner of a wide variety of sexual activities both legal and illegal.

After the world's first technological war nothing was, or could ever be, the same again. Empires, classes, political systems: all the old structures were either fractured or had collapsed altogether. In art and literature new voices said new things, and old voices said different things. Sex became a subject which mainstream writers demanded freedom to explore. It was a freedom which had to be fought for – there are still skirmishes – but sex was in the open. While writers such as James Joyce pushed language to its limits to explore new aspects of conventional sexuality, in *Ulysses* (first published in Paris in 1922), other writers used conventional language to explore the extreme limits of sexuality itself. The American writer Edith Wharton (1862–1937) took one of the darkest of all sexual topics, incestuous love, as the subject for her short story *Beatrice Palmato*.

Then suddenly he drew back her wrapper entirely, whispered: 'I want you all, so that my eyes can see all that my lips can't cover,' and in a moment she was free, lying before him in her fresh young nakedness, and feeling that indeed his eyes were covering it with fiery kisses. But Mr Palmato was never idle, and while this sensation flashed through her one of his arms had slipped under her back and wound itself around her so that his hand again enclosed her left breast. At the same moment the other hand softly separated her legs, and began to slip up the old path it had so often travelled in darkness. But now it was light, she was uncovered, and looking downward, beyond his dark silver-sprinkled head, she could see her own parted knees, and outstretched ankles and feet. Suddenly she remembered Austin's rough advances, and shuddered.

The mounting hand paused, the dark head was instantly raised. 'What is it, my own?'

'I was—remembering—last week—' she faltered, below her breath.

'Yes, darling. That experience is a cruel one – but it has to come once in all women's lives. Now we shall reap its fruit.'

But she hardly heard him, for the old swooning sweetness was creeping over her. As his hand stole higher she felt the secret bud of her body swelling, yearning, quivering hotly to burst into bloom. Ah, here was his subtle forefinger pressing it, forcing its tight petals softly apart, and laying on their sensitive edges a circular touch so soft and yet so fiery that already lightnings of heat shot from that palpitating centre all over her surrendered body, to the tips of her fingers, and the ends of her loosened hair.

The sensation was so exquisite that she could have asked to have it indefinitely prolonged; but suddenly his head bent lower, and with a deeper thrill she felt his lips pressed upon that quivering invisible bud, and then the delicate firm thrust of his tongue, so full and yet so infinitely subtle, pressing apart the close petals, and forcing itself in deeper and deeper through the passage that glowed and seemed to become illumined at its approach. . . .

'Ah—' she gasped, pressing her hands against her sharp nipples, and flinging her legs apart.

Instantly one of her hands was caught, and while Mr Palmato, rising, bent over her, his lips on hers again, she felt his fingers pressing into her hand that strong fiery muscle that they used, in their old joke, to call his third hand.

'My little girl,' he breathed, sinking down beside her, his muscular trunk bare, and the third hand quivering and thrusting upward between them, a drop of moisture pearling at its tip.

She instantly understood the reminder that his words conveyed, letting herself downward along the divan until her head was in a line with his middle she flung herself upon the swelling member, and began to caress it insinuatingly with her tongue. It was the first time she had ever seen it actually exposed to her eyes, and her heart swelled excitedly: to have her touch confirmed by sight enriched the sensation that was communicating itself through her ardent twisting tongue. With panting breath she wound her caress deeper and deeper into the thick firm folds, till at length the member, thrusting her lips open, held her gasping, as if at its mercy; then, in a trice, it was withdrawn, her knees were pressed apart, and she saw it before her, above her, like a crimson flash, and at last, sinking backward into new abysses of bliss, felt it descend on her, press open the secret gates, and plunge into the deepest depths of her thirsting body. . . .

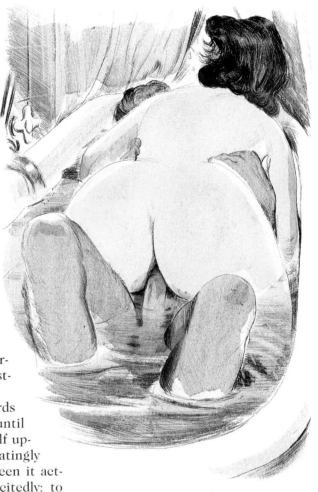

ABOVE *In the bath*, book illustration by G. de Sainte-Croix (active 1949–59 in France); drypoint, hand-coloured in aquatint.

I f Frank Harris had not published *My Life and Loves* (in Paris in 1925) the world of letters would have been poorer (and duller), but the author's reputation would have stood rather higher. This was after all the radical editor of the *Saturday Review* who defended the Boers, who spoke out against the war with Germany, who went to Brixton Prison fighting for the freedom of the press. Harris (1856–1931) was also the loyal ally of Oscar Wilde and a close friend of Bernard Shaw for forty years. Shaw's perceptive assessment of him ran as follows:

Harris suffered deeply from repeated disillusions and disappointments. Like Hedda Gabler he was tormented by a sense of the sordidness in the common-place realities which form so much of the stuff of life, and was not only disappointed in people who did nothing splendid, but savagely contemptuous of people who did not want to have anything splendid done . . .

Frank, too, was a man of splendid visions, unreasonable expectations, fierce appetites which he was unable to relate to anything except to romantic literature, and especially to the impetuous rhetoric of Shakespear. It is hardly an exaggeration to say that he ultimately quarrelled with everybody but Shakespear. . . .

It was Harris's tendency to romanticize and idealize everything – especially what he called 'the greatest of all influences', sex – which has led those who understood him less well than Shaw to dub him a liar, or at the very least a fantasist. As we have seen before, remembered sexual incidents, even when the intention is to be truthful, hover between reality and the world of dreams. Did Frank really talk to his young lover Grace about Montaigne? Yes, he probably did.

BELOW An illustration in watercolour over sepia ink by an unknown Italian artist, c. 1935.

I put my arms round her legs and, lifting her up, carried her to the bed. The next moment I had thrown up her clothes and buried my face between her thighs.

'What are you doing?' she cried, but as I began kissing love's sweet home and the little red button, involuntarily she opened her thighs and gave herself to the new sensations. As I felt her responding, I drew her nearer to me a little roughly and opened her thighs fully. There never was a more lovely sex, and already the smaller inside lips were all flushed with feeling, while soon pearling love-drops oozed down on my lips.

I kept on, knowing that such a first experience is unforgettable and soon she abandoned herself recklessly, and her hand came down on my head and directed me now higher, now lower, according to her desire.

When the love-play had gone on four or five times and I stood up to rest, she said gravely: 'You are a dear and gave me great pleasure, but do you like it?'

'Of course,' I said. 'Even old Montaigne knew that the pleasure we give the loved one is more than that we get.'

'Oh, that's my feeling,' she said, 'but how am I to give you pleasure?' In answer, I took out my sex. She touched it curiously, drawing back the skin and pushing it forward: 'Does that give you pleasure?'

I nodded. 'But this,' and I put my hand on her sex, 'could give me much more.'

'Unquestionably obscure, lewd, lascivious and indecent' was how a judge of the New York Supreme Court described *My Life and Loves*. The ringing phrase would have made a good selling line on a dust-jacket, but it is hardly an accurate description of the work. The sex in *My Life and Loves* is not simply a record of the author's experience, it is part of a philosophy of life which Harris develops from the very beginning. For example, in chapter three of Volume One (there were five volumes in all) we have a commonplace enough description of Frank's wet dreams and sexual investigations as a schoolboy.

> I could not sleep that night for thinking of Lucille's sex. When I fell asleep I dreamed of Lucille, dreamed that she had yielded to me and I was pushing my sex into hers; but there was some obstacle and while I was pushing, pushing, my seed spirted in an orgasm of pleasure – and at once I awoke and putting down my hand, found that I was still coming: the sticky, hot, milklike sperm was all over my hairs and prick.
>
> I got up and washed and returned to bed; the cold water had quieted me; but soon by thinking of Lucille and her soft, hot, hairy 'pussy,' I grew randy again and in this state fell asleep. Again I dreamed of Lucille and again I was trying, trying in vain to get into her when again the spasm of pleasure overtook me; I felt my seed spirting hot and – I awoke.
>
> But lo! when I put my hand down, there was no seed, only a little moisture just at the head of my sex – nothing more. Did it mean that I could only give forth seed once? I tested myself at once; while picturing Lucille's sex, its soft hot roundness and hairs, I caressed my sex, moving my hand faster up and down till soon I brought on the orgasm of pleasure and felt distinctly the hot thrills as if my seed were spirting, but nothing came, hardly even the moisture.

This description of sexual awakening is followed by an effect which is the exact opposite of the blindness which children were once told would afflict them if they played with themselves.

> It was the awakening of sex-life in me, I believe, that first revealed to me the beauty of inanimate nature.
>
> A night or two later I was ravished by a moon nearly at the full that flooded our playing field with ivory radiance, making the haystack in the corner a thing of supernal beauty.
>
> Why had I never before seen the wonder of the world, the sheer loveliness of nature all about me? From this time on I began to enjoy descriptions of scenery in the books I read, and began, too, to love landscapes in painting.
>
> Thank goodness! the miracle was accomplished, at long last, and my life enriched, ennobled, transfigured as by the bounty of God! From that day on I began to live an enchanted life, for at once I tried to see beauty everywhere and at all times of day and night caught glimpses that ravished me with delight and turned my being into a hymn of praise and joy.

My Life and Loves may be 'lascivious' (and a lot more besides), but it is certainly not 'obscene', 'lewd' or 'indecent'. Two paragraphs

BELOW An etching by 'Rainier, E.', the pseudonym of Carl Breuer-Courth, Germany, c. 1920.

A niece of the late Queen of Sheba
Was promiscuous with an amoeba.
This queer blob of jelly
Would lie in her belly
And, quivering, murmur, 'Ich liebe!'

NORMAN DOUGLAS (1868–1952)

after the last extract, Harris makes a very revealing comment about himself: 'Dimly I became conscious that if this life were sordid and mean, petty and unpleasant, the fault was in myself and in my blindness. I began then for the first time to understand that I myself was a magician and could create my own fairyland, ay, and my own heaven, transforming this world into the throne-room of a god.'

Frank Harris was no ordinary romantic in search of perfection: he sought it in every sphere of his life – as an editor, as a writer, and of course in bed. *A ménage à trois* with a mature French woman and her adopted daughter affords him a glimpse, at least, of sexual perfection.

I gave a big lunch to people of importance in the theatre and in journalism and invited Jeanne and referred everything to her and drew her out, throning her, and afterwards returning to her house to dinner. While she was changing and titivating, I took Lisette in my arms and kissed her with hot lips again and again while feeling her budding breasts, till she put her arms round my neck and kissed me just as warmly; and then I ventured to touch her little half-fledged sex and caress it, till it opened and grew moist and she nestled up to me and whispered: 'Oh! how you excite me!'

'Have you ever done it to yourself?' I asked. She nodded with bright dancing eyes. 'Often, but I prefer you to touch me.' For the first time I heard the truth from a girl and her courage charmed me. I could not help laying her on the sofa, and turning up her clothes: how lovely her limbs were, and how perfect her sex. She was really exquisite, and I took an almost insane pleasure in studying her beauties, and parting the lips of her sex [with] kisses: in a few moments she was all trembling and gasping. She put her hand on my head to stop me. When I lifted her up, she kissed me. 'You dear,' she said with a strange earnestness, 'I want you always. You'll stay with us, won't you?' I kissed her for her sweetness.

When Jeanne came out of the cabinet, we all went into the dining-room, and afterwards Lisette went up to her room after kissing me, and I went to bed with Jeanne, who let me excite her for half an hour; and then mounting me milked me with such artistry that in two minutes she brought me to spasms of sensation, such as I had never experienced before with any other woman. Jeanne was the most perfect mistress I had met up to that time, and in sheer power of giving pleasure hardly to be surpassed by any of western race.

An unforgettable evening, one of the few evenings in my life when I reached both the intensest pang of pleasure with the even higher aesthetic delight of toying with beautiful limbs and awakening new desires in a lovely body and frank honest spirit.

The only woman I really love, is the Unknown who haunts my imagination – seduction in person, for she possesses all the incompatible perfections I've never yet found in any one woman. She must be intensely sensuous, yet self-controlled; soulful, yet a coquette: to find her, that's the great adventure of life and there's no other.

GUY DE MAUPASSANT (1850–93)
SPEAKING TO FRANK HARRIS

A true obsessive in his search for sexual perfection, Frank is mortified by any flaw.

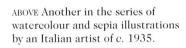

'It's your naughtiness saves you,' I responded, 'and your wonderful beauty of figure; your little breasts are tiny-perfect, taken with your strong hips and the long limbs and the exquisite triangle with the lips that are red, crimson-red as they should be, and not brown like most, and so sensitive, curling at the edges and pearling with desire.'

Suddenly she put her hand over my mouth. 'I won't listen,' she pouted, wrinkling up her nose – and she looked so adorable that I led her to the sofa and soon got busy kissing, kissing the glowing crimson lips that opened at once to me, and in a minute or two were pearly wet with the white milk of love and ready for my sex.

But in spite of the half-confession, the antagonism between us continued, though it was much less than it had been. I could not get her to give herself with passion, or to let herself go frankly to love's ultimate expression, even when I had reduced her to tears and sobbings of exhaustion. 'Please not, boy! Please, no more,' was all I could get from her, so that often and often I merely had her and came to please myself and then lay there beside her talking, or threw down the sheets and made her lie on her face so that I could admire the droop of the loins and the strong curve of the bottom. Or else I would pose her sideways so as to bring out the great swell of the hip and the poses would usually end with my burying my head between her legs, trying with lips and tongue and finger and often again with my sex to bring her sensations to ecstasy and if possible to love-speech and love-thanks! Now and again I succeeded, for I had begun to study the times in the month when she was most easily excited. But how is it that so few women ever try to give their lover the utmost sum of pleasure?

ABOVE Another in the series of watercolour and sepia illustrations by an Italian artist of c. 1935.

In giving an account of Frank Harris in an anthology of erotica, the thumbnail sketch of the man which emerges is, perhaps, less sympathetic than it should be, especially to women. Some of his lovers became lifelong friends, like Enid Bagnold, who said 'his talk made you feel as though you were living in heaven'. Many other women, who were not lovers, regarded Harris as a loyal and devoted friend. As usual, it is better to leave the last word on the subject to Frank: 'All that is amiable and sweet and good in life, all that ennobles and chastens I have won from women. Why should I not sing their praises, or at least show my gratitude by telling of the subtle intoxication of their love that has made my life an entrancing romance?'

For more than thirty years after its first publication in 1928 an English person wishing to read *Lady Chatterley's Lover* had to purchase a copy abroad. The famous trial in which the jury – to their eternal credit – decided that the book was not obscene had several positive results. Among these, and by no means the least important, was the extraordinary publicity the case received. As a direct result the book became a bestseller overnight and was read by countless thousands of people who would not otherwise have done so. If D. H. Lawrence's vast new readership expected smut they were mistaken. *Lady Chatterley's Lover* is a tender, moral book and – for all its idiosyncrasies and quaintness – one of the finest books about sexual love ever written. In the foreword to the Paris edition of 1928, D. H. Lawrence (1885–1930) said that the point of his novel was to enable 'men and women to be able to think sex, fully, completely, honestly and cleanly. Even if we cannot act sexually to our complete satisfaction, let us at least think sexually, complete and clear.' Lawrence was in fact rather prudish about sex: he loathed bawdiness and anything which (as he saw it) detracted from the sacredness of our sexuality.

Lady Chatterley's Lover is the story of Connie, who finds true love and fulfilment with her husband's gamekeeper. In this extract Connie summarizes her frustration, and her past sexual experience. Michaelis is her former lover.

BELOW The first of a sequence of studies of a young woman, Paris, c. 1930; photographer unknown.

When Connie went up to her bedroom she did what she had not done for a long time: took off all her clothes, and looked at herself naked in the huge mirror. She did not know what she was looking for, or at, very definitely, yet she moved the lamp till it shone full on her.

And she thought, as she had thought so often, what a frail, easily hurt, rather pathetic thing a human body is, naked, somehow a little unfinished, incomplete!

She had been supposed to have rather a good figure, but now she was out of fashion: a little too female, not enough like an adolescent boy. She was not very tall, a bit Scottish and short; but she had a certain fluent, down-slipping grace that might have been beauty. Her skin was faintly tawny, her limbs had a certain stillness, her body should have had a full, down-slipping richness; but it lacked something.

Instead of ripening its firm, down-running curves, her body was flattening and going a little harsh. It was as if it had not had enough sun and warmth; it was a little greyish and sapless.

Disappointed of its real womanhood, it had not succeeded in becoming boyish, and unsubstantial, and transparent; instead it had gone opaque.

Her breasts were rather small, and dropping pear-shaped. But they were unripe, a little bitter, without meaning hanging there. And her belly had lost the fresh, round gleam it had had when she was young, in the days of her German boy, who really loved her physically. Then it was young and expectant, with a real look

of its own. Now it was going slack, and a little flat, thinner, but with a slack thinness. Her thighs, too, they used to look so quick and glimpsy in their female roundness, somehow they too were going flat, slack, meaningless. . . .

She looked in the other mirror's reflection at her back, her waist, her loins. She was getting thinner, but to her it was not becoming. The crumple of her waist at the back, as she bent back to look, was a little weary; and it used to be so gay-looking. And the longish slope of her haunches and her buttocks had lost its gleam and its sense of richness. Gone! Only the German boy had loved it, and he was ten years dead, very nearly. How time went by! Ten years dead, and she was only twenty-seven. The healthy boy with his fresh, clumsy sensuality that she had then been so scornful of! Where would she find it now? It was gone out of men. They had their pathetic, two-seconds spasms like Michaelis; but no healthy human sensuality, that warms the blood and freshens the whole being.

Still she thought the most beautiful part of her was the long-sloping fall of the haunches from the socket of the back, and the slumberous, round stillness of the buttocks. Like hillocks of sand, the Arabs say, soft and downward-slipping with a long slope. Here the life still lingered hoping. But here too she was thinner, and going unripe, astringent.

After her first blissful lovemaking with the gamekeeper Mellors – when they both obey instincts they hardly understand – Connie returns to his cottage. But even in Eden, even in the enchanted forest, not everything is perfect.

And she went with him to the hut. It was quite dark when he had shut the door, so he made a small light in the lantern, as before.

'Have you left your underthings off?' he asked her.

'Yes!'

'Ay, well, then I'll take my things off too.'

He spread the blankets, putting one at the side for a coverlet. She took off her hat, and shook her hair. He sat down, taking off his shoes and gaiters, and undoing his cord breeches.

'Lie down then!' he said, when he stood in his shirt. She obeyed in silence, and he lay beside her, and pulled the blanket over them both.

'There!' he said.

And he lifted her dress right back, till he came even to her breasts. He kissed them softly, taking the nipples in his lips in tiny caresses.

'Eh, but tha'rt nice, tha'rt nice!' he said, suddenly rubbing his face with a snuggling movement against her warm belly.

And she put her arms round him under his shirt, but she was afraid of his thin, smooth, naked body, that seemed so powerful, afraid of the violent muscles. She shrank, afraid.

And when he said, with a sort of little sigh: 'Eh, tha'rt nice!' something in her quivered, and something in her spirit stiffened in resistance: stiffened from the terribly physical intimacy, and

OPPOSITE and BELOW Two more studies of a young woman, Paris, c. 1930, by an unknown photographer.

I would censor genuine pornography,
vigorously . . . you can recognize it by
the insult it offers, invariably, to sex
and to the human spirit.

D. H. Lawrence (1885–1930)

from the peculiar haste of his possession. And this time the sharp ecstasy of her own passion did not overcome her; she lay with her hands inert on his striving body, and do what she might, her spirit seemed to look on from the top of her head, and the butting of his haunches seemed ridiculous to her, and the sort of anxiety of his penis to come to its little evacuating crisis seemed farcical. Yes, this was love, this ridiculous bouncing of the buttocks, and the wilting of the poor, insignificant, moist little penis. This was the divine love! After all, the moderns were right when they felt contempt for the performance; for it was a performance. It was quite true, as some poets said, that the God who created man must have had a sinister sense of humour, creating him a reasonable being, yet forcing him to take this ridiculous posture, and driving him with blind craving for this ridiculous performance. Even a Maupassant found it a humiliating anti-climax. Men despised the intercourse act, and yet did it.

Cold and derisive her queer female mind stood apart, and though she lay perfectly still, her impulse was to heave her loins, and throw the man out, escape his ugly grip, and the butting over-riding of his absurd haunches. His body was a foolish, impudent, imperfect thing, a little disgusting in its unfinished clumsiness. For surely a complete evolution would eliminate this performance, this 'function'.

And yet when he had finished, soon over, and lay very very still, receding into silence, and a strange motionless distance, far, farther than the horizon of her awareness, her heart began to weep. She could feel him ebbing away, ebbing away, leaving her there like a stone on a shore. He was withdrawing, his spirit was leaving her. He knew.

And in real grief, tormented by her own double consciousness and reaction, she began to weep. He took no notice, or did not even know. The storm of weeping swelled and shook her, and shook him.

'Ay!' he said. 'It was no good that time. You wasn't there.' – So he knew! Her sobs became violent.

'But what's amiss?' he said. 'It's once in a while that way.'

'I . . . I can't love you,' she sobbed, suddenly feeling her heart breaking.

'Canna ter? Well, dunna fret! There's no law says as tha's got to. Ta'e it for what it is.'

He still lay with his hand on her breast. But she had drawn both her hands from him.

His words were small comfort. She sobbed aloud. . . .

Yet, as he was drawing away, to rise silently and leave her, she clung to him in terror.

'Don't! Don't go! Don't leave me! Don't be cross with me! Hold me! Hold me fast!' she whispered in blind frenzy, not even knowing what she said, and clinging to him with uncanny force. It was from herself she wanted to be saved, from her own inward anger and resistance. Yet how powerful was that inward resistance that possessed her!

He took her in his arms again and drew her to him, and suddenly she became small in his arms, small and nestling. It was gone, the resistance was gone, and she began to melt in a marvel-lous peace. And as she melted small and wonderful in his arms, she became infinitely desirable to him, all his blood-vessels seemed to scald with intense yet tender desire, for her, for her softness, for the penetrating beauty of her in his arms, passing into his blood. And softly, with that marvellous swoon-like caress of his hand in pure soft desire, softly he stroked the silky slope of her loins, down, down between her soft warm buttocks, coming nearer and nearer to the very quick of her. And she felt him like a flame of desire, yet tender, and she felt herself melting in the flame. She let herself go. She felt his penis risen against her with silent amazing force and assertion and she let herself go to him. She yielded with a quiver that was like death, she went all open to him. And oh, if he were not tender to her now, how cruel, for she was all open to him and helpless!

She quivered again at the potent inexorable entry inside her, so strange and terrible. It might come with the thrust of a sword in her softly-opened body, and that would be death. She clung in a sudden anguish of terror. But it came with a strange slow thrust of peace, the dark thrust of peace and a ponderous, pri-mordial tenderness, such as made the world in the beginning. And her terror subsided in her breast, her breast dared to be gone in peace, she held nothing. She dared to let go everything, all herself, and be gone in the flood.

And it seemed she was like the sea, nothing but dark waves ris-ing and heaving, heaving with a great swell, so that slowly her whole darkness was in motion, and she was ocean rolling its dark, dumb mass. Oh, and far down inside her the deeps parted and rolled asunder, in long, far-travelling billows, and ever, at the quick of her, the depths parted and rolled asunder, from the cen-tre of soft plunging, as the plunger went deeper and deeper, touching lower, and she was deeper and deeper and deeper dis-closed, the heavier the billows of her rolled away to some shore, uncovering her, and closer and closer plunged the palpable unknown, and further and further rolled the waves of herself away from herself, leaving her, till suddenly, in a soft, shuddering con-vulsion, the quick of all her plasm was touched, she knew herself touched, the consummation was upon her, and she was gone. She was gone, she was not, and she was born: a woman. . . .

When awareness of the outside began to come back, she clung to his breast, murmuring 'My love! My love!' And he held her silently. And she curled on his breast, perfect.

But his silence was fathomless. His hands held her like flowers, so still and strange. 'Where are you?' she whispered to him. 'Where are you? Speak to me! Say something to me!'

He kissed her softly, murmuring: 'Ay, my lass!'

But she did not know what he meant, she did not know where he was. In his silence he seemed lost to her.

'You love me, don't you?' she murmured.

'Ay, tha knows!' he said.

'But tell me!' she pleaded.

'Ay! Ay! 'asn't ter felt it?' he said dimly, but softly and surely. And she clung close to him, closer. He was so much more peace-

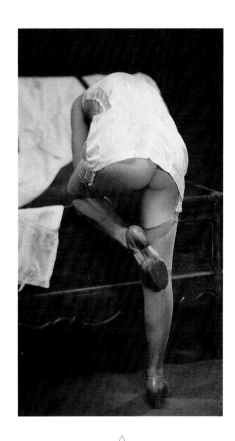

ABOVE Another in the sequence of studies of a young woman, Paris, c. 1930.

ful in love than she was, and she wanted him to reassure her.

'You do love me!' she whispered, assertive. And his hands stroked her softly, as if she were a flower, without the quiver of desire, but with delicate nearness. And still there haunted her a restless necessity to get a grip on love.

'Say you'll always love me!' she pleaded. . . .

'I love thee that I can go into thee,' he said.

'Do you like me?' she said, her heart beating.

'It heals it all up, that I can go into thee. I love thee that tha opened to me. I love thee that I came into thee like that.'

He bent down and kissed her soft flank, rubbed his cheek against it, then covered it up. . . .

'Th'art good cunt, though, aren't ter? Best bit o' cunt left on earth. When ter likes! When tha'rt willin'!'

'What is cunt?' she said.

'An' doesn't ter know? Cunt! It's thee down theer; an' what I get when I'm i'side thee, and what tha gets when I'm i'side thee; it's a' as it is, all on't.'

'All on't,' she teased. 'Cunt! It's like fuck then.'

'Nay nay! Fuck's only what you do. Animals fuck. But cunt's a lot more than that. It's thee, dost see: an' tha'rt a lot besides an animal, aren't ter? – even ter fuck? Cunt! Eh, that's the beauty o' thee, lass!'

She got up and kissed him between the eyes, that looked at her so dark and soft and unspeakably warm, so unbearably beautiful.

'Is it?' she said. 'And do you care for me?'

He kissed her without answering.

'Tha mun goo, let me dust thee,' he said.

His hand passed over the curves of her body, firmly, without desire, but with soft, intimate knowledge.

As she ran home in the twilight the world seemed a dream; the trees in the park seemed bulging and surging at anchor on a tide, and the heave of the slope to the house was alive.

In writing *Lady Chatterley's Lover* Lawrence created a new language to describe sex: he needed to. No one had ever written like that before, no novelist of genius had ever been brave enough to describe the things he describes, and bring such creative insights to the subject.

After Lawrence the floodgates opened and the bad and the mediocre swept in along with the good, but he was the first. And even now he moves us with the truth of what he says. We can smile at the naivety and what now seems in some senses old-fashioned, but still he moves us.

The thunder had ceased outside, but the rain which had abated, suddenly came striking down, with a last blench of lightning and mutter of departing storm. Connie was uneasy. He had talked so long now, and he was really talking to himself, not to her. Despair seemed to come down on him completely, and she was feeling happy, she hated despair. She knew her leaving him,

ABOVE and OPPOSITE Two further studies from the sequence of a young Parisian woman, c. 1930.

We fucked a flame into being. Even the flowers are fucked into being between the sun and the earth.

FROM *LADY CHATTERLEY'S LOVER*
D. H. LAWRENCE (1885–1930)

which he had only just realized inside himself, had plunged him back into this mood. And she triumphed a little.

She opened the door and looked at the straight heavy rain, like a steel curtain, and had a sudden desire to rush out into it, to rush away. She got up, and began swiftly pulling off her stockings, then her dress and underclothing, and he held his breath. Her pointed keen animal breasts tipped and stirred as she moved. She was ivory-coloured in the greenish light. She slipped on her rubber shoes again and ran out with a wild little laugh, holding up her breasts to the heavy rain and spreading her arms, and running blurred in the rain with the eurhythmic dance-movements she had learned so long ago in Dresden. It was a strange pallid figure lifting and falling, bending so the rain beat and glistened on the full haunches, swaying up again and coming belly-forward through the rain, then stooping again so that only the full loins and buttocks were offered in a kind of homage towards him, repeating a wild obeisance. . . .

She was nearly at the wide riding when he came up and flung his naked arm round her soft, naked-wet middle. She gave a shriek and straightened herself, and the heap of her soft, chill flesh came up against his body. He pressed it all up against him, madly, the heap of soft, chilled female flesh that became quickly warm as flame, in contact. The rain streamed on them till they smoked. He gathered her lovely, heavy posteriors one in each hand and pressed them in towards him in a frenzy, quivering motionless in the rain. Then suddenly he tipped her up and fell with her on the path, in the roaring silence of the rain, and short and sharp, he took her, short and sharp and finished, like an animal.

He got up in an instant, wiping the rain from his eyes.

'Come in,' he said, and they started running back to the hut. He ran straight and swift: he didn't like the rain. But she came slower, gathering forget-me-nots and campion and bluebells, running a few steps and watching him fleeing away from her.

When she came with her flowers, panting to the hut, he had already started a fire, and the twigs were crackling. Her sharp breasts rose and fell, her hair was plastered down with rain, her face was flushed ruddy and her body glistened and trickled. Wide-eyed and breathless, with a small wet head and full, trickling, naïve haunches, she looked another creature.

He took the old sheet and rubbed her down, she standing like a child. Then he rubbed himself, having shut the door of the hut. The fire was blazing up. She ducked her head in the other end of the sheet, and rubbed her wet hair.

'We're drying ourselves together on the same towel, we shall quarrel!' he said.

She looked up for a moment, her hair all odds and ends.

'No!' she said, her eyes wide. 'It's not a towel, it's a sheet.'

And she went on busily rubbing her head, while he busily rubbed his.

Still panting with their exertions, each wrapped in an army blanket, but the front of the body open to the fire, they sat on a log side by side before the blaze, to get quiet. Connie hated the feel of the blanket against her skin. But now the sheet was all wet.

She dropped her blanket and kneeled on the clay hearth, holding her head to the fire, and shaking her hair to dry it. He watched the beautiful curving drop of her haunches. That fascinated him today. How it sloped with a rich down-slope to the heavy roundness of her buttocks! And in between, folded in the secret warmth, the secret entrances!

He stroked her tail with his hand, long and subtly taking in the curves and the globe-fullness.

'Tha's got such a nice tail on thee,' he said, in the throaty caressive dialect. 'Tha's got the nicest arse of anybody. It's the nicest, nicest woman's arse as is! An' ivery bit of it is woman, woman sure as nuts. Tha'rt not one o' them button-arsed lasses as should be lads, are ter! Tha's got a real soft sloping bottom on thee, as a man loves in 'is guts. It's a bottom as could hold the world up, it is!'

All the while he spoke he exquisitely stroked the rounded tail, till it seemed as if a slippery sort of fire came from it into his hands. And his finger-tips touched the two secret openings to her body, time after time, with a soft little brush of fire.

'An' if tha shits an' if tha pisses, I'm glad. I don't want a woman as couldna shit nor piss.'

Connie could not help a sudden snort of astonished laughter, but he went on unmoved.

'Tha'rt real, tha art! Tha'art real, even a bit of a bitch. Here tha shits an' here tha pisses: an' I lay my hand on 'em both an' like thee for it. I like thee for it. Tha's got a proper, woman's arse, proud of itself. It's none ashamed of itself, this isna.'

He laid his hand close and firm over her secret places, in a kind of close greeting.

'I like it,' he said. 'I like it! An' if I only lived ten minutes, an' stroked thy arse an' got to know it, I should reckon I'd lived *one* life, see ter! Industrial system or not! Here's one o' my lifetimes.'

She turned round and climbed into his lap, clinging to him. 'Kiss me!' she whispered.

And she knew the thought of their separation was latent in both their minds, and at last she was sad.

She sat on his thighs, her head against his breast, and her ivory-gleaming legs loosely apart, the fire glowing unequally upon them. Sitting with his head dropped, he looked at the folds of her body in the fire-glow, and at the fleece of soft brown hair that hung down to a point between her open thighs. He reached to the table behind, and took up her bunch of flowers, still so wet that drops of rain fell on to her.

'Flowers stops out of doors all weathers,' he said. 'They have no houses.'

'Not even a hut!' she murmured.

With quiet fingers he threaded a few forget-me-not flowers in the fine brown fleece of the mount of Venus.

'There!' he said. 'There's forget-me-nots in the right place!'

She looked down at the milky odd little flowers among the brown maiden-hair at the lower tip of her body.

'Doesn't it look pretty!' she said.

'Pretty as life,' he replied.

ABOVE The final photograph from the sequence of studies of a young woman in Paris, c. 1930.

The erotica of the 1930s and early 1940s was dominated by two writers: the Frenchwoman Anaïs Nin and the American Henry Miller. They were friends, and together with several other members of their bohemian expatriate circle they wrote erotica for 'a dollar a page' to make ends meet. They lived in Paris, and the city exerted such a strong influence on both writers that it is almost like a character in their work. Here is Anaïs Nin:

It was a soft rainy afternoon, with that gray Parisian melancholy that drove people indoors, that created an erotic atmosphere because it fell like a ceiling over the city, enclosing them all in a nerveless air, as in an alcove; and everywhere, some reminder of the erotic life – a shop, half-hidden, showing underwear and black garters and black boots; the Parisian woman's provocative walk; taxis carrying embracing lovers.

Balzac's house stood at the top of a hilly street in Passy, overlooking the Seine. First they had to ring at the door of an apartment house, then descend a flight of stairs that seemed to lead to a cellar but opened instead on a garden. Then they had to traverse the garden and ring at another door. This was the door of his house, concealed in the garden of the apartment house, a secret and mysterious house, so hidden and isolated in the heart of Paris.

The woman who opened the door was like a ghost from the past – faded face, faded hair and clothes, bloodless. Living with Balzac's manuscripts, pictures, engravings of the women he had loved, first editions, she was permeated with a vanished past, and all the blood had ebbed from her. Her very voice was distant, ghostly. She slept in this house filled with dead souvenirs. She had become equally dead to the present. It was as if each night she laid herself away in the tomb of Balzac, to sleep with him.

She guided them through the rooms, and then to the back of the house. She came to a trap door, slipped her long bony fingers through the ring and lifted it for Elena and Pierre to see. It opened on a little stairway.

This was the trap door Balzac had built so that the women who visited him could escape from the surveillance or suspicions of their husbands. He, too, used it to escape from his harassing creditors. The stairway led to a path and then to a gate that opened on an isolated street that in turn led to the Seine. One could escape before the person at the front door of the house had enough time to traverse the first room.

For Elena and Pierre, the effect of this trap door so evoked Balzac's love of life that it affected them like an aphrodisiac. Pierre whispered to her, 'I would like to take you on the floor, right here.'

The ghost woman did not hear these words, uttered with the directness of an apache, but she caught the glance which accompanied them. The mood of the visitors was not in harmony with the sacredness of the place, and she hurried them out.

The breath of death had whipped their senses. Pierre hailed a taxi. In the taxi he could not wait. He made Elena sit over him,

BELOW and OPPOSITE Two of a series of thirty lithographs, entitled *Idylle Printanière*, hand-coloured in crayon by the artist Rojan or Rojankowski, 1933.

with her back to him, the whole length of her body against his, concealing him completely. He raised her skirt.

Elena said, 'Not here, Pierre. Wait until we get home. People will see us. Please wait. Oh, Pierre, you're hurting me! Look, the policeman stared at us. And now we're stopped here, and people can see us from the sidewalk. Pierre, Pierre, stop it.'

But all the time that she feebly defended herself, and tried to slip off, she was conquered by pleasure. Her efforts to sit still made her even more keenly aware of Pierre's every movement. Now she feared that he might hurry his act, driven by the speed of the taxi and the fear that it would stop soon in front of the house and the taxi driver would turn his head towards them. And she wanted to enjoy Pierre, to reassert their bond, the harmony of their bodies. They were observed from the street. Yet she could not draw away, and he now had his arms around her. Then a violent jump of the taxi over a hole in the road threw them apart. It was too late to resume the embrace. The taxi had stopped. Pierre had just enough time to button himself. Elena felt they must look drunk, disheveled. The languor of her body made it difficult for her to move.

Pierre was filled with a perverse enjoyment of this interruption. He enjoyed feeling his bones half-melted in his body, the almost painful withdrawal of the blood. Elena shared his new whim, and later they lay on the bed caressing each other and talking.

Miller's Paris is a very different place from the city Anaïs Nin has just described. In *Tropic of Cancer* (1934), although he concedes it is exciting he calls it 'a foul sink' and a 'whore', and is eternally ambivalent about it:

The world of Matisse is still beautiful in an old-fashioned bedroom way. There is not a ball bearing in evidence, nor a boiler, plate, nor a piston, nor a monkey wrench. It is the same old world that went gaily to the Bois in the pastoral days of wine and fornication. I find it soothing and refreshing to move amongst these creatures with live, breathing pores whose background is stable and solid as light itself. I feel it poignantly when I walk along the Boulevard de la Madeleine and the whores rustle beside me, when just to glance at them causes me to tremble. Is it because they are exotic or well-nourished? No, it is rare to find a beautiful woman along the Boulevard de la Madeleine. But in Matisse, in the exploration of his brush, there is the trembling glitter of a world which demands only the presence of the female to crystallize the most fugitive aspirations. To come upon a woman offering herself outside a urinal, where there are advertised cigarette papers, rum, acrobats, horse races, where the heavy foliage of the trees breaks the heavy mass of walls and roofs, is an experience that begins where the boundaries of the known world leave off. . . . Even as the world falls apart the Paris that belongs to Matisse shudders with bright, gasping orgasms, the air itself is steady with a stagnant sperm, the trees tangled like hair. On its wobbly axle the wheel rolls steadily downhill;

there are no brakes, no ball bearings, no balloon tires. The wheel is falling apart, but the revolution is intact. . . .

It is worth exploring the differences between these two pieces of writing before comparing their treatment of explicitly sexual scenes. Paris is an eroticized city for both of them, a place where the ghosts of the great affect the living. That is enough for her; she catches the mood and follows its influences. Miller, in contrast, has to analyse and dissect, hacking at the idea with robust prose that is almost poetry. Her prose never shocks – it glides like silk across the idea, defining it that way.

Tropic of Cancer is an erotic book in that one of its main topics is sex, but it is not intended to excite the reader sexually. To compare the two writers – and a woman's erotica with a man's – it is better to look at the work each of them produced for a dollar a page. In both extracts, the subject of the erotic writing is the effect of visual erotica. Here is Anaïs Nin.

She could think only of erotic images in connection with him, his body. If she saw a penny movie on the boulevards that stirred her, she brought her curiosity or a new experiment to their next meeting. She began to whisper certain wishes in his ear.

Pierre was always surprised when Elena was willing to give him pleasure without taking it herself. There were times after their excesses when he was tired, less potent, and yet wanted to repeat the sensation of annihilation. Then he would stir her with caresses, with an agility of the hands that approached masturbation. Meanwhile her own hands would circle around his penis like a delicate spider with knowing fingertips, which touched the most hidden nerves of response. Slowly, the fingers closed upon the penis, at first stroking its flesh shell; then feeling the inrush of dense blood stretching it; feeling the slight swell of the nerves, the sudden tautness of the muscles; feeling as if they were playing upon a stringed instrument. . . . Then he would be drugged by her hands, close his eyes and abandon himself to her caresses. Once or twice he would try, as if in sleep, to continue the motion of his own hands, but then he lay passively, to feel better the knowing manipulations, the increasing tension. 'Now, now,' he would murmur. 'Now.' This meant that her hand must become swifter to keep pace with the fever pulsing within him. Her fingers ran in rhythm with the quickening blood beats, as his voice begged, 'Now, now, now.'

Blind to all but his pleasure, she bent over him, her hair falling, her mouth near his penis, continuing the motion of her hands and at the same time licking the tip of the penis each time it passed within reach of her tongue – this, until his body began to tremble and raised itself to be consumed by her hands and mouth, to be annihilated, and the semen would come, like little waves breaking on the sand, one rolling upon another, little waves of salty foam unrolling on the beach of her hands. Then she enclosed the spent penis tenderly in her mouth, to cull the precious liquid of love.

His pleasure gave her such a joy that she was surprised when he began to kiss her with gratitude, as he said, 'But you, you didn't have any pleasure.'

'Oh, yes,' said Elena, in a voice he could not doubt.

In this extract from *Opus Pistorum*, Henry Miller shows a visiting American his Paris flat.

Ann thinks that my apartment is very quaint and very cozy. Everything about it is so private, she says . . . she doesn't know about the parades that troop in and out of here at the most inappropriate times. Such a place would be just the thing for a woman who wished to conduct an affair, wouldn't it? And are there many such in the neighborhood? Of course she was merely wondering. . . .

Ann wants to know Paris better, and she has a list of questions as long as your arm. Where is this? Where does one find that?

LEFT The warm tones and sensitive lighting heighten the erotic impact of this photograph, one of a series of exceptionally fine studio nudes by an unknown photographer, Paris, c. 1930.

Which is the best neighborhood for thus and so? And for this first half hour that she's in my place she sits and scribbles into a notebook all the answers. She still has a lot of Paris to see before she goes home, she exclaims, and she wants to know the city from all angles. Now, where does one buy those awful postcards?

I tell her where she can buy dirty pictures. . . . Although how she's been here as long as she has and not met the hawkers I don't know. Then she wants to know if they are actually as bad as they're supposed to be . . . or are they just . . . risqué? She's never seen any, of course. . . . Well, would she like to see some.

RIGHT and OPPOSITE Two further photographic studies in the series by an unknown Parisian photographer of c. 1930.

Oh, I have some? Now, that's embarrassing . . . but she supposes that it's part of life. Yes, she ought to see them; one's education should be well rounded. . . .

I show her the ones of Anna, give her the whole handful of them and let her go through them. She blushes as soon as she glances at the first one. Oh . . . they are rather strong, aren't they? She looks at them all very quickly and then looks at them all again, very slowly. . . . She becomes warm, glances at the fireplace, and loosens her sweater. She drinks many glasses of wine. . . .

Getting her out of her clothes after that isn't very hard at all. A few feels and she's ready for anything . . . or so she thinks. Once I've got my hand under her skirt it's clear sailing. She spreads her thighs when I feel them up and lets me take off her pants without as much as a raised eyebrow. And she's really gotten into the spirit of those pictures, the bitch . . . she's so juicy between the legs that her pants are soaked, and that big cunt of hers is like a firebox. . . .

Ann rolls back and forth on the couch while I feel her up. Oh, what would Sam think, what would he do, if he saw her now! She sticks her fist into my pants and grabs my dick. What would Sam think! This is really shameful of her . . . coming here to be fucked by me, leaving poor Sam to himself. She ought to be at home screwing her husband rather than here giving it to me. . . .

Finally I let her get a taste of what she wants to feel. I kiss her squarely on the cunt, slide my tongue over the lips and in . . . her thighs swing wide, like a double gate that will never close again, and she gasps when I suck the juicy, hot fruit . . . Oh, what a feeling! . . . My tongue can go in deeper . . . I can suck harder . . . she'll spread her legs further. . . .

While Miller uses strong language and staccato rhythms to achieve his effect, Anaïs Nin moves the action forward gently, with long, dreamily orchestrated sentences. Both writers create an artificial world, but whereas Miller wants the sex scenes to be immediate and 'real', it is always clear in the writing of Anaïs Nin that we are stepping into never-never land. Her erotica is an invitation to share her fantasies. Dreaming and sleep are recurring motifs in *Delta of Venus*: 'the dream that had grown between them', 'a dream of enveloping caresses', or more explicit fantasies.

Miller's work is fuelled by his fantasies, of course, but they are male fantasies presented in a realistic way. This is his Rabelaisian version of the dream sequence.

Toots is curled in front of the doorway, stinking drunk and asleep. She doesn't wake up when I shake her . . . she moans and begins to make a racket, so Anna and I take her by the heels and drag her in . . . Anna is laughing.

Toots lies sprawled in the center of the floor with her legs apart and her dress up to her belly. She's wearing pants but her bush sticks out around the edges between her thighs. Anna tickles her and she kicks her feet.

Anna gets a crazy idea. She wants to undress Toots and she thinks I ought to fuck her while she's asleep! My God, the purity of women! . . . There's something in a woman's make-up that makes them a fuck of a lot more interested in other women than you think they ought to be. Take two men and one woman, and one of the men passed out, and the chances are ninety to one that the only one who got his prick played with would be the one who was still on his feet. It's certain that if anything happened to the lush, it would be the woman's idea.

Anna unfastens Toots's dress and takes it off carefully over her head. Then she sits down with her skirt tucked up in such a way that I can see her cunt and begins to feel Toots up. It's more curiosity than anything else . . . she wants to see what the cunt

Sid has a dong on that looks like something you ought to go after with a horse and a lariat, but that's just the kind Ann is looking for.

FROM *OPUS PISTORUM*
HENRY MILLER (1891–1980)

ABOVE and OPPOSITE Two more of the imaginative and effective studio photographs by an unknown Parisian photographer, c. 1930.

does when she feels somebody's hands on her . . . but it looks damned queer. She knows all the best places, too, being a woman. . . .

Toots doesn't do anything at first. She lies like a rock while Anna gives her teats a squeeze and a pinch and takes off her brassiere. Anna tickles her belly and her crotch . . . she begins to feel her thighs and rub them.

'I feel like one of those damned Lesbians,' Anna says. She means it . . . she tries to laugh, but her voice sounds strange. I pour myself a drink and sit down to watch . . . on top of having Anna suck my prick in a taxi, this business gives me a bastard of a dong.

Anna doesn't touch Toots's fig. She rubs all around it, pulls Toots's pants down and almost off, reaches between her thighs to give her ass a feel. Toots half wakes and wiggles . . . she reaches for Anna's hand and holds it . . . then pushes it across her con. Anna giggles but she's blushing in a way I never saw her blush before. She plays with Toots's bonne-bouche, touching the upper part of the split but not putting her fingers into it.

'She's dreaming of you,' she says.

Toots must be dreaming of something . . . she closes her legs and holds Anna's hand between them, then opens them as far as they will spread.

'So this is what it's like to be a man,' says Anna. 'I used to wonder . . .' She slips her finger into Toots's abricot-fendu and moves it around.

Which of the two writers produced the better erotica? That can only be a matter of individual taste. It has to be said that as magnificent as *Tropic of Cancer* and *Tropic of Capricorn* were, some of Miller's hack work, written in difficult times, was not. But whether it was written for 'a dollar a page' or because he wanted to, his work is always bursting with humour and life. Anaïs Nin wrote some beautiful erotica but humour was not among the ingredients she used. She could also write powerfully when she wanted. If the selection of her work included here for reasons of comparison gives the impression that her erotica is always gentle, this final extract with its fierce climax and fearsome bullring metaphors should correct the balance.

Martha, completely naked, was behaving like a demon, climbing over him, in a frenzy of hunger for his body.

FROM *DELTA OF VENUS* ANAÏS NIN (1903–77)

He was in France without papers, risking arrest. For greater security Elena hid him at the apartment of a friend who was away. They met every day now. He liked to meet her in the darkness, so that before they could see each other's face, their hands became aware of the other's presence. Like blind people, they felt each other's body, lingering in the warmest curves, making the same trajectory each time; knowing by touch the places where the skin was softest and tenderest and where it was

She arrived at his apartment moist and trembling. The lips of her sex were as stiff as if they had been caressed, her nipples hard, her whole body quivering, and as he kissed her he felt her turmoil and slipped his hand directly to her sex. The sensation was so acute that she came.

FROM *DELTA OF VENUS*
ANAÏS NIN (1903–77)

ABOVE and OPPOSITE Two of the series of thirty lithographs, *Idylle Printanière*, by Rojan or Rojankowski, 1933.

stronger and exposed to daylight; where, on the neck, the heartbeat was echoed; where the nerves shivered as the hand came nearer to the center, between the legs.

His hands knew the fullness of her shoulders so unexpected in her slender body, the tautness of her breasts, the febrile hairs under her arm, which he had asked her not to shave. Her waist was very small, and his hands loved that curve opening wider and wider from the waist to the hips. He followed each curve lovingly, seeking to take possession of her body with his hands, imagining the color of it.

Only once had he looked at her body in full daylight, in Caux, in the morning; and then he had delighted in the color of it. It was pale ivory, and smooth, and only towards the sex this ivory became more golden, like old ermine. Her sex he called 'the little fox', whose hair bristled when his hand reached out for it.

His lips followed his hands; his nose, too, buried in the odors of her body, seeking oblivion, seeking the drug that emanated from her body.

Elena had a little mole hidden away in the folds of secret flesh between the legs. He would pretend to be seeking it when his fingers ran up between the legs and behind the fox's bush, pretend to be wanting to touch the little mole and not the vulva; and as he caressed the mole, it was only accidentally that he touched the vulva, so light, just lightly enough to feel the quick plantlike contraction of pleasure which his fingers produced, the leaves of the sensitive plant closing, folding over the excitement, enclosing its secret pleasure, whose vibrato he felt.

Kissing the mole and not the vulva, while sensing how it responded to the kisses given a little space away, traveling under the skin, from the mole to the tip of the vulva, which opened and closed as his mouth came near. He buried his head there, drugged by the sandalwood smells, seashell smells; by the caress of her pubic hair, the fox's bush, one strand losing itself inside of his mouth, another losing itself among the bed clothes, where he found it later, shining, electric. Often their pubic hairs mingled. Bathing afterwards, Elena would find strands of Pierre's hair curled among hers, his hair longer, thicker and stronger.

Elena let his mouth and hands find all kinds of secret shelters and nooks, and rest there, falling into a dream of enveloping caresses, bowing her head over his when he placed his mouth on her throat, kissing the words she could not utter. He seemed to divine where she wanted a kiss to fall next, what part of her body demanded to be warmed. Her eyes fell on her own feet, and then his kisses went there, or below her arm, or in the hollow of her back, or where the belly ran into a valley, where the pubic hairs began, small and light and sparse.

Pierre stretched out his arm as a cat might, to be stroked. He threw his head back at times, closed his eyes, and let her cover him with moth kisses that were only a promise of more violent ones to come. When he could no longer bear the silky light touches, he opened his eyes and offered his mouth like a ripe fruit to bite, and she fell hungrily on it, as if to draw from it the very source of life.

When desire had permeated every little pore and hair of the body, then they abandoned themselves to violent caresses. At times she could hear her bones crack as he raised her legs above her shoulders, she could hear the suction of the kisses, the rain-drop sound of the lips and tongues, the moisture spreading in the warmth of the mouth as if they were eating into a fruit which melted and dissolved. He could hear her strange muffled croon-ing sound, like that of some exotic bird in ecstasy; and she, his breath, which came more heavily as his blood grew denser, richer.

When his fever rose, his breath was like that of some legendary bull galloping furiously to a delirious goring, a goring without pain, a goring which lifted her almost bodily from the bed, raised her sex in the air as if he would thrust right through her body and tear it, leaving her only when the wound was made, a wound of ecstasy and pleasure which rent her body like lightning, and let her fall again, moaning, a victim of too great a joy, a joy that was like a little death, a dazzling little death that no drug or alcohol could give, that nothing else could give but two bodies in love with each other, in love deep within their beings, with every atom and cell and nerve, and thought.

〇

Love and death and the relationship between the two was a recurring theme in Lawrence Durrell's work: 'Kisses them-selves became charged with the deliberate affirmation which can come only from the foreknowledge and presence of death.' These words were to be well understood by the millions of men and women who became unwilling actors in the inevitable second act of the Great War – World War II. Like many other writers and artists – Poe, Baudelaire, Maupassant, Rops – Durrell knew that it was a pale horse, Death, which stalked the erotic.

In 1938, with the clouds of war darkening over the city, Henry Miller helped Durrell to publish *The Black Book* in Paris. Miller was an appropriate – if improbable – midwife, since the style in which it is written owes a good deal to him. Durrell later called his early novel 'a savage charcoal sketch of spiritual and sexual etiolation', a book concerned with the 'real problems of the Anglo-Saxon psyche'. Whatever else it does, *The Black Book* certainly gives us some insights into the psyche of the twenty-six-year-old Lawrence Durrell.

It would have been good to die at any moment then, for love and death had somewhere joined hands.

FROM *THE ALEXANDRIA QUARTET*
LAWRENCE DURRELL (1912–90)

Flesh robot with cold thighs and fingers of icicle gripping the wheel of the black car, everything is forgotten. It is no use telling me of her inadequacy, her limitations; no good saying her mouth is an ash tray crammed with the butts of reserve, funk, truism, revulsion. I admit it. I admit everything with a great grin of snow. But it is no use. If I can find her moist and open between two sheets anywhere among the seven winds, you can have everything that lives and agonizes between the twin poles. Seriously, I switch off the dashboard and let my soul ride out on to the dark, float-

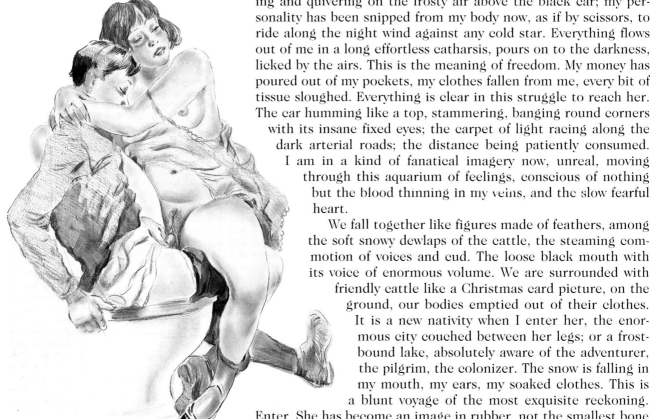

ABOVE *'Loo'd'*, a drawing by the
artist Rojan or Rojankowski
(active 1930–50).

ing and quivering on the frosty air above the black car; my personality has been snipped from my body now, as if by scissors, to ride along the night wind against any cold star. Everything flows out of me in a long effortless catharsis, pours on to the darkness, licked by the airs. This is the meaning of freedom. My money has poured out of my pockets, my clothes fallen from me, every bit of tissue sloughed. Everything is clear in this struggle to reach her. The car humming like a top, stammering, banging round corners with its insane fixed eyes; the carpet of light racing along the dark arterial roads; the distance being patiently consumed.

I am in a kind of fanatical imagery now, unreal, moving through this aquarium of feelings, conscious of nothing but the blood thinning in my veins, and the slow fearful heart.

We fall together like figures made of feathers, among the soft snowy dewlaps of the cattle, the steaming commotion of voices and cud. The loose black mouth with its voice of enormous volume. We are surrounded with friendly cattle like a Christmas card picture, on the ground, our bodies emptied out of their clothes. It is a new nativity when I enter her, the enormous city couched between her legs; or a frost-bound lake, absolutely aware of the adventurer, the pilgrim, the colonizer. The snow is falling in my mouth, my ears, my soaked clothes. This is a blunt voyage of the most exquisite reckoning. Enter. She has become an image in rubber, not the smallest bone which will not melt to snow under the steady friction of the penis. The hot thaw spreads raw patches of grass under us: every abstraction now is bleeding away into the snow – death, life, desire. It is so fatal, this act among the cattle. We are engrossed bobbins on a huge loom of terror, knowing nothing, wishing to know nothing of our universe, its machinery. When she comes it's all pearls and icicles emptied from her womb into the snow. The penis like a dolphin with many muscles and black humour, lolling up to meet the sun. The fig suddenly broken into a sticky tip that is all female. She is laughing hideously. The car is standing among the cattle, no less intelligent than they. Under me is no personality any more but a composite type of all desire. Enter. I do not recognize my arctic sister. Under my heart the delicate tappets of a heart; my penis trapped in an inexorable valve, drawing these shapes and chords out of me inexhaustible, like toothpaste. The cattle are kindly and interested in a gentlemanly way; the car urbane as a metal butler. Under my thews, trapped in bracts and sphincters, a unique destruction. She is weeping. Her spine has been liquefied, drawn out of her. She is filleted, the jaw telescoped with language, eyes glassy. Under my mouth a rouged vagina speaking a barbaric laughter and nibbling my tongue. It is all warm and raw: a spiritual autumn with just that scent of corruption, that much death in it, to make it palatable. A meal of game well-hung pig-scented tangy. Such a venison, more delicate than the gums of babies or little fishes. Open to me once like that and the Poles are shaken out of their orbits, the sky falls down in a fan of planets. I am the owner of the million words, the ciphers, the dead vocabularies. In this immense ceiling of swan's-down there is nothing left but a laughter that opens heaven: a half-life, running on the batteries. I am eating the snow and drinking your tears. Stand against the hedge to snivel and make water while the shivers run down your spine. You are beautiful all of a sudden. Your fear makes me merry. *A very merry Christmas to you and yours.* I am saying it insanely over and again. A very merry Christmas to you and yours. She runs at me suddenly with blunt fists raised, shouting wildly. Enormous dark eyes with the green and red lights growing from them. The cattle draw back softly on the carpet. Her tears punch little hot holes in the snow. I am happy. You will go about from now on with an overripe med-lar hanging out between your legs, your womb burst like the tip of the Roman fig. But even this brutality goes when I feel the bones against me, malleable and tender as gum; the eager whim-pering animal dressed in cloth opening up to me, wider and wider, softer than toffee, until the bland sky is heavy with falling feathers, angels, silk, and there is a sword softly broken off in my bowels. I am lying here quite ruined, like a basketful of spilt eggs, but happy. Vulnerable, but lying in you here, at peace with myself: the tides drawing back from me, gathering up the dirt and scurf of things, the thawed pus and venom, and purifying me. I am at peace. It is all falling away from me, the whole of my life emptied out in you like a pocketful of soiled pennies. The faces of the world, Lobo and Marney, the children, Peters, the car, Gracie, the enormous snow, statues, history, mice, divinity. It is for ever, you are saying wildly, with green lips, red lips, white lips, blue lips, green lips. It is for ever. Our lives stop here like a strip of cinema film. This is an eternal still life, in the snow, two crooked bodies, eating the second of midnight and snivelling. We will die here in this raw agony of convalescence, by the ice-bound lake, the city lying quiet among its litter of whimpering, blind steeples.

They must be saying good nights now all over the world. I am saying good-bye to part of my life, no, part of my body. It is irra-tional. I do not know what to say. If I take your hand it is my own hand I am kissing. The aquarium again, with everything slowed down to the tempo of deep water. Good-bye to my own body under the windmill, weeping in the deep snow, nose, ankle, wrist made of frosty iron again. Help me. O eloquent, just and mighty death. The great anvil of the frost is pounding us. The cattle are afraid. Let me put my hand between your legs for warmth. Speak to my fingers with your delicate mouth, your pillow of flesh. I am a swimmer again, moving in a photograph with great, uncertain, plausible gestures towards you.

I have said good night and drawn the car out slowly homeward. There is no feeling in my hands or feet. As though the locomotive centres had been eaten away. Tired.

Hot scent of oil along the great arterial road. There is not a frac-tion of my life which is not left behind with you, back there, in the snows.

BELOW An example from a series of drawings by the Viennese artist 'AL', published in Vienna in 1935.

Eroticism is assenting to life even up to the point of death.

GEORGES BATAILLE (1897–1962)

PART FIVE

Fantasy or reality?

ABOVE and OPPOSITE Original illustrations by the French artist Suzanne Ballivet (active 1930–45) from *Initiation Amoureuse*: etchings with aquatint.

A happier face of sexuality reveals itself in *Initiation Amoureuse*, published with charming illustrations by Suzanne Ballivet in 1943. The anonymous author of this novella describes the gentle wooing of a young bride by her intelligent (and preternaturally patient) husband. This hymn to foreplay proceeds as gently as we would expect.

I repeat my caresses of the night before on the stunning beauty of her naked bosom: gentle manual pressure, multiple fondling with my fingers, teasing with my tongue and sucking with my lips. And these caresses, emboldened by a new conquest, venture as far as her stomach, which quivers under my lips; like a minuscule lake, a little saliva shines in the hollow of her navel. Thérèse lets me do this, her arms inert, indifferent in appearance; but when my tongue, sliding across her stomach, slowly climbs towards her breasts, I see them swell with voluptuous expectation, heave with increased respiration and raise their hardened tips. . . .

Languidly, her lips and tongue trace a thousand interweaving arabesques on my body. Then, with the supple grace of a wild animal, she comes close enough to me to press her breasts against my stomach and takes pleasure in brushing their two pointed tips against my body. Their delicate flesh feels slightly cooler than the rest of her skin. Sometimes she brings them up as far as my mouth and holds them there a moment to let me taste their flushed sweetness. Sometimes she retreats as far as my navel where she hides the little red fruit for a second; then it's back to my lips to tirelessly continue her game. But when she slithered towards me on her stomach, across the bed, the sheet slid off her rump, within close range of my hand. It is still only partly naked, however enough to reveal the small of her back in its harmonious entirety and the beginning of a narrow valley. Soon I push the sheet back; the double profile emerges entirely in its abundant, but svelte fullness. Will Thérèse protest against the inquisitiveness of this action? For a moment, I fear that she will, since right away her bottom has tensed, ready to refuse me; but almost as soon, it relaxes, accepting its nudity under my gaze. All the same, I don't wish to abuse my victory. Resisting the urge to grab my voluptuous prize, I content myself with greedily eyeing the perfection of its curves and its mysterious line of shadow.

Eventually tiring of stroking me, Thérèse has allowed her head to fall on to my stomach. This movement of a broken, but some-what erratic doll has pushed her bottom towards me. So adjust-ing my position a little in order to reach, with both hands, the coveted riches, I begin to stroke them as lightly as possible with my fingers. The same reflex as before: the tensing action of a modesty that would still deny me, followed by the relaxation of a body which is accepting of – and curious about – new sensual delights. My hands, now bolder, knead the yielding amplitude of her twin buttocks.

At first I follow the length of her bottom. Leaving the small of her back, my hands climb the double hill, coming down again towards the dimples which denote the beginning of her thighs. And once there, I often let my errant finger brush against the silky fleece, so close to her warm sex. But fearing my impatience, just as soon I flee this provoking contact and return to the small of her back in order to resume my amorous comings and goings. At other times, my hands move from left to right and back again, squeezing and releasing the twin globes of flesh. Flesh which is both firm and pliable at the same time and whose texture is infinitely soft to the touch. Flesh which is cooler at its peaks but warmly perspiring in its shadowy crevice. Flesh that comes alive as I stroke it, which sometimes tightens to protect the intimacy of its secret valley, but which, by contrast, relaxes in confident and visible sensuality when my hands bring these matching spheres together. In my ardent love for my wife, her enjoyment under my touch is as sweet to me as if it were my own; tirelessly I multiply my caresses. Evening is almost here when Thérèse asks me to stop, her eyes heavy with a voluptuous weariness.

Initiation Amoureuse succeeds as erotica by herding its readers together like voyeuristic old goats and leading them into the bed-room of two newly-weds. Nevertheless the book has a serious point, which it makes well, and in this respect it is in the tradition of *L'École des filles*: titillation with education.

Timidly, my hand returns, gliding over the inside of her thigh and feeling the astonishingly incorporeal softness of her skin. As I progress, the muscles become less firm, the surface of the skin becomes softer still and, with no transition, I feel the folds of her sex and the fine fleece which surrounds it. But suddenly her legs snap shut, trapping my hand. Once more it is a refusal, modesty's invincible reflex, which every time denies me the ultimate intima-cy of her flesh. Exasperated, I want to give up my disappointing incursion and pull back my imprisoned hand. But Thérèse holds me there: 'No, stay. Wait a little.' And her thighs relax their grip, then open all together. So I am able to place my entire hand on her sex, offered to me at last, my palm resting where her fleece is thickest, my fingers where her flesh opens up like a red flower in full bloom. For a long time, I make no move, savouring the sensu-al pleasure of this warm encounter, and the heady sensation of having stormed love's secret bastion. Under my perfectly still

. . . *I knew*
Of no more subtle master under
  heaven
Than is the maiden passion for a
  maid.

FROM *GUINEVERE*
ALFRED LORD TENNYSON (1809–92)

hand, the naked intimacy of this flesh is animated by long shivers, whose waves travel the length of my wife's quivering body as far as our closely kissing lips.

The only sound to disturb the absolute silence of the night is that of our mouths, merging and separating. Thérèse's shivers become more rare and are drawn out. Abandoning, for a moment, her appeased flesh, my fingers wander over her smooth stomach and go back up under her dressing gown, seeking the tips of her breasts. Soon they come down again, but now, like will-o'-the-wisps, do no more than skim her sex, without touching its more intimate flesh. Like a light flame, they dance over her fleece, graze the shadowy, downy edges, sliding up as far as her bottom, feeling their way along its mysterious divide. Then they make the dancing journey back once more to their point of departure, tirelessly continuing the light tickle of their coming and going. Little by little, however, they become more insistent, more penetrating. Pushing aside the frizzy curls which have tangled there in their erratic way, my fingers come into contact once more with the innermost lips of her sex. Soon it is only this part they stimulate, and then only its most tender details, with an increasingly strong rhythm.

Thérèse has ceased to kiss me, completely absorbed by the intensely erotic sensations which cause her to tremble anew. She attempts to untie the triple knot of her belt. Then, impatient, she tears at it and, throwing off her clothing, offers up her completely nude body to the luminous softness of the night. The folds of her sex become wet with desire and my excited fingers increase their stimulation. Then her legs spread wider, yielding her wildly contracting sex to me and, with her two hands firmly clasping her breasts, she throws herself back, her eyes rolled upwards.

ABOVE and OPPOSITE More etchings by Suzanne Ballivet (active 1930–45) from *Initiation Amoureuse.*

A much older tradition than the libertine literature of the eighteenth century underlies *Initiation Amoureuse*: the medieval concept of Courtly Love. Thérèse herself has intimations of this.

'Listen darling, if you're so worried by our passion, we'll put a broadsword between us; you know, like Tristan and Isolde in the Forest of Morois. Come here and I'll tell you that beautiful story, which I've read so often I know it by heart.'

She makes me sit down on the edge of the big, low bed and, standing before me, she recites Bédier's prose to me, richer in poetry than many poems I know: 'Under a bower of green branches, strewn with fresh grass, Isolde is the first to lie down; Tristan

lies next to her and places his sword between their bodies . . .'
Thérèse recounts to me, without any hesitations, the old king's
visit, the lovers' awaking and their sin. Then she stops talking,
her hands held out to me, to claim her reward, her loose hair,
falling in two long golden tresses, framing her face. I remain
seated before her, entranced by this vision of medieval purity
that awaits my every whim. . . .

A hundred times, my lips have kissed her body all over, my
hands have felt and stroked it, turning it this way and that; but
now many details, hardly noticed before, intoxicate me with their
perfection. The immaculate whiteness of her slender waist, the
svelte generosity of her hips, the clean curve of her thighs and
the elegant length of her legs. My hungry lips and tongue go to
these novel attractions first of all, but then they linger over the
fleshy globes and warm shadows of her bottom which, up until
now, only my hands have explored. And I amuse myself by letting
my tongue play over the two adorable dimples which accentuate
this bottom. They are like two brazen arrows which a treacherous
hand has drawn there, to point the way towards her most secret
parts. Then I turn her beautiful body over once more, which
writhes sensually in my arms, and I run my lips over her elegant
thighs and smooth stomach. Meanwhile, Thérèse's breasts, pointing their tiny pink tips, cry out to me silently, provocatively,
seeming to reproach me for abandoning them. I answer their
call. A repeat of yesterday's caresses was only just enough to
assuage the impatience of their long wait.

Thérèse's body responds passionately, but with complete sin-
cerity, incapable of feigning a sensation it does not know. Some
caresses that I believe to be of a more acute sensuality, provoke
no reaction, but on the other hand, some, applied almost unconsciously, cause her to quiver with excitement. At times her entire
supple body writhes on the bed, as if maddened by the impossible
urge to offer itself, all at once, to the urgency of my touch. But
when my fingers or my mouth, travelling the length of
her stomach, try to penetrate the most intimate
parts of her sex, she denies me access by an abrupt
constriction of her thighs. No doubt she fears
that a repeat of the preceding night's lustful
spasm might cause in her an irresistible attraction towards my body, a body she would like
to first explore, before offering up the most
precious gift her own flesh possesses.

Guessing her thoughts, I resist the impulse to throw her legs wide and smother
her sex with kisses, and I resume
my exploration in other regions
of her body. Soon I return, however, even thirstier for her forbidden juices; once more my
mouth settles upon her irresistible blond fleece, and once more,
Thérèse's legs snap shut, preventing me
from going any further. But little by little I feel

her resistance weakening, and suddenly, with a great shudder, she admits defeat. Her legs slowly open half-way, still hesitant, but yielding to the pressure of my caresses; then they open altogether, offering my lips the naked redness of her own.

Careless of Thérèse's modesty (who is now, in any case, weary of my restraint) I pull her body close to the edge of the bed, within easier reach of my mouth. Then in a frenzy of tender madness, I lovingly punish her virginal flesh, alternately giving it long sucks with my lips and then letting my tongue dance over it. Or then, with my entire mouth, I completely envelop it in a lingering kiss which travels from the creases of her buttocks to the top of her sex to end on the soft curve of her stomach.

In the end I have to stop, shattered by the maddening tension in my loins; Thérèse stretches back, as if tearing herself awake from a dream. Suddenly more conscious, she pushes me gently away and quickly hides her sex with her hand: 'We are going too far . . .' She sits up on the edge of the bed, her hand clasped shiveringly tight between her legs, once more shut; picking up an item of her clothing which is lying around on the carpet, she tries to cover her nakedness. But she makes a bad job of it. Still quite dazed by such a prolonged pleasuring, she is at once both comically and touchingly clumsy. Despite her efforts to cover herself, first a breast appears, then the blond tuft of her sex.

Alone in their château, with every need attended to by unseen servants, the young lovers are also following patterns even more ancient than the medieval rituals of Courtly Love. We are of course in Fairyland, spying upon lovers in an enchanted castle.

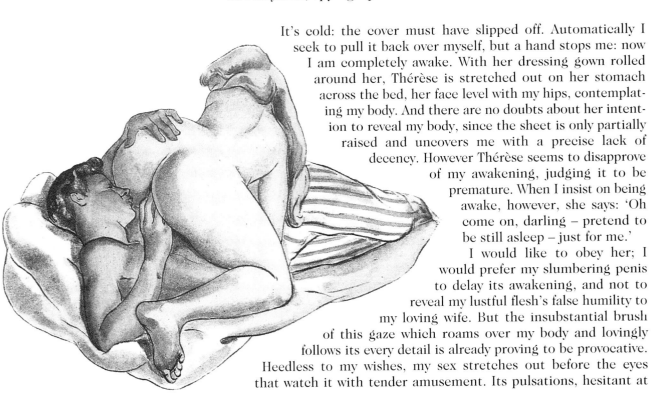

It's cold: the cover must have slipped off. Automatically I seek to pull it back over myself, but a hand stops me: now I am completely awake. With her dressing gown rolled around her, Thérèse is stretched out on her stomach across the bed, her face level with my hips, contemplating my body. And there are no doubts about her intention to reveal my body, since the sheet is only partially raised and uncovers me with a precise lack of decency. However Thérèse seems to disapprove of my awakening, judging it to be premature. When I insist on being awake, however, she says: 'Oh come on, darling – pretend to be still asleep – just for me.'

I would like to obey her; I would prefer my slumbering penis to delay its awakening, and not to reveal my lustful flesh's false humility to my loving wife. But the insubstantial brush of this gaze which roams over my body and lovingly follows its every detail is already proving to be provocative. Heedless to my wishes, my sex stretches out before the eyes that watch it with tender amusement. Its pulsations, hesitant at

first, become faster and stronger. A sudden uprising makes
Thérèse laugh. But she recoils, a little afraid, letting her head fall
back on to my chest. I can only see her hair, a little wild, but I
guess that her eyes are still fixed on my sex. After a little time
she returns to it, her cheek, sliding down my body, rubs the surface of my stomach in a slow caress. Then suddenly I am shuddering at the incredibly soft touch of her warm kiss, enveloping the
naked tip of my phallus.

. . . Beneath the screaming tension of my erect sex, I can hear
the imperious, rumbling summons of an approaching orgasm,
and, instantly more alert, I can perceive the dangers of an unpar-
donable profanity, which nothing could excuse. So I tear myself
briskly from my wife's overly erotic mouth. Then I pounce upon
her, burying my face in the shadowy place where buttocks and
vulva join.

Has she understood the cause of my panic? What does it really
matter? In a few days, all our thoughts will have been unbur-
dened to each other.

All the same, I don't want her to think that she has provoked
my retreat by some clumsiness of hers that was painful to me. So
to allay any possible worries she might have, I amuse myself by
exploring every little nook and cranny of her genitals with the
point of my tongue. She tries to defend herself against this game
by closing her legs tight, and it helps us to keep those exquisite
paroxysms at bay. Thérèse soon bursts out laughing, tickled by
my tongue and the efforts she makes to avoid it. I pretend to
stop. Her muscles relax, and before she's had a chance to recover, parting the globe of her buttocks with both hands, I rudely
give her a great, slicing lick. She whips round, quite angry, and
chases me away, but she soon starts to laugh again and shaking a
finger at me, says:

'Ça alors! Tu dépasses les bornes! [You're overstepping the
mark!] And cover yourself up with the sheets, you really are indecent!'

'Well whose fault is that? I was sleeping perfectly innocently
this morning!'

For a moment we squabbled, each trying to deny responsi-
bility, Thérèse comparing me to a woman-eating Bluebeard, and I
accusing her of being like some monstrously greedy ogress, prey-
ing on sleeping children at dawn. To end the dispute we retreat
to our respective bathrooms.

Finally – as characters in fables come to deserve and the reader
comes to expect – there is a happy ending.

As if she was discovering it for the first time, Thérèse contem-
plates my body with an astonished smile; her caressing fingers
stroke it with the lightest touches and she scatters quick little
kisses all over it. She holds me like this for a long time, without
getting tired of looking at me, touching me or licking me. Then,
keeping me tight and upright between her legs, she makes me
turn sideways. With her hands, she passionately starts to follow
the two outlines of my body's profiles: one sliding down my back

*For manners are not idle, but the fruit
Of loyal nature and of noble mind.*

FROM *GUINEVERE*
ALFRED LORD TENNYSON (1809–92)

OPPOSITE and ABOVE Two more
original etchings by Suzanne
Ballivet (active 1930–45) from
Initiation Amoureuse.

Upon a bed of roses she was laid,
As faint through heat, or dight to
pleasant sin,
And was arrayed, or rather
disarrayed,
All in a veil of silk and silver thin,
That hid no whit her alabaster skin,
But rather showed more white, if more
might be:
More subtle web Arachne cannot spin,
Nor the fine nets, which oft we woven
see
Of scorched dew, do not in th'air more
lightly flee.

FROM *THE FAERIE QUEEN*
EDMUND SPENSER (1552–99)

and cupping my buttocks, the other, in a parallel motion, straying over my stomach and my sex.

Little by little, however, her touch becomes more precise, more deliberate, seeking out my most sensitive areas, returning to them insistently. I beg Thérèse to stop her over-intense pleasuring, whose dangers I already know. But she just smiles at my anguish, priding herself with her inventive affection, and the confession of my weakness, far from stopping her, makes her more passionate still. I can feel that intoxicating, inexorable surge of sensuality rising inside me. I know that any moment now, no sense of modesty will contain it, not even the shame of ejaculating under that curious and avid gaze. However a short giddy spell comes to the aid of my flagging will. The walls seemed to oscillate around me in the heavy air and I let myself fall on the cushions that strew the ground, thus escaping, very much in spite of myself, Thérèse's ecstatically amorous hands. She throws me a disappointed glance, but noticing my pallor, encircles my neck with her arms and presses my head against her stomach, which the narrow bolero has uncovered. . . .

Crouching, naked, between Thérèse's legs, I want to undress her as well. The trousers she wears have become physically intolerable to me. With a little movement of her hips she helps me uncover her bottom and they slip off. She allows me to part her legs and she lets me untangle the entwined blond curls with my fingers. She lets me half-open the most secret part of her. Falling back on the divan, her thighs spread wide, she arches her back in a heaving offering of her sex; then she greedily gives herself up to the multiple caresses of my lips and tongue, which are made drunk by the rising sap of her desire.

Finally I straighten up to regain my breath; as I am on my knees between her legs, our sexes meet.

Then I stroke her open flesh with my glans, as slowly as the tension of my aching need will allow.

Long strokes, which start at the crease of my wife's bottom, then caress the length of her crimson valley, causing her most tender spot to quiver, and finally end in the most fleecy part of her thatch. As her pleasure is intensified, so Thérèse's breasts shudder with her more rapid panting. Stretched towards me, her body rises and falls, obeying the instinctive need to intensify and accelerate the slippery rubbing of our sexes.

A cry escapes her: 'Oh, take me! Take me now!'

And yet I hesitate. Dominating the turmoil of my senses, one scruple holds me back: the fear of tearing that flesh whose fragile sweetness I know so well; compassion for the sensibilities of that virgin body which wants to give itself to the brutal appeasement of my desire. Astonished by my hesitation, and a little disappointed perhaps, Thérèse remains motionless, slumped on the divan. Then she sits up a little way, puts her arms around me, clutching my buttocks with her hands.

At the moment my glans, departing the crease of her bottom on the upstroke, reaches her secret flesh once more, she pulls me violently towards her in a passionate gesture and buries me inside of her.

On her features I can read the extraordinarily rapid succession of her emotions: a fleeting tension in her face, a misting of her eyes, then finally a flash of joyful pride. After another moment she smiles at me, a little wistfully perhaps, but nonetheless with great tenderness. Then, closing her eyes, she lets herself fall back, with no other cry than one of pure love:

'My husband! My beloved husband!'

---◊---

In 1945, refusing to walk any further after a two-day forced march towards Kiel, Maurice Sachs and his male lover were shot by an SS officer. He had played many parts in his time: novitiate for the priesthood, chronicler of Paris in the Twenties, husband, collaborator, Gestapo spy. Sachs considered himself 'thoroughly defiled'. It was the right time to bring down the curtain. Maurice Sachs had been a friend of Jean Cocteau in Paris, and of many of the other homosexuals who contributed so much to the world of art and letters. This extract from his autobiography speaks for all of them.

It was at this period that I experienced the first strong passion of my life. It was for a boy whom I shall call Octave. We had met at the Collège de Luza. At home, my good behavior astonished everyone; there was no need to forbid me anything now. Indeed, as soon as dinner was over, I locked myself in my room and wrote enormous letters to Octave. I was happy: he loved me too. . . .

Blond, muscular, covered with freckles, Octave had something rather animal about him; he was if not younger, at least shorter than I, but I showed utter submission toward him, for unconsciously I had perhaps already developed a certain inferiority complex that has hampered my emotional involvements ever since, leading me to that victimization to which those who must buy love are subjected.

How had this affair begun? I no longer remember very clearly. It seems to me that I took the first step, I mean, that I wrote first. He answered, even before we had made

BELOW An illustration for his autobiographical account of homosexuality *Le Livre Blanc* by Jean Cocteau (1889–1963).

any gesture toward each other more affectionate than those customary among schoolmates. And that was the paradoxical thing about our situation: we treated each other as 'comrades' and wrote each other so passionately that anyone would have assumed, had they read what we wrote, that we were making love every day; for we used a conventional vocabulary, as children and uneducated people always do when they are surprised by their own feelings. But such pleasures preoccupied us singularly little. Doubtless they seemed the necessary fulfillment to such ardor, but we were not in any hurry to achieve it.

During recess periods, we kept apart from the others and talked endlessly (and it seems to me today, quite intelligently for our age). Sometimes we held hands, and given our extreme youth, this did not seem at all improper. Soon, the tone of our letters mounting, Octave got in the habit of spending an hour at my house in the afternoon.

We lay together on the couch in my bedroom, rather like puppies, while playing in the fashion of lovers. I remember those afternoons with deep emotion. Enthusiasm and innocence sorted well together, and so deep was the wellspring of tenderness we felt that I don't recall we felt any real guilt at all. And if I kept the door shut, it was rather out of modesty, out of respect for this emotion which I thought deserved secrecy, and out of fear that I would be accused of laziness, for my love in itself seemed innocent and beautiful. And if I felt some sense of inferiority, it was only toward this friend of whom I considered myself unworthy, for I thought him more handsome, more charming, more sensitive than myself.

I shall not claim that this relationship was entirely chaste. But I recall that we were not at all eager to seal it in the pleasure of the flesh, so greatly did we enjoy the exaltation of those embraces without any declared purpose, without ulterior motive. The day we touched each other more intimately we added nothing to our happiness, for at that age tenderness can still do without possession.

If the reader grants with me that the whole of our life is nothing more than an attempt to fulfill the dreams of our youth, he will understand that it is possible to search throughout the whole of one's life for a happiness one has enjoyed as a child.

For me, the memory of Octave and the endless, perhaps futile search for another Octave all too like the original confirmed me in my homosexual appetites and I no longer believe myself capable of other pleasures of the heart and of the body. Doubtless there is some infantilism in this, as the psychiatrists call it, and doubtless I would have rediscovered these innocent pleasures that Octave afforded me, so gentle yet so sensual, much more certainly in the arms of a woman my own age twenty years later.

But this is beyond my powers. I do not *believe*, in other words I do not believe that a woman can ever be Octave. She cannot even pretend to be.

ABOVE A drawing by Jean Cocteau (1889–1963).

The writing of Violette Leduc (1907–72) is fierce, sad stuff. But it is a voice which Albert Camus – publisher of her first novel – thought we should hear. This extract from her autobiographical novel *La Bâtarde*, although it takes place in a girls' dormitory, is a very long way from the jolly hockey-sticks world of Angela Brazil.

Her hand undressed my arm, halted near the vein in the crook of the elbow, fornicated there among the traceries, moved downward to the wrist, right to the tips of the nails, sheathed my arm once more in a long suède glove, fell from my shoulder like an insect, and hooked itself into the armpit. I was stretching my neck, listening for what answers my arm gave the adventuress. The hand, still seeking to persuade me, was bringing my arm, my armpit, into their real existence. The hand travelled over the chatter of white bushes, over the last frosts on the meadows, over

BELOW *Abbandono*, contemporary photograph by Giovanni Zuin.

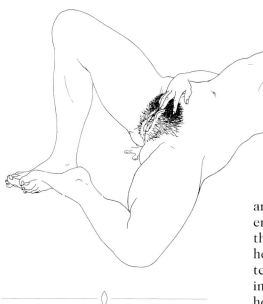

ABOVE A brilliantly executed drawing by Mario Tauzin, active in Paris in the 1920s. The artist's controlled use of line, careful exaggeration, and stylistic tricks such as luring the viewer's eye to the erotic focus with shading, owe much to the *shunga* tradition of Japan.

the first buds as they swelled to fullness. Spring that had been chirping with impatience under my skin was now bursting forth into lines, curves, roundnesses. Isabelle, stretched out upon the darkness, was fastening my feet with ribbons, unravelling the swaddling bands of my alarm. With hands laid flat upon the mattress, I was immersed in the self-same magic as she. She was kissing what she had caressed, and then, lightly, her hand ruffled and whisked with the feathers of perversity. The octopus in my entrails quivered. Isabelle was drinking at my breast, the right, the left, and I drank with her, sucking the milk of darkness when her lips had gone. The fingers were returning now, encircling and testing the warm weight of my breast. The fingers were pretending to be waifs in a storm; they were taking shelter inside me. A host of slaves, all with the face of Isabelle, fanned my brow, my hands.

She knelt up in the bed.

'Do you love me?'

I led her hand up to the precious tears of joy.

Her cheek took shelter in the hollow of my groin, I shone the torch on her, and saw her spreading hair, saw my own belly beneath the rain of silk. The torch slipped, Isabelle moved suddenly toward me.

As we melted into one another we were dragged up to the surface by the hooks caught in our flesh, by the hairs we were clutching in our fingers; we were rolling together on a bed of nails. We bit each other and bruised the darkness with our hands.

Slowing down, we trailed back beneath our plumes of smoke, black wings sprouting at our heels. Isabelle leaped out of bed.

I wondered why Isabelle was doing her hair again. With one hand she forced me to lie on my back, with the other, to my distress, she shone the pale yellow beam of the torch on me.

I tried to shield myself with my arms.

'I'm not beautiful. You make me feel ashamed,' I said.

She was looking at our future in my eyes, she was gazing at what was going to happen next, storing it in the currents of her blood.

She got back into bed, she wanted me.

I played with her, preferring failure to the preliminaries she needed. Making love with our mouths was enough for me: I was afraid, but my hands as they signalled for help were helpless stumps. A pair of paint brushes was advancing into the folds of my flesh. My heart was beating under its molehill, my head was crammed with damp earth. Two tormenting fingers were exploring me. How masterly, how inevitable their caress. . . . My closed eyes listened: the finger lightly touched the pearl. I wanted to be wider, to make it easier for her.

The regal, diplomatic finger was moving forward, moving back, making me gasp for breath, beginning to enter, arousing the tentacles in my entrails, parting the secret cloud, pausing, prompting once more. I tightened, I closed over this flesh of my flesh, its softness and its bony core. I sat up, I fell back again. The finger which had not wounded me, the finger, after its grateful exploration, left me. My flesh peeled back from it.

'Do you love me?' I asked.

I wanted to create a diversion.

'You mustn't cry out,' Isabelle said.

I crossed my arms over my face, still listening under my lowered eyelids.

Two thieves entered me. They were forcing their way inside, they wanted to go further, but my flesh rebelled.

'My love . . . you're hurting me.'

She put her hand over my mouth.

'I won't make any noise,' I said.

The gag was a humiliation.

'It hurts. But she's got to do it. It hurts.'

I gave myself up to the darkness and without wanting to, I helped. I leaned forward to help tear myself, to come closer to her face, to be nearer my wound: she pushed me back on the pillow. She was thrusting, thrusting, thrusting. . . . I could hear the smacking noise it made. She was putting out the eye of innocence. It hurt me: I was moving on to my deliverance, but I couldn't see what was happening.

We listened to the sleeping girls around us, we sobbed as we sucked in our breath. A trail of fire still burned inside me.

'Let's rest,' she said.

--------------------------◊--------------------------

The *Story of O* appeared in Paris in 1954. Its origins are still unclear, but we know that it was written by a woman who used the pseudonym 'Pauline Réage'. Uniquely, for a book dealing with bondage, flagellation and the outer limits of sexual behaviour, *Story of O* has received serious critical attention and praise. A lot of this has to do with the cool, elegant prose which distances the novel from obscenity.

Her lover one day takes O for a walk, but this time in a part of the city – the Parc Montsouris, the parc Monceau – where they've never been together before. After they've strolled awhile along the paths, after they've sat down side by side on a bench near the grass, and got up again, and moved on towards the edge of the park, there, where two streets meet, where there never used to be any taxi-stand, they see a car, at that corner. It looks like a taxi, for it does have a meter. 'Get in,' he says; she gets in. It's late in the afternoon, it's autumn. She is wearing what she always wears: high heels, a suit with a pleated skirt, a silk blouse, no hat. But she has on long gloves reaching up to the sleeves of her jacket, in her leather handbag she's got her papers, and her compact and lipstick. The taxi eases off, very slowly; nor has the man next to her said a word to the driver. But on the right, on the left, he draws down the little window-shades, and the one behind

ABOVE and OPPOSITE Photographs by
China Hamilton, Suffolk, England.

too; thinking that he is about to kiss her, or so as to caress him, she has slipped off her gloves. Instead, he says: 'I'll take your bag, it's in your way.' She gives it to him, he puts it beyond her reach; then adds: 'You've too much clothing on. Un-hitch your stockings, roll them down to just above your knees. Go ahead,' and he gives her some elastics to hold the stockings in place. It isn't easy, not in the car, which is going faster now, and she doesn't want to have the driver turn around. But she manages anyhow, at last; it's a queer, uncomfortable feeling, the contact of silk of her slip upon her naked and free legs, and the unattached garters are sliding loosely back and forth across her skin. 'Undo your garter-belt,' he says, 'take off your panties.' There's nothing to that, all she has to do is get at the hook behind and raise up a little. He takes the garter-belt from her hand, he takes the panties, opens her bag, puts them away inside it; then he says: 'You're not to sit on your slip or on your skirt, pull them up and sit on the seat without anything in between.' The seat-covering is a sort of leather, slick and chilly; it's a very strange sensation, the way it sticks and clings to her thighs. Then he says: 'Now put your gloves back on.' The taxi goes right along and she doesn't dare ask why René is so quiet, so still, or what all this means to him: she so motionless and so silent, so denuded and so offered, though so thoroughly gloved, in a black car going she hasn't the least idea where. He hasn't told her to do anything or not to do it, but she doesn't dare either cross her legs or sit with them held together. One on this side, one on that side, she rests her gloved hands on the seat, pushing down.

'Here we are,' he says all of a sudden. Here we are: the taxi comes to a stop on a fine avenue, under a tree – those are plane trees – in front of a small mansion, you could just see it, nestled away between courtyard and garden, the way the Faubourg Saint-Germain mansions are. There's no streetlight nearby, it is dark inside the cab, and outside rain is falling. 'Don't move,' said René. 'Don't move a muscle.' He extends his hand towards the neck of her blouse, unties the ribbon at the throat, then unbuttons the buttons. She leans forward ever so little, and believes he is about to caress her breasts. But no; he's got a small penknife out, he's only groping for the shoulder-straps of her brassiere, he cuts the straps, removes the brassiere. He has closed her blouse again and now, underneath, her breasts are free and nude, like her belly and thighs are nude and free, like all of her is, from waist to knee.

'Listen,' he says. 'You're ready. Here's where I leave you. You're going to get out and go to the door and ring the bell. Someone will open the door, whoever it is you'll do as he says. You'll do it right away and willingly of your own accord'. . . .

And so O enters an alternative world, a novitiate, abandoning one life and all its trappings, to wear new clothes and live by strict new

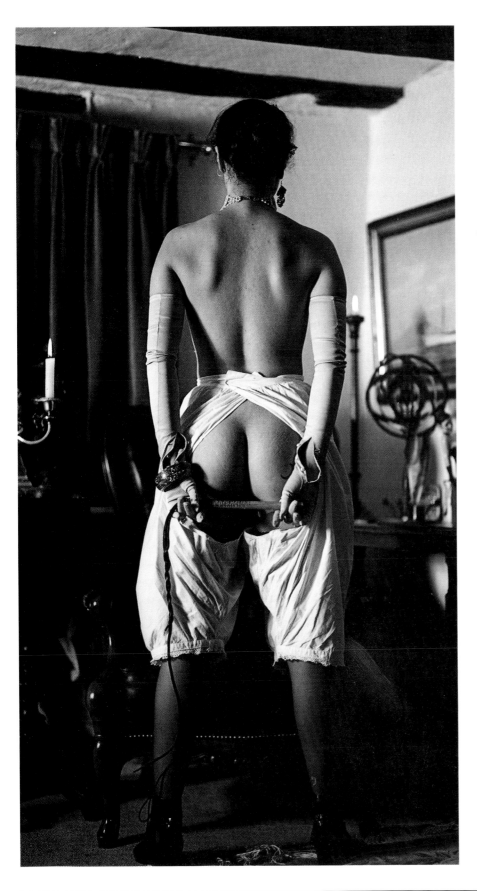

Nay, slay me now; nay, for I will be
    slain
Pluck thy red pleasure from the teeth of
    pain,
Break down thy vine 'ere yet grape-
    gatherers prune,
Stay me 'ere day can slay desire
    again;
Ah God, ah God, that day should be so
    soon.

FROM THE ORCHARD
ALGERNON SWINBURNE (1837–1909)

rules: she does this of her own free will and all because of love. Or, since this famous erotic novel has alternative beginnings, O steps through the looking glass into a sado-masochistic pantomime, produced in a madhouse and utterly devoid of humour. In this scene she learns obedience.

The stranger, whom she still dared not look at, after he had glided his hands over her breasts and down her buttocks, then asked her to spread her legs. 'Do as you're told,' said René, against whose chest her back was leaning and who was holding her erect; and his right hand was caressing one of her breasts, his left held her shoulder. The stranger had seated himself on the edge of the bed, by means of the hairs growing on them had taken hold of and gradually opened the labia guarding the entrance to her crack. René nudged her forward in an effort to facilitate the task, but no, that wasn't quite it, then he understood what the other

RIGHT A photograph by China Hamilton, Suffolk, England.

was after and slipped his right arm around her waist, thus improving his grip. Under this caress, which she had never hitherto accepted without a struggle and without an overpowering feeling of shame, from which she would escape as quickly as she could, so quickly that it scarcely had the opportunity to register its effects, and which seemed a sacrilege to her, because it seemed to her sacrilegious that her lover be on his knees when she ought to be on hers – of a sudden she sensed that she was not going to escape this caress, not this time, and she saw herself doomed. For she moaned when that strange mouth pushed aside the fold of flesh whence the inner corolla emerges, moaned when those strange lips abruptly set her afire then retreated to let a strange tongue's hot tip burn her still more; she moaned louder when strange lips seized her anew; she sensed the hidden point harden and protrude to be taken between strange teeth and tongue in a long sucking bite that held her and held her still; she reeled, lost her footing, and found herself upon her back, René's mouth upon her mouth; his two hands pinned her shoulders to the mattress whilst two other hands gripping her calves were opening and flexing her legs. Her own hands – they were behind and under her back (for at the same moment he had thrust her towards the stranger René had bound her wrists by joining the two wristbands' catches) – her hands were brushed by the sex of the man who was rubbing himself in the crease between her buttocks; that sex now rose and shot swiftly to the depths of the hole in her belly. In answer to that first blow she emitted a cry as when under the lash, acknowledged each succeeding blow with a cry, and her lover bit her mouth. It was as though snatched forcefully away that the man quit her, hurled backwards as though thunderstruck, and from his throat there also came a cry. René detached O's hands, eased her along the bed, and tucked her away under the blanket. The stranger got up and the two men went towards the door. In a flash, O saw herself immolated, annihilated, cursed. She had groaned under the stranger's mouth as never she had under René's, cried before the onslaught of the stranger's member as never her lover had made her cry. She was profaned and guilty. If he were to abandon her, it would be rightfully. But no: the door swung to again, he was still there, was staying with her, he walked towards her, lay full length down beside her, beneath the fur blanket, slipped himself into her wet and burning belly and, holding her thus embraced, said to her: 'I love you.'

The costumes and rituals, which are such an essential part of the sexuality explored in the book, are described with scrupulous attention to detail: colours, textures and shapes are all defined, all carefully chosen. After an elaborate toilette O learns that concepts such as jealousy and possession have no place in her new world. As each new dignity and supposed right is stripped away from our heroine, with only love remaining at the centre and that always untouched, we become aware that a curious sense of morality pervades the book.

If I do prove her haggard
Though that her jesses were my dear
*   heart strings*
I'd whistle her off and let her down the
*   wind,*
To prey at fortune.

FROM *OTHELLO*
WILLIAM SHAKESPEARE (1564–1616)

Ah beautiful, passionate body
That never has ached with a heart!
On thy mouth though the kisses are
    bloody,
Though they sting till it shudder and
    smart
More kind than the love we adore is
They hurt not the heart nor the brain
Of bitter and tender Dolores
Our Lady of Pain.

FROM *DOLORES*
ALGERNON SWINBURNE (1837–1909)

She bathed, did her hair; upon contact with her bruised buttocks the tepid water made her shiver, she had to sponge herself but not rub to avoid reviving the fiery pain. She painted her mouth, but not her eyes, powdered herself and, still naked, but with her eyes lowered, came back into the cell. René was looking at Jeanne, who had entered and who was standing quietly by the head of the bed, she too with lowered eyes, she, too, mute. He told her to dress O. Jeanne took the green satin bodice, the white petticoat, the gown, the green clogs and, having hooked O's bodice in front, began to lace it up tight in back.

The bodice was stoutly whaleboned, long and rigid, something from the days when wasp-waists were in fashion, and was fitted with gussets upon which the breasts lay. The tighter it was drawn, the more prominently O's breasts rose, pushed up by the supporting gussets, and the more sharply upward her nipples were tilted. At the same time, as her waist was constricted, her womb and buttocks were made to swell out. The odd thing is that this veritable cuirass was exceedingly comfortable and, up to a certain point, relaxing. In it, one felt very upright, but, without one being able to tell just how or why unless it was by contrast, it increased one's consciousness of the freedom or rather the availability of the parts it left unencompassed. The wide skirt and the neckline, sweeping down from her shoulders to below and the whole width of her breasts, looked on the girl clad in it, not so much like an article of clothing, a protective device, but like a provocative one, a mechanism for display. When Jeanne had tied a bow in the laces and knotted it for good measure, O took her gown from the bed. It was in one piece, the petticoat tacked inside the skirt like an interchangeable lining, and the bodice, cross-laced in front and secured in back by a second series of laces, was thus, depending on how tightly it was done up, able to reproduce more or less exactly the subtler lines of the bust. Jeanne had laced it very tight, and O caught a glimpse of herself through the open door to the bathroom, her slender torso rising like a flower from the mass of green satin billowing out from her hips as if she were wearing a hoop-skirt. The two women were standing side by side. Jeanne reached to correct a pleat in the sleeve of the green gown, and her breasts stirred beneath her gauze kerchief, breasts whose nipples were long, whose halos were brown. Her gown was of yellow faille. René, who had approached the two women, said to O: 'Look.' And to Jeanne: 'Lift your dress.' With both hands she lifted the stiff crackling silk and the linen lining it to reveal a golden belly, honey-smooth thighs and knees, and a black, closed triangle. René put forth his hand and probed it slowly, with his other hand exciting the nipple of one breast, till it grew hard and yet darker. 'That's so you can see,' he told O. O saw. She saw his ironic but concentrated face, his intent eyes scanning Jeanne's half-opened mouth and the back-bent throat girdled by the leather collar. What pleasure could she, O, give him, that this woman or some other could not give him too? 'Hadn't you thought of that?' he asked. No, she'd not thought of that. She had slumped against the wall between the two doors; her spine was straight, her arms trailed limply.

LEFT A contemporary photograph
by Alexandre Dupouy, Paris.

There was no further need for ordering her to silence. How could
she have spoken? He may perhaps have been moved by her
despair, for he relinquished Jeanne to take O in his arms, hugging her to him, calling her his love and his life, saying again and
again that he loved her. The hand with which he was caressing
her throat and neck was moist with the wetness and smell of
Jeanne. And then? And then the despair in whose tide she had
been drowning ebbed away: he loved her, ah yes, he did love her.
He did indeed have the right to take pleasure with Jeanne, to

seek it with others, he loved her. 'I love you,' she whispered in his ear, 'I love you,' in so soft a whisper he could just barely hear.

'I love you.'

It wasn't until he saw the sweetness flow back into her and the brightness into her eyes that he took leave of her, happy.

However, whenever we are tempted to take the *Story of O* too seriously, the Demon Prince – sometimes complete with mask and tasteful accessories – springs from the stage trapdoor. 'Sir Stephen' is the master of ceremonies, an Englishman related by marriage to O's lover René. If we take a midpoint between James Bond, Vincent Price and the Marquis de Sade we begin to glimpse him. As an Englishman he is, of course, a connoisseur of the three S's: Sartorial elegance, Sodomy and Sadism. In this extract a new player is introduced.

OPPOSITE and BELOW Contemporary photographs by China Hamilton, Suffolk, England.

The dressing-table wasn't a dressing-table properly speaking but, next to a ledge in the wall upon which were ranged bottles and brushes, a wide, low Restoration table and upon it a mirror where O, in her little armchair, could see all of herself. While speaking to her, Sir Stephen roved to and fro in the room behind her back; now and again his reflection moved across the mirror, behind O's reflection, but his image seemed faraway, for the silvering of the mirror was a bit fuzzy and the surface of the glass wavy. O, her hands limp and knees spread, would have liked to seize the reflection, make it halt in order to answer more easily. For, in the precisest English, Sir Stephen was putting question after question to her, the last questions O would ever have dreamt of hearing him put to her, if ever he would have put any at all. He had hardly begun, however, when he interrupted himself and arranged O so that she was leaning back, almost lying in the chair; her left leg hooked over an arm of the chair, her right bent a little at the knee, in all that excess of light she offered herself and Sir Stephen a reflected view of her body as perfectly open as if an invisible lover had withdrawn from her and left her belly agape. Sir Stephen resumed his questioning, with a judge's firmness and the skill of a confessor. O not only saw him speak, she saw herself answer. Had she, since returning from Roissy, had she belonged to other men than René and himself? No. Had she desired to belong to others whom she might have met? No. Did she caress herself at night at such times as she was alone? No. Had she female friends by whom she might allow herself to be caressed, or whom she might caress? No (this no was more hesitant). But were there female friends whom she desired? Well, yes, Jacqueline, except that the word 'friend' would be overdoing it. Thereupon Sir Stephen asked her if she had any photographs of Jacqueline, for in describing Jacqueline as her 'companion', she had given Sir Stephen to understand that she had made Jacqueline's acquaintance at the studio. The photographs, however: he helped her get up to go and fetch them. René, out of breath after running up the four flights, found them in the living room: O standing before the large table upon which, bright black and white, shining like puddles of water in the night, were all the pictures of Jacqueline; Sir Stephen, half-seated on the edge of the table, taking them one by one as O handed them to him, and one by one setting them back on the table and, with his other hand, holding O's womb. As of that instant, Sir Stephen, who had said hello to René without letting go of her – she even felt him bury his fingers deeper in her – ceased to address her, addressed René instead. She clearly saw why: the understanding between the two men: René there, it reasserted itself: it was an understanding reached about her, but apart from her, she was simply its occasion or subject, there were no further questions to put to her, no further replies for her to make, what she was to do and even what she was to be was being decided over her head. Noon was approaching. The sun, falling vertically upon the table, was causing the prints to curl at the edge. O wanted to move them into the shade, to flatten them to prevent them from being spoiled; her hands fumbled, she was near to pleasure's critical point, so persistently did Sir Stephen's fingers probe her. She dropped the pictures, did indeed melt, moan, and found herself lying flat on her back across the table amidst the scattered photographs where Sir Stephen, having jerked his hand free, had thrust her, legs spread and dangling. Her feet didn't reach the floor, one of her slippers fell off, landed noiselessly on the white carpeted floor. Her face lay in the sun's path, she shut her eyes.

The introduction of Jacqueline changes the pattern of the fable.

Jacqueline liked pleasure, and found it both agreeable and practical to receive it from a woman, in whose hands she ran no risks.

Five days after having unpacked her suitcases and with O's help arranged what had been in them, and when René had brought them home for the third time, towards ten o'clock, and had gone – for he had left, as he had the two times before – she appeared in O's doorway, naked and still damp from her bath; she said: 'You're sure he won't come back?' and without even waiting for her answer, slipped into the big bed. She let herself be embraced and caressed, her eyes shut; she did not repay O in kind, she did nothing at all, at first she hardly reacted, hardly moaned, but then began to, then did moan louder and finally emitted a cry. She fell asleep, the light of the pink lamp falling on her face, her body stretched across the bed, knees apart, torso a bit to one side, hands open. The sweat glistened in the cleft between her breasts. O drew the covers over her, turned out the light. Two hours later, when she took Jacqueline again, in the darkness, Jacqueline submitted quietly. . . .

Is this the beginning of a revolt? The angels in heaven revolted, why not in hell? In fact it is only a change of pattern.

She, O, she was fit for the hunt, she was a naturally trained bird of prey that would rise and strike and bring home the quarry, every time. And indeed . . . It was at this point, as with beating

heart she thought again of Jacqueline's delicate and so very pink lips behind the blonde fur of her sex, of the still more delicate, still pinker ring hidden between her buttocks, the ring she'd dared force only three times, it was at this point she heard Sir Stephen stir in his room. She knew he could see her, even though she could not see him, and once again she felt that she was fortunate to be exposed thus, openly, constantly, fortunate in this prison wherein his constant gaze enclosed her.

Sir Stephen permits O to caress Jacqueline because he likes to watch them secretly. The 'bird of prey' metaphor is particularly apt: an owl mask is the identity O always adopts in their masked orgies. And remember there are no random motifs here: each thread is woven carefully and obsessionally into the fabric to contribute to the pattern. The relationship between the falconer and his beautiful creature, the fierce and uncompromising love, the mutual dependence – and of course the cruel talons, the blood, the leather thongs – are emblematic of this extraordinary novel.

———————————◊———————————

The 1960s were a period of hopeful, feverish experimentation. The newly affluent young and their rock star prophets tried out religion, drugs, music and sex – often simultaneously. *A Long Letter from F* by the poet and singer Leonard Cohen (b. 1934) bears a superficial resemblance to the drug-inspired language of psychedelic pop lyrics, but has a beauty and coherence they seldom – if ever – achieved. What self-induced or accidental trauma frees F's mind from the mundane is never quite clear: we only know that he is writing his letter during a session of occupational therapy.

I was your adventure and you were my adventure. I was your journey and you were my journey, and Edith was our holy star. This letter rises out of our love like the sparks between dueling swords, like the shower of needles from flapping cymbals, like the bright seeds of sweat sliding through the center of our tight embrace, like the white feathers hung in the air by razored bushido cocks, like the shriek between two approaching puddles of mercury, like the atmosphere of secrets which twin children exude. I was your mystery and you were my mystery, and we rejoiced to learn that mystery was our home. Our love cannot die. Out of history I come to tell you this. Like two mammoths, tusk-locked in earnest sport at the edge of the advancing age of ice, we preserve each other. Our queer love keeps the lines of our manhood hard and clean, so that we bring nobody but our own self to our separate marriage beds, and our women finally know us.

    Mary Voolnd has finally admitted my left hand into the creases of her uniform. She watched me compose the above paragraph, so I let it run on rather extravagantly. Women love excess in a man because it separates him from his fellows and makes him

ABOVE A drypoint etching from France, c. 1960.

———————◊———————

ABOVE Another French drypoint etching of c. 1960.

lonely. All that women know of the male world has been revealed to them by lonely, excessive refugees from it. Raging fairies they cannot resist because of their highly specialized intelligence.

—Keep writing, she hisses.

Mary has turned her back to me. The balloons are shrieking like whistles signaling the end of every labor. Mary pretends to inspect a large rug some patient wove, thus shielding our precious play. Slow as a snail I push my hand, palm down, up the tight rough stocking on the back of her thigh. The linen of her skirt is crisp and cool against my knuckles and nails, the stockinged thigh is warm, curved, a little damp like a loaf of fresh white bread.

—Higher, she hisses.

I am in no hurry. Old friend, I am in no hurry. I feel I shall be doing this throughout eternity. Her buttocks contract impatiently, like two boxing gloves touching before the match. My hand pauses to ride the quiver on the thigh.

—Hurry, she hisses.

Yes, I can tell by the tension in the stocking that I am approaching the peninsula which is hitched to the garter device. I will travel the whole peninsula, hot skin on either side, then I will leap off the nipple-shaped garter device. The threads of the stocking tighten. I bunch my fingers together so as not to make premature contact. Mary is jiggling, endangering the journey. My forefinger scouts out the garter device. It is warm. The little metal loop, the rubber button – warm right through.

—Please, please, she hisses.

Like angels on the head of a pin, my fingers dance on the rubber button. Which way shall I leap? Toward the outside thigh, hard, warm as the shell of a beached tropical turtle? Or toward the swampy mess in the middle? Or fasten like a bat on the huge soft over-hanging boulder of her right buttock? It is very humid up her white starched skirt. It is like one of those airplane hangars wherein clouds form and it actually rains indoors. Mary is bouncing her bum like a piggy bank which is withholding a gold coin. The inundations are about to begin. I choose the middle.

—Yesssss.

Delicious soup stews my hand. Viscous geysers shower my wrist. Magnetic rain tests my Bulova. She jiggles for position, then drops over my fist like a gorilla net. I had been snaking through her wet hair, compressing it between my fingers like cotton candy. Now I am surrounded by artesian exuberance, nipply frills, numberless bulby brains, pumping constellations of mucous hearts. Moist Morse messages move up my arm, master my intellectual head, more, more, message dormant portions of dark brain, elect happy new kings for the exhausted pretenders of the mind. I am a seal inventing undulations in a vast electric aquacade, I am wires of tungsten burning in the seas of bulb, I am creature of Mary cave, I am froth of Mary wave, bums of nurse Mary applaud greedily as she maneuvers to plow her asshole on the edge of my arm bone, rose of rectum sliding up and down like the dream of banister fiend.

—Slish slosh slish slosh.

Are we not happy? Loud as we are, no one hears us, but this is a tiny miracle in the midst of all this bounty, so are the rainbow crowns hovering over every skull but tiny miracles. Mary looks at me over her shoulder, greeting me with rolled-up eyes white as eggshells, and an open goldfish mouth amazed smile. In the gold sunshine of OT everyone believes he is a stinking genius, offering baskets, ceramic ashtrays, thong-sewn wallets on the radiant altars of their perfect health.

———◊———

Erica Jong has said: 'I wrote *Fear of Flying* in a mad rush, heart racing, adrenaline pumping, wanting to tell the truth about women whatever it cost me.' Millions of readers are very happy that Erica Jong (b. 1942) took that chance in 1973. In a preface written to mark twenty years of continual reprinting the author said that her novel 'had become a rallying cry for women who wanted the right to have fantasies as rich and raunchy as those of men'. The heroine of *Fear of Flying*, the intrepid Isadora Wing, explores every aspect and application of erotic fantasy in her search for fulfilment.

I shut my eyes tightly and pretended that Bennett was Adrian. I transformed B into A. We came – first me, then Bennett – and lay there sweating on the awful hotel bed. Bennett smiled. I was miserable. What a fraud I was! Real adultery couldn't be worse than these nightly deceptions. To fuck one man and think of another and keep the deception a secret – it was far, far worse than fucking another man within your husband's sight. It was as bad as any betrayal I could think of. 'Only a fantasy,' Bennett would probably say. 'A fantasy is only a fantasy, and *everyone* has fantasies. Only psychopaths actually act out all their fantasies; normal people don't.'

But I have more respect for fantasy than that. You are what you dream. You are what you daydream. Masters and Johnson's charts and numbers and flashing lights and plastic pricks tell us everything about sex and nothing about it. Because sex is all in the head. Pulse rates and secretions have nothing to do with it. That's why all the best-selling sex manuals are such gyps. They teach people how to fuck with their pelvises, not with their heads.

What did it matter that technically I was 'faithful' to Bennett? What did it matter that I hadn't screwed another guy since I met him? I was unfaithful to him at least ten times a week in my thoughts – and at least five of those times I was unfaithful to him while he and I were screwing.

Maybe Bennett was pretending I was someone else, too. But so what? That was *his* problem. And doubtless 99 per cent of the people in the world were fucking phantoms. They probably were. That didn't comfort me at all. I despised my own deceitfulness and I despised myself. I was already an adulteress, and was only holding off the actual consummation out of cowardice. That

The bonds of wedlock are so heavy that it takes two to carry them – sometimes three.

ALEXANDRE DUMAS (1802–70)

———◊———

ABOVE An illustration by G. de Sainte-Croix (active 1949–59 in France); drypoint, hand-coloured in aquatint.

———◊———

made me an adulteress *and* a coward (cowardess?). At least if I fucked Adrian I'd only be an adulteress (adult?).

Fear of Flying is a witty, bawdy, hopeful book, peppered with astute insights and savage satire. Before Isadora was with the unsatisfactory Bennett, there was the unsatisfactory Brian.

Our marriage went from bad to worse. Brian stopped fucking me. I would beg and plead and ask what was wrong with me? I began to hate myself, to feel ugly, unloved, bodily odoriferous – all the classic symptoms of the unfucked wife; I began to have fantasies of zipless fucks with doormen, derelicts, countermen at the West End Bar, graduate students – even (God help me!) professors. I would sit in my 'Proseminar in Eighteenth-Century English Lit.' listening to some creepy graduate student drone on and on about Nahum Tate's revisions of Shakespeare's plays, and meanwhile I would imagine myself sucking off each male member (hah) of the class. Sometimes I would imagine myself actually fucking Professor Harrington Stanton, a fiftyish proper Bostonian with a well-

RIGHT and OPPOSITE *Sogno* and *Curiosità*, two photographs by Giovanni Zuin.

connected New England family behind him – a family renowned for politics, poetry, and psychosis. Professor Stanton had a wild laugh and always called James Boswell Bozzy – as if he drank with him nightly at the West End (which, indeed, I suspected him of doing). Somebody once referred to Stanton as 'very brilliant but not quite plugged in.' It was apt. Despite being well-connected socially, he flickered on and off between sanity and insanity, never staying in one state long enough for you to know where you stood. How *would* Professor Stanton fuck? He was fascinated with eighteenth-century dirty words. Perhaps he would whisper 'coun,' 'cullion,' 'crack' (for 'cunt,' 'testicles,' 'pussy') in my ear as we screwed? Perhaps he would turn out to have his family crest tattooed on his foreskin? I would be sitting there chuckling to myself at these fantasies and Professor Stanton would beam at me, thinking I was chuckling at one of his own wisecracks.

But what was the use of these pathetic fantasies? My husband had stopped fucking me. He thought he was working hard enough as it was. I cried myself to sleep every night, or else went into the bathroom to masturbate after he fell asleep. I was twenty-one and a half years old and desperate. In retrospect, it all seems so simple. Why didn't I find someone else? Why didn't I have an affair or leave him or insist on some sort of sexual freedom arrangement? But I was a good girl of the fifties. I had grown up finger-fucking to Frank Sinatra's *In the Wee Small Hours of the Morning*. I had never slept with any man but my husband. I had petted 'above the waist' and 'below the waist' according to some mysterious unwritten rules of propriety. But an affair with another man seemed so radical that I couldn't even consider it. Besides, I was sure that Brian's failure to fuck me was *my* fault, not his.

Erica Jong's achievement in cramming so many facets of the sexual debate into such a readable, funny novel should not be underestimated. Furthermore, in creating a heroine with whom readers can identify she has made it a genuinely enabling book. In this final extract, male writing about female sexuality receives close scrutiny, as do sex education and Steve Applebaum.

Sex. I was terrified of the tremendous power it had over me. The energy, the excitement, the power to make me feel totally crazy! What about that? How do you make that jibe with 'playing hard to get'?

I never had the courage to ask my mother directly. I sensed, despite her bohemian talk, that she disapproved of sex, that it was basically unmentionable. So I turned to D. H. Lawrence, and to *Love Without Fear*, and to *Coming of Age in Samoa*. Margaret Mead wasn't much help. What did I have in common with all

ABOVE and BELOW Illustrations by G. de Sainte-Croix (active 1949–59 in France); drypoint, hand-coloured in aquatint.

those savages? (Plenty, of course, but at the time I didn't realize it.) Eustace Chesser, M.D., was good on all the fascinating details ('How to Manage the Sex Act,' penetration, foreplay, afterglow), but he didn't seem to have much to say about *my* moral dilemmas: how 'far' to go? inside the bra or outside? inside the pants or outside? inside the mouth or outside? When to swallow, if ever. It was all so complicated. And it seemed so much more complicated for *women*. Basically, I think, I was furious with my mother for not teaching me how to be a woman, for not teaching me how to make peace between the raging hunger in my cunt and the hunger in my head.

So I learned about women from men. I saw them through the eyes of male writers. Of course, I didn't think of them as *male* writers. I thought of them as *writers*, as authorities, as gods who knew and were to be trusted completely.

Naturally I trusted everything they said, even when it implied my own inferiority. I learned what an orgasm was from D. H. Lawrence, disguised as Lady Chatterley. I learned from him that all women worship 'the Phallos' – as he so quaintly spelled it. I learned from Shaw that women never can be artists; I learned from Dostoyevsky that they have no religious feeling; I learned from Swift and Pope that they have too *much* religious feeling (and therefore can never be quite rational); I learned from Faulkner that they are earth mothers and at one with the moon and the tides and the crops; I learned from Freud that they have deficient superegos and are ever 'incomplete' because they lack the one thing in this world worth having: a penis.

But what did all this have to do with me – who went to school and got better marks than the boys and painted and wrote and spent Saturdays doing still lifes at the Art Students League and my weekday afternoons editing the high-school paper (Features Editor; the Editor-in-Chief had never been a girl – though it also never occurred to us then to question it)? What did the moon and tides and earth-mothering and the worship of the Lawrentian 'phallos' have to do with me or with my life?

I met my first 'phallos' at thirteen years and ten months on my parents' avocado-green silk living-room couch, in the shade of an avocado-green avocado tree, grown by my avocado green-thumbed mother from an avocado pit. The 'phallos' belonged to Steve Applebaum, a junior and art major when I was a freshman and art major, and it had a most memorable abstract design of blue veins on its Kandinsky-purple underside. In retrospect, it was a remarkable specimen: circumcised, of course, and huge (what is huge when you have no frame of reference?), and with an impressive life of its own. As soon as it began to make its drumlin-like presence known under the tight zipper of Steve's chinos (we were necking and 'petting-below-the-waist' as one said then), he would slowly unzip (so as not to snag it?) and with one hand (the other was under my skirt and up my cunt) extract the huge purple thing from between the layers of his shorts, his blue Brooks-Brothers shirttails, and his cold, glittering, metal-zippered fly. Then I would dip one hand into the vase of roses my flower-loving mother always kept on the coffee table, and with a right hand moistened with water and the slime from their stems, I would proceed with my rhythmic jerking off of Steve. How exactly did I do it? Three fingers? Or the whole palm? I suppose I must have been rough at first (though later I became an expert). He would throw his head back in ecstasy (but controlled ecstasy: my father was watching TV in the dining room) and would come into his Brooks-Brothers shirttails or into a handkerchief quickly produced for the purpose. The technique I have forgotten, but the feeling remains. Partly, it was reciprocity (tit for tat, or clit for tat), but it was also power. I knew that what I was doing gave me a special kind of power over him – one that painting or writing couldn't approach. And then I was coming too – maybe not like Lady Chatterley, but it was something.

———————— ◊ ————————

Today, as we approach the end of the millennium, there is an explosion of new erotic fiction. A thousand voices, beautiful and thrilling, vicious and tuneless, clamour to be heard. Pens expert and clumsy explore every erogenous crevice, and the technology of word processing facilitates the birth of the good, the bad and the ugly without discrimination.

Subniv Babuta's first novel, *The Still Point*, was published in 1991. An extract from it makes a fitting conclusion to this anthology, pointing as it does to a hopeful future for erotic literature while recalling that the first humane writing about sexuality came out of India. Two young Westerners make love in today's India, while nine centuries earlier the old temple architect and sculptor Srivastava has a vision of their lovemaking.

Out of a misty dream
Our path emerges for a while, then
*   closes*
Within a dream.

FROM *VITAE SUMMA BREVIS*
ERNEST DOWSON (1867–1900)

Max knew he was being watched. But he often had this feeling when making love to Imogen, and it was never anything more than a figment of his imagination. He was, once again, above her. He could see her perfectly, his own shadow shielding her face from the fierce sun above them. Max bent down and kissed her, searching her mouth with his tongue. Moments later, he pulled away, and let his tongue begin to explore her neck, which Imogen stretched to its full length as she arched her body backwards. She tasted bitter, and the saline savour, coupled with the aroma rising from lower down, quickened Max's desire. As he traced a path with his tongue between her breasts, he slid his whole body down. Over the ridges he continued, sucking the skin until the blood rose to the surface. Imogen held onto Max's shoulders, restraining him. Then she released him, and he worked his way down, pushing his tongue into the crevices formed beneath each breast, then going on to trace intricate invisible patterns on Imogen's stomach. He felt her hands urging him to go lower, but he waited, resting his cheek on her waist. Max closed his eyes, breathing in the juices deeply, feeding on their promise. Then, almost imperceptibly, he began to descend. Max's tongue moved from the smooth surface of Imogen's womb, into a tiny thicket of soft hair. Slowly and deliberately, he licked each strand dry. Eventually, he reached the crevice between his lover's legs and, frantically, Imogen pressed his head into her, twisting strands of his hair in her fingers. With his tongue, Max pushed aside the soft folds of flesh, feeling at last the warm fluid flowing over his lips.

Imogen relaxed. As soon as she relinquished her hold over herself, the tiny disparate fires that the firefly had set alight inside her suddenly gathered force, and exploded. Wave after wave of fire rushed through Imogen's body. She held Max's head down, drawing it in with her thighs. As he sucked deeper and deeper, so Imogen surrendered to the raging within her.

Srivastava felt the dream slipping from him. The image of the lovers was beginning to fade, and he knew that soon he must leave this place and return to the world of his labours. He was satisfied that he now possessed the visions he would sculpt. He turned to leave the hall through the archway he had entered. But something held Srivastava back. On an impulse, the old man turned back again, and keeping his eyes fixed on the empty alcove on the wall, walked over to it. He touched the smooth plaster. It was still soft and supple, and the sculptor's finger left a tiny trench where he had traced it. Srivastava caressed the wet wall softly, as if stroking a delicate animal. As his eyes looked

RIGHT *Anja*, a sculpture in alabaster by the contemporary German artist Arpad Safranek.

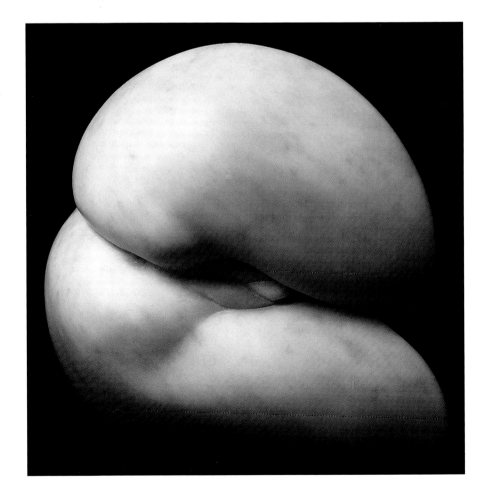

down, he noticed a pebble at its base. Instinctively, he bent down and picked it up. Its sharp point formed a perfect nib with which to inscribe the plaster. Srivastava smoothed the wall with his hand just below the base of the alcove. Here, deliberately, and with a craftsman's practised care, he took the pebble and began to cut the intricate outlines of Sanskrit characters into the stonework. The pebble sliced easily through the smooth skin. One by one the shapes appeared. Srivastava knew that such a liberty with the Prince's temple would be forbidden him in reality, but here, in his sleeping vision, the old man was master. With a steady hand, Srivastava finished off the word that he had been compelled to write. VIDHI. As the sculptor stepped back to examine his handiwork, his lips formed the sound. 'Vidhi,' he whispered silently to himself. Destiny.

Max pushed further and further into the soft flesh. Imogen had begun to convulse gently, pulling him in, then pushing him away in a regular rhythm. Her hands grasped Max firmly, afraid that he might withdraw. He could feel her gasping for breath. But now Imogen pulled him up sharply, guiding his head the full length of her body, forcing him to shift his body awkwardly and rise once more onto her. As he covered her, Max felt Imogen pull his still glistening mouth hungrily onto her own. At the same time, her hand searched lower down, beneath their waists. Gradually, her firm sensitive fingers tightened on Max, guiding him once again inside her. He felt her thighs shuddering against him. Her gasping became desperate, yet she refused to release her lover's mouth. Her heart pounded with a deafening rhythm.

As Max thrust, and thrust again, Imogen rushed to the edge of the precipice, and looked down into the chasms of fire at her feet. Yet she clung for a moment longer. Together, they would plunge into the inferno. Each tiny movement brought Max closer. He felt her waiting for him. Higher and higher he pushed. Still she waited. Finally, Max too could see the edge of the precipice: as he caught sight of the blazing sea beneath the cliff, he rushed forward with a final explosion of energy, grabbed Imogen as she waited on the edge, and leapt into the chasm.

For a moment, the two bodies, fused together on the dusty patch of grass, stopped. All sound ceased. The breeze did not blow, the dust froze. Even the birds, hiding from the sun in shady nooks, arrested their fidgeting. The shadows on the ground, lengthening each second, held their shapes one instant longer. Into the stillness a shot was fired. The noise tore through the silence, and sound rushed back in through the hole in the vacuum. Birds, startled by the explosion, took off, flapping their wings frantically. The sand began its meanderings once more, blown into flurries and eddies by a new wind. The sun continued on its relentless journey, and the shadows lengthened once more.

Imogen felt the surge deep inside her, and screamed silently. Though audible to no human ear, her cry reached every corner of the derelict temple. The carvings, motionless and inert, safe within their alcoves, heard the song, and for a moment their own sculpted passion came to life.

ABOVE Torso by A. Klinkenberg, contemporary.

The authors

Subniv Babuta (b. 1958) Indian novelist (page 155).

Georges Bataille (1897–1962) French writer and librarian (page 127).

Charles Baudelaire (1821–67) French poet, author of *Les Fleurs du Mal* (page 64).

Aubrey Beardsley (1872–98) *see under* List of Artists *below* (page 80).

William Blake (1757–1827) English poet and painter, author of *Songs of Innocence* and *Songs of Experience* (page 29).

George Gordon, Lord Byron (1788–1824) British poet, author of *Childe Harold* and *Don Juan* (page 40).

Nicolas Chorier Late seventeenth–early eighteenth-century French lawyer and writer (page 20).

John Cleland (1709–89) English writer (page 25).

Leonard Cohen (b. 1934) Canadian poet and singer (page 149).

Aleister Crowley (1875–1947) English magician, 'The Great Beast' (page 76).

Lord Alfred Douglas (1870–1945) 'Bosie', son of the Marquess of Queensberry and lover of Oscar Wilde, whose downfall was brought about by the Marquess (page 74).

Norman Douglas (1868–1952) British novelist who settled in Italy (page 103).

Ernest Dowson (1867–1900) British poet, friend of Yeats (page 155).

Alexandre Dumas *père* (1802–70) French novelist, author of *The Three Musketeers* (page 151).

Lawrence Durrell (1912–90) British novelist and poet, author of *The Alexandria Quartet* (page 125).

Gustave Flaubert (1821–80) French novelist, author of *Madame Bovary* (page 56).

John Fletcher (1579–1625) English dramatist who may have collaborated with Shakespeare (page 19).

Thomas Hardy (1840–1928) English poet and novelist, author of the 'Wessex' novels including *The Mayor of Casterbridge* and *Tess of the D'Urbervilles* (page 59).

Frank Harris (1856–1931) Writer and newspaper editor; born in Ireland, he lived in London and America (pages 102, 103, 104, 106).

Robert Herrick (1591–1674) English poet (pages 14, 15).

Erica Jong (b. 1942) American novelist and poet; her best-known work is *Fear of Flying* (page 151).

Rudyard Kipling (1865–1936) British writer and poet, born in India; author of the *Jungle Books* (page 66).

D. H. Lawrence (1885–1930) British novelist, author of *Sons and Lovers* and *Women in Love* as well as *Lady Chatterley's Lover* (pages 107, 109, 112, 113).

Violette Leduc (1907–72) French writer; her best-known work is *La Bâtarde* (page 137).

Guy de Maupassant (1850–93) French short story writer and novelist (page 105).

Henry Miller (1891–1980) American writer resident in Paris, author of *Tropic of Cancer* and *Tropic of Capricorn* (pages 117, 119, 121).

Honoré Gabriel Riquetti, Comte de Mirabeau (1749–91) French writer and political figure of the Revolution (page 33).

Anaïs Nin (1903–77) French writer, brought up in New York; she published a seven-volume *Diary* (pages 116, 118, 122, 124).

Sir Thomas Overbury (1581–1613) English poet and essayist, courtier at the court of King James I (page 62).

Cora Pearl (1837–86) English courtesan who lived in Second-Empire Paris (pages 56, 59, 60, 62).

Matthew Prior (1664–1721) English diplomat and poet (page 25).

Marcel Proust (1871–1922) French novelist, author of *Remembrance of Things Past* (page 97).

John Wilmot, Earl of Rochester (1647–80) Libertine, poet, courtier at the court of King Charles II (pages 10, 11, 13, 24, 38).

Pierre de Ronsard (1524–85) French Renaissance poet (page 18).

Maurice Sachs (d. 1945) Parisian writer and spy, friend of Cocteau and his circle (page 135).

Saki (H. H. Munro) (1870–1916) English writer of sardonic short stories (pages 80, 90, 93, 95).

William Shakespeare (1564–1616) English dramatist and poet, the greatest playwright in the English language (page 143).

George Bernard Shaw (1856–1950) Irish playwright and theatre critic, author of *St Joan* and *Pygmalion* (page 102).

Edmund Spenser (1552–99) Elizabethan poet whose greatest work was *The Faerie Queen* (page 134).

Lytton Strachey (1880–1932) English biographer, author of *Eminent Victorians* (pages 96, 97, 98).

Algernon Charles Swinburne (1837–1909) British poet (pages 141, 144).

Alfred Lord Tennyson (1809–92) British poet, admired by Queen Victoria; he became Poet Laureate in 1850 (pages 129, 133).

Edith Wharton (1862–1937) American writer, later resident in France; author of *The Age of Innocence* (page 100).

Walt Whitman (1819–92) American poet, author of *Leaves of Grass* (page 74).

Oscar Wilde (1854–1900) English playwright of Irish ancestry, author of *The Importance of Being Earnest*; jailed for homosexuality, he died in exile in France (page 75).

John Wilkes (1727–97) English journalist and politician, member of the infamous Hellfire Club (page 23).

The artists

Eugène Agelou Late nineteenth-century French photographer (page 92).

AL (active 1930s) Viennese illustrator (page 127).

Paul Edouard-Henri Avril (1849–1928) French artist, born in Algeria (page 75).

Suzanne Ballivet (active 1930–45) French book illustrator (pages 128–33).

Franz von Bayros (1866–1924) German painter and illustrator (page 76).

Aubrey Beardsley (1872–98) British draughtsman and illustrator who contributed to *The Yellow Book* (pages 6, 78, 79).

C. Bernard Late nineteenth-century French watercolourist (page 39).

Louis André Berthomme Saint-André (1905–77) French illustrator (pages 72, 73).

Antoine Borel (1743–1810) Parisian painter, engraver and draughtsman (pages 16, 18, 25, 26, 31).

Bruno Braquehais Mid-nineteenth-century mute French photographer (page 43).

Carl Breuer-Courth ('Rainier, E.') Early twentieth-century German painter and illustrator (page 103).

Agnolo Bronzino (1503–72) Florentine Late Renaissance painter who worked for Cosimo I de' Medici (page 2).

Jean Cocteau (1889–1963) French draughtsman, novelist, dramatist, film-maker and poet (pages 135, 136).

Achille Deveria (1800–57) French painter and illustrator (page 65).

Michael Martin Drolling (1786–1851) Parisian painter, pupil of J.-L. David (pages 17, 21).

Louis-Jules Duboscq-Soleil Late nineteenth-century French photographer (pages 48, 61).

Alexandre Dupouy Contemporary Parisian photographer (page 145).

Peter Fendi (1796–1842) Austrian artist, court painter at Vienna (page 69).

Artur Fischer (1872–1948) German painter, active in Berlin (page 11).

Emmanuel de Ghendt (1738–1815) French engraver (page 35).

Eric Gill (1882–1940) British graphic artist and typographer (page 100).

Heinrich or Hendrick Goltzius (1558–1617) Dutch engraver and painter (page 10).

Alexis Gouin Mid-nineteenth-century French photographer (page 57).

Monica Guevara Contemporary graphic artist (page 160).

China Hamilton (b. 1946) English photographer, graphic designer, painter, musician and healer (pages 140–2, 146–8).

A. Klinkenberg Contemporary German artist and sculptor (page 157).

Henri Monnier (1799–1875) French watercolourist (page 64).

Félix Jacques-Antoine Moulin (active 1849–61) Parisian photographer (pages 49, 55, 60).

Georg Emmanuel Opitz (1775–1841) Austrian painter and illustrator (pages 44, 45, 46, 53).

Man Ray (1890–1976) American surrealist photographer who settled in France, co-founder with Marcel Duchamp of the Dada movement (page 8)

Rojan or Rojankowski (active 1930–50) Polish-French illustrator (pages 116, 118, 124, 126).

Johann Heinrich Romberg (1763–1840) German watercolourist (pages 27, 28, 32).

Félicien Rops (1833–98) Belgian symbolist painter (page 71).

Thomas Rowlandson (1756–1827) British caricaturist and draughtsman (page 41).

Arpad Safranek Contemporary German sculptor and photographer (pages 156, 160).

G. de Sainte-Croix (active 1949–59) French book illustrator (pages 98, 101, 151, 154).

Egon Schiele (1890–1918) Austrian expressionist painter, imprisoned for 'pornographic' work; he died young in the influenza epidemic after the Great War (page 9).

Mario Tauzin (active 1910/20) Parisian draughtsman (page 138).

Denon Vivant Late eighteenth-century French etcher and engraver (pages 36, 37).

Gerda Wegener (b. 1889) Danish commercial artist who worked in Paris between the wars (pages 83, 97, 99).

Giovanni Zuin Contemporary Italian photographer (pages 137, 152, 153).

Sources and acknowledgements

Bibliographical details of the excerpts in this anthology are given below, with copyright notices and permissions indicated where appropriate. Every effort has been made to acknowledge the copyright owner of the material used. Where this has proved impossible, the copyright owner is invited to contact Eddison Sadd Editions.

Pages 10, 11, 13, 24, 38: John Wilmot, Earl of Rochester, *The Imperfect Enjoyment; Signior Dildo; A Ramble in St James's Park; Love and Life; The Disabled Debauchee.*

Pages 14, 15: Robert Herrick, *Upon the Nipples of Julia's Breast; Upon Julia's Sweat.*

Pages 14, 16: *L'Ecole des filles* ('School of Venus'), 1655. Trans. © 1972 Donald Thomas, Panther. Reproduced by permission of HarperCollins Publishers Ltd, London.

Page 18: Pierre de Ronsard, *A son Ame* ('To his Soul').

Page 19: John Fletcher, *Love's Emblems.*

Pages 20, 22, 23: Nicolas Chorier, *Satyra Sotadica*, 1660. English trans. in British Library, 1682, 1740, 1786; original in Bibliothèque Nationale, Paris.

Page 24: John Wilkes, *An Essay on Women.*

Pages 25, 28, 31: John Cleland, *Fanny Hill – Memoirs of a Woman of Pleasure*, 1749. British Library. (Also published by Penguin Books/Mayflower.)

Page 25: Matthew Prior, *Nanny Blushes.*

Pages 33, 37: Honoré Gabriel Riquetti, Comte de Mirabeau, *Ma Conversion*. Trans. © Holloway House Publishing Co., Los Angeles, 1972. (Also published by Star Books/W. H. Allen, London.)

Page 40: Lord Byron, *We'll Go No More A-roving.*

Page 40: *The Lustful Turk*, 1828. British Library.

Page 43: 'Walter', *My Secret Life*, 1850s. British Library. Reprinted by Grove Press Inc., New York.

Pages 56, 59, 60, 62: Cora Pearl, *The Memoirs of Cora Pearl*. © 1983 William Blatchford, Granada. Reproduced by permission of HarperCollins Publishers Ltd, London.

Page 59: Thomas Hardy, *The Ruined Maid.*

Page 64: *The Romance of Lust*, ed. William Simpson Potter, 4 vols., 1873–6.

Pages 67, 69: *The Pearl* magazine, 1879–80.

Pages 69, 70: *The Oyster* magazine, c.1880.

Pages 71, 72: *The Boudoir: Voluptuous Confessions of a French Lady of Fashion*, early 1880s. British Library. (Also published by Star Books/W. H. Allen, London; Grove Press Inc., New York.)

Page 74: Walt Whitman, *Calamus.*

Page 74: Lord Alfred Douglas, *Two Loves.*

Pages 75, 77: Oscar Wilde et al., *Teleny or The Reverse of the Medal*, 1893. British Library. (Also published by Grove Press Inc., New York.)

Page 76: Aleister Crowley, *White Stains.*

Page 80: Aubrey Beardsley, *Under the Hill*. British Library.

Pages 80, 81, 84: *Eveline*, 1904. British Library. (Also published by Star Books/W. H. Allen, London.)

Pages 87, 88, 91, 95: *Pleasure Bound Afloat*, 1908; *The Confessions of Nemesis Hunt*, 1910; *Maudie*, 1909. British Library.

Pages 96, 97, 98: Lytton Strachey, *Ermyntrude and Esmeralda*, 1912. Reproduced by permission of The Society of Authors, London, as agents of the Strachey Trust.

Page 100: Edith Wharton, *Beatrice Palmato* (short story). © The Author's Estate.

Page 102: George Bernard Shaw, from the Preface to the Grove Press edition of *The Collected Works of Frank Harris.*

Pages 102, 103, 104, 106: Frank Harris, *My Life and Loves*. Copyright © 1925 Frank Harris, © 1953 Nellie Harris, © 1963 by Arthur Leonard Ross as Executor of the Frank Harris Estate. Copyright renewed © 1991 by Ralph G. Ross and Edgar M. Ross. Used by permission of Grove Press Inc., New York.

Page 103: Norman Douglas, limerick.

Pages 107, 109, 112, 113: D. H. Lawrence, *Lady Chatterley's Lover*, 1928. Reprinted by permission of Laurence Pollinger Ltd, London, and the Estate of Frieda Lawrence Ravagli. Published by Penguin Books Ltd, London, and Penguin USA, New York.

Pages 116, 118, 122, 124: Anaïs Nin, *Delta of Venus, Erotica*. Copyright © The Anaïs Nin Trust, 1977, reprinted by permission of Penguin Books Ltd (publ. 1990) and of Harcourt, Brace & Company, USA.

Pages 117, 119, 121: Henry Miller, *Tropic of Cancer*. Copyright © 1934 The Estate of Henry Miller. Reproduced with permission of Grove Press Inc., New York. *Opus Pistorum.* © 1983 The Estate of Henry Miller. Reproduced with permission of Grove Press

Inc., New York.

Page 125: Lawrence Durrell, *The Black Book*, 1938. Copyright © The Estate of Lawrence Durrell 1938, 1973, reproduced with permission of Faber and Faber Ltd, London, and Curtis Brown Ltd, London, on behalf of The Estate of Lawrence Durrell. *The Alexandria Quartet*, 1957–60.

Pages 128, 129, 130, 132, 133: *Initiation Amoureuse*, Buenos Aires, 1943. Reproduced by courtesy of The Erotic Print Society, London.

Pages 129, 133: Alfred Lord Tennyson, *Guinevere.*

Page 134: Edmund Spenser, *The Faerie Queen*, 1589–96.

Page 135: Maurice Sachs, *Witches' Sabbath*, © 1965 Stein & Day, trans. Richard Howard.

Page 137: Violette Leduc, *La Bâtarde*, trans. Derek Coltman. © The Author's Estate. Reproduced by permission of Peter Owen Publishers, London, and Gallimard, Paris.

Pages 139, 142, 144, 147, 148: Pauline Réage, *Story of O*. Published by Société Nouvelle des Editions J.-J. Pauvert, Paris, 1954. (Also published by Corgi, London, and Ballantine, New York.)

Pages 141, 144: Algernon Charles Swinburne, *The Orchard; Dolores.*

Page 143: William Shakespeare, excerpt from *Othello*, c.1604.

Page 149: Leonard Cohen, 'A Long Letter from F', from *Beautiful Losers*, © Leonard Cohen 1967. Reproduced by permission of Black Spring Press Ltd, London, and Stranger Music Inc., Los Angeles. All rights reserved.

Pages 151, 152, 153: Erica Jong, *Fear of Flying*. © Erica Mann Jong 1973. Reproduced by permission of Reed Books Ltd, UK, and Henry Holt & Co., New York.

Page 155: Subniv Babuta, *The Still Point*. © The Author, 1991. Reproduced by permission of Weidenfeld & Nicolson, London.

Page 155: Ernest Dowson, *Vitae Summa Brevis.*

Most of the art used to illustrate this anthology is reproduced by kind permission of The Erotic Print Society, London. For the exceptions Eddison Sadd would like to thank and acknowledge the following:

The National Gallery, London (page 2); Copyright © Photo Réunion des Musées Nationaux (page 7); Copyright © Man Ray Trust/ADAGP, Paris and DACS, London 1995 (page 8); The Metropolitan Museum of Art, New York, Bequest of Schofield Thayer, 1982 (1984.433.311) (page 9); Copyright © DACS, London, 1996 from *Le Livre Blanc*, 1930 (pages 135, 136); The Klinger Collection (pages 11, 81, 86, 87, 94, 95, 102, 104, 105, 106 and 127); Il Collezionista (page 30). All the photographs (except that on page 8) are reproduced courtesy of the Akehurst Bureau, London.

Collecting erotic art

By James Maclean

At its best, erotic art is one of the most direct manifestations of our response to the life force. It is a celebration of our most fundamental and enjoyable instincts; a celebration which can enhance the experience of those fortunate enough to have access to it.

This genre of art is the only surviving area of man's creativity in which objects of exceptional power and beauty have been secreted away – for diverse cultural reasons – from the scrutiny of the vast majority of people. It has an earthy candour not often found in other, more formal artistic categories such as portraiture or still-life; it can give us a valuable insight into the sexual politics of the day or afford access to the secret world of an artist's innermost thoughts.

Because of censorship and repression, much erotic art has been destroyed; the rest usually remains hidden from public view. In the nineteenth century, rich individuals such as the Russian Prince Galitzin accumulated such a magnificent hoard of erotic works that it occupied two catalogues and several hundred pages when dispersed by auction sale in 1887. The widow of the great explorer and collector of erotica, Sir Richard Burton, on the other hand, incinerated his important collection when he died in 1890, and only two years earlier a London publisher, Henry Vizetelly, had been imprisoned as an old man for printing Zola's *La Terre*, despite the protests of the artistic and literary world of the time. The Royal Collection, the Vatican and a number of major museums around the world have great but concealed collections. The *sub rosa*, under-the-counter attitudes that persist in most museums about their erotic treasures are therefore doubly infuriating. Few, if any, major museums would have the bravery to put on a comprehensive exhibition of erotic works.

Historically, the market for erotic art has been clandestine and all but non-existent; the market-place remains tiny thanks to a noticeable reluctance on the part of most media to let their readers or viewers be exposed to this sort of thing. But there *are* ways to build a collection.

It is worth viewing auction sales when possible, but this is a time-consuming, though pleasant, occupation: very few auction houses have specialist sales of erotica.

Some picture dealers and antiquarian booksellers specialize in erotic art, but these again need to be winkled out. Some publishers of facsimile prints spend years of research assembling enough material to grant their membership access to limited editions of the world's finest existing erotica. These are produced, often in small numbers, using the newest technology but with faithfulness to the quality and character of the originals. The prints offered by The Erotic Print Society, for example, span a period from the sixteenth century to the present day. Their first portfolio of prints by a contemporary artist, Monica Guevara (above), has proved to be an enormous success. The majority of the drawings and prints in this anthology are from the collection of The Erotic Print Society.

Another way of collecting erotica is to buy high-quality prints of the work of contemporary photographers from specialist photographic galleries such as the Akehurst Bureau in London. Finally, you can of course become part of the age-old – and very important – system of artistic patronage by simply buying the work of young artists. Arpad Safranek of Viersen in Germany produces bronzes (left) of the exquisite alabaster sculpture on page 156. Only if contemporary artists of talent are encouraged will our culture leave a legacy of erotic art for future generations to enjoy.

The Erotic Print Society can be contacted at EPS (Dept EB1) Admail 366, London SW1H 9EP, UK. Their 48-page colour catalogue costs £5/$8 including postage. Members also enjoy a regular Review containing articles that are both authoritative and interesting, as well as essays on the lighter side of collecting erotic art.

James Maclean, formerly of Sotheby's, is a leading expert on erotic art.